ISBN 978-1-7363798-4-4

StumpStrong

Strength In Roots

Nicki Pascarella

In memory of my grandparents, Robert Stauffer and Martha Brickell Stauffer. I miss them with all my heart.

And to my parents, Bill and Bonnie. Thank you for encouraging me to chase my dreams.

Nicki

Prologue

"A woman's guess is much more accurate
than a man's certainty."

Rudyard Kipling, *Plain Tales From The Hills*

TO: PAMoore@gmail
FROM: Cassfldhock@gmail
SUBJECT: Happy Birthday Mom
DATE: September 26, 2019

Hi Mom,

Happy Birthday! I just finished this assignment for my History class. We had to tell a story about an ancestor. I thought it would be the perfect present for you. Eat lots of cake and kiss Zoomie for me.

Love you the absolute most!
Cassie

The Visitor
US History
by
Cassandra Moore
9/26/19

On December 31st, 1944, a bump in the night awoke my great-great-grandmother, Sarah McClimate Stauffer. She sat upright and listened. Since it was New Year's Eve, and she was a superstitious Scottish woman, she believed the strange noises to be the dark First Footer. Thank goodness, because as long as this inaugural visitor was a dark-haired man, and he stepped foot across their threshold, his arrival would ward off ill-luck for the coming year. She hoped their guest was incredibly handsome and carried shortcake.

She concentrated on the strange sound. Unfortunately, what had started as soft knocking had turned to frantic scratching.

"Wait a minute. It kin't be," she whispered. Startled, she aggressively shook my sound asleep great-great-grandfather into a state of semi-lucidity. "Horace! Git up! Robert's at the front door and he's hurt."

My groggy great-great-grandfather, Horace Patchin Stauffer, sat up rubbed at his carroty-colored hair, and faced his distraught wife. He took a moment to compose himself before explaining that their son couldn't be visiting because he was flying a bombing mission over Germany.

My always correct great-great-grandmother was relentless in her request. "I'm telling ye, Robert's at the front door. He's been shot n' needs help. Horace, go down and let him in!" She uttered an exasperated grunt before continuing. "Fur God's sake, if ye don't answer the door, Horace, then I will. Why are ye arguin' with me?"

Despite his pragmatic German nature, my great-great-grandfather gave in to her Scottish whims. He knew it would have saved him time and allowed him to get back to his slumber sooner if he had acquiesced at her first request, but being aroused in the middle of dreams has a way of making even the most intelligent husband challenge reason. As he reluctantly dragged himself down the steep stairs of their farmhouse, he noticed the faint sound of knocking, or was it scratching? Robert was there. But how? Rural Burnside, Pennsylvania, was a world away from the European front. Were the letters from England wrong?

Upon opening the door, my great-great-grandfather experienced a moment of vindication. The night was undisturbed, and their front porch was empty. Seconds later, a heavy gust of wind slapped him in the face. Next, a second brutal punch, knocked the wind out of him. That was the precise moment he realized that his heroic son had taken a final journey home.

The hardest thing Great-great-grandpa Horace ever did was climb that narrow, suffocating stairwell to tell Great-great-grandma Sarah that their son had died and it was only his spirit that had reached out to them. She met him at their bedroom door, her eyes filled with tears because moments before, the tragic message had also revealed itself to her.

That night, mourning the loss of the kindest and most gentle of their seven children, my heartbroken ancestors held each other and grieved.

Meanwhile, in a field somewhere in Germany, my seriously injured great-grandfather called his mother by her given name. "Sarah, I've been hit. It hurts so much. I'm sorry. I'm dying. I love you, Mom!"

..........*.....*

TO: Cassfldhock@gmail
FROM: PAMoore@gmail
SUBJECT: Re: Happy Birthday Mom
DATE: September 26, 2019
Cassie,

Loved it!!!! I'm going to share it with your Grandma Susan and Uncle Jimmy.

I hope you receive an A+++! Zoomie says, Hi.

Love you to the Moon,

Mom

Chapter 1

---

*"I've just read that I'm dead. Don't forget
to delete me from your list of
subscribers."*

Rudyard Kipling

TO: Lmartin@PEA.com
FROM: PAMoore@gmail
SUBJECT: Assaulted at work
DATE: October 5, 2019

Ms. Leigh Ann Martin, Esq.,

Yesterday Missy McMann contacted you on my behalf and filled you in on my recent assault. She suggested that since I suffered damage to my vocal cords and am currently unable to speak, I write a detailed account of yesterday's incident. I will leave it to you to delete the extraneous details.

FYI—I hereby declare on oath, the events in the attached document are true, and Dr. Anne Westbrook, East City High's Student Services Supervisor, is an evil cunt!

Sincerely,
Patricia Anne Moore

ATTACHMENT
Ms. Martin,

On October 4th, at approximately ten a.m., a sixteen-year-old sociopath tried to kill me. The most horrifying part was, he almost succeeded. Lying helpless on my cold classroom floor while staring into the questioning eyes of my charges was a new low, even for me. Three years of crap-ass luck culminated in my waking up in a hospital room this morning.

I will start at the beginning. Yesterday morning, I switched on my hairdryer, and it blew a lone strand of my hair into the air before shutting off and taking the power on the second floor of my grandparents' one-hundred-twelve-year-old house along with it.

In the unelectrified dark of the early dawn, I had difficulty finding the flashlight in my nightstand drawer. After a fruitless search, I remembered my ex-husband telling me he kept a Fenix in the basement file cabinet. I made my way down two flights of stairs, eventually finding it in a drawer alongside a shoebox of old cassette tapes. The stream of light emanating from it revealed long-lost memorabilia that had belonged to my late grandfather. The exciting discovery distracted me from finding the correct fuse in a timely manner. Thus, I found myself racing the clock.

As I attempted to speed up my morning routine, my inner spaz emerged. For starters, I spilled my coffee all over the counter. Next, I realized that Zoomie, my jokester of a Blue Merle Shetland Sheepdog, had carried my shoes away from their usual spot. Then, loaded down with my school bags, I tore my skirt as it caught on the rough edge of my front door.

Finally, I had to navigate both the traffic in my small town and the three lanes of vehicles practically at a standstill on the bridge into the city. I have no idea how I made it to work on time, but I did, without a moment to spare.

For the first two periods of the day, I played cheerleader. I encouraged, I begged, I even bribed my class of fifteen Alternative Education students to do their work. Considering that the only difference between my morning preparing for school—and that of the unlucky Wile E. Coyote—was the appearance of a five-hundred-pound anvil, my classroom ran smoothly. Let me rephrase that. It functioned as efficiently as a classroom of at-risk students with inadequate resources can. That is, until Tanner Jones, a sixteen-year-old delinquent diagnosed with Attention Deficit Disorder and a learning disability—undiagnosed with a nasty disposition and criminal tendencies—told me he wanted popcorn. I don't think it unusual for a teenager to want popcorn. In fact, before yesterday, I occasionally enjoyed partaking in the buttery treat. The problem was, I didn't have any.

"Tanner, please do your work. I don't have any popcorn right now. If you get your work done, I'll bring you some tomorrow," I promised.

"I want popcorn, now!'' he demanded, his blue eyes flashing.

"I don't have any right now, but if you do a good job on your worksheet, I'll go to the store tonight and get you some. How does that sound?" I thought it more than generous since the little miscreant was, as usual, making unreasonable demands and behaving like a spoiled brat.

Despite my coddling, a possessed demonic voice came from the freckled-faced teen. "I said, I want popcorn now!"

I contemplated my options. The problem being, as a teacher, I only had a few. One—I could give in to the kid's demand, which is rarely the best choice. However, even if I wanted to acquiesce, I couldn't because I didn't have popcorn. Two—I could call for an administrator to come and remove him from my classroom. But at that moment, it seemed to be a more severe solution than his behavior warranted. Three—I could continue explaining that I didn't have popcorn. Although I wasn't sure that rationalizing with him for the next five hours would do either of us any good. Four—I could assume that he didn't have the skills to appropriately ask for what he wanted, and model the correct behavior with a yummy praise sandwich. As you know, this is often the choice a good teacher makes.

"Tanner, I like the way you concentrated on organizing your backpack when you came in this morning, so tomorrow when I have popcorn, you could ask nicely by saying—"

I didn't get to finish modeling a polite request or end my sandwich with a slice of praise because Tanner looked me in the eyes and growled, "Now!"

I analyzed my dilemma and concluded that Tanner Jones was a little jerk who was trying to exert control over me while capitalizing on the additional bonus of escaping his school work. I skipped to option number five—Disengage.

I composed myself and calmly said, "Tanner, we will discuss this later." Then I attempted to walk away.

I never imagined that turning my back to the little jerk would be the most dangerous decision of my life. The next thing I knew, he had his hands around my throat. It is important to note he outweighed me by at least forty pounds and towered over me by a good six inches.

At first, I panicked, then I tried to recall the basic self-defense lessons I learned decades ago at a women's gym. When my memory failed, I instinctively pushed all my body weight into Tanner. We both stumbled backward, hitting a desk, and his hands released me. I took in a gulp of air and tried to step away. A second later, something tightened around my neck. Terror set in when I realized he was strangling me with the lanyard holding my ID badge. I used my fingers to create a barrier between my neck and the lanyard, but it was pointless because the strap dug into my skin.

I shoved my body weight back into Tanner again. Unfortunately, this time he was prepared. I couldn't throw him off balance, I couldn't free myself, and I couldn't breathe.

On a side note, you may want to warn Union members that the easy-release clasps you recommend that teachers wear are a bullshit waste.

When faced with the fear of death, my life did, in a way, flash before my eyes. It wasn't scenes or memories. It was a few quick, incomplete thoughts. *Goodbye, Cassie! Who will take care of Zoomie? Sorry, Mike.*

After this, I experienced the oddest sensation. I stopped fighting, and my body relaxed. I know it sounds crazy, but I felt peaceful.

Tanner's voice faded out. "From now on, give me what I want b—"

When I came to, two teachers had Tanner in the hallway, and the rest of my class was gathered around my supine body, talking in unison.

"You okay, missus?"

"You dead, missus?"

"That was scary!"

"Ms. Moore, damn! Next time just give him popcorn."

One voice stood out above all the others. "Missus, we tried to save you, and I ran to get help. Tanner is a crazy fuck," said my lone female student, Diamond Washington.

Since the inappropriate-for-school language seemed to fit the horror of the life and death nadir I found myself in, I chose not to address it at that moment.

As I am sure you are aware, both factual news and exaggerated gossip travel at warp speed in a public high school. Pretty soon, adults filled my classroom. I was oddly calm and preparing to reassure everyone that, although rattled, I was uninjured. Instead, I emitted a strange scratchy sound. I'm ashamed to admit my weakness, but following the discovery of my lost voice, I broke down and sobbed like a terrified child.

My friend, who teaches upstairs, had been alerted to my misfortune through the speedy, although often inaccurate, and always unofficial, twenty-first-century school communication system of Snapchat. Mathematics instructor Missy McMann darted to the basement to see if the social media rumors of my death were indeed true. Finding me alive, she wrapped her arm around my shoulders and walked me to the school infirmary.

The horrified school nurse examined me, then placed me in the back room, where she told me to rest on one of the cots. My tears had dried and left a throbbing headache in their wake. The sweet nurse swaddled me in a warm blanket. Thank God, because I was so cold.

"Patti, I called Mike," Nurse Jenkins explained. "He's on his way to pick you up."

I panicked. *No! Please, no! Not Mike. He can't see me like this!* Since I couldn't talk, I shook my aching head from side to side to let her know that she had made an error in judgment in contacting my ex-husband.

Please hurry up, Mike! I prayed a moment later.

Although Nurse Jenkins ignored my protests concerning the phone call, she acknowledged my chattering teeth. She settled two more blankets over me. Exhausted, traumatized, and finally warm, I fell asleep.

I awoke to Principal Alan Anderson's voice.

"Patricia," he whispered. "I just got off the phone with Dr. Westbrook. She denied my request to have Tanner suspended."

A student who had been physically violent wasn't going to be removed from the classroom? Attempting to process this, I stared at my principal until Nurse Jenkins knocked on the frame of the open sickroom door. Her hand covered the mouthpiece of an old-school phone. "Alan, Patricia, Dr. Westbrook's on the phone." She cringed. "Sorry. She wants to talk to you, Patricia."

Still in a brain fog, I reached for the phone.

Before handing it to me, Nurse Jenkins held the receiver to her ear to relay a message. "Anne, she's awake, but her vocal cords are injured, and she's going to need to go to the hospital. You can talk to her but she can't respond." The nurse rolled her eyes as she listened to the loud voice at the other end. Finally, she said, "Here's Patricia." She shook her head and handed me the phone.

I took a deep breath and held it to my ear. I attempted a "hello" out of habit and etiquette, although it came out as a garbled groan.

From the other end came Anne's shrill. "Patricia, are you there?" She waited five seconds before saying, "I can't hear you." When I still didn't respond, she demanded, "If you are there answer me."

What the hell? I grunted.

She responded with, "I'm sure you are fine. Schedule an IEP team meeting immediately. Call Tanner's parents right now, and get them into school tomorrow. We need to make sure that you followed his IEP and that you didn't do something to trigger his behavior. This stuff happens because teachers—"

Ms. Martin, I assume that you are aware that an IEP is a legal document outlining individual programming for special needs students attending public schools. Part of my job is writing and implementing these important documents, so I know firsthand that they don't include allowing unprovoked assaults on teachers.

Anyway, I didn't finish listening to my reprimand. I handed the phone to the nurse. As she left the room she muttered a frustrated-sounding, "Goodbye" to Westbrook. I looked to Principal Anderson for words of wisdom.

"I could hear most of that." He shook his head in what I assumed was disgust. "I'm sending you home. Mike is in the front office waiting for you. First, get yourself to the hospital and have a doctor check you out. Then write out every detail of your day. I advise you to call your union attorney."

After experiencing a sensation akin to someone punching me in the chest, I found myself in the emergency room. The doctor positioned numerous pads and wires on my body and then connected me to an EKG machine. A few hours later, my friend Tina's husband, the emergency room nurse, Cody Smith, assured me that my heart was healthy, although my vocal cords were not.

Yesterday was the worst day of my life.

Patricia Anne Moore

…..…..*…..*

TO: PAMoore@gmail
FROM: Lmartin@PEA.com
SUBJECT: Re: Assaulted at work
DATE: October 6, 2019
Dear Patricia,

I appreciate your thorough account of the incident. However, I only need the details of what transpired in your classroom. I have attached a list of approved medical providers for your reference.

Please provide me a list of any other concerns you have about student and staff safety. My preliminary investigation indicates that Dr. Westbrook recently cut many of your resources. I will meet with Superintendent Mitchell and be in touch soon.

Sincerely,

Leigh Ann

Chapter 2

---

*"Get up, an' take my scarf, an' bandage
these bullet-holes I got."*

Zane Grey, *The Mysterious Rider*

October 17, 2019

Dear Diary,

You have been assigned the task of keeping my crazy at bay. Let me warn you, it won't be an easy undertaking. I'm a hot mess! Two weeks ago, I was knocked down and assaulted by one of my alternative education students, and I still have the damaged vocal cords to show for it.

Today, feeling annoyed, skeptical, and humiliated, I once again found myself lying on the ground. This time I was splayed out under a wooden signpost announcing the office of *Dr. Jacob Greene, Psy.D.* The gold-leafed nameplate hung between two brass hooks, and it swung back and forth in the breeze. It quivered and laughed, mocking my miserable existence.

I suppose I was both nervous and cursed because I tripped on the front stoop leading to my new psychotherapist's office. It was an epic slapstick style fall that resulted in a cracked cell phone, a scraped knee, and a humiliating ass-in-the-air view for the construction workers across the street. A string of profanity ending with a resounding, "You have got to be shitting me!" spewed forth as I stood, pulled down my skirt, picked up and examined my cell phone, chased down my water bottle, and looked over my shoulder at the street work going on behind me. At first, I felt relief that none of the men were paying attention. Since they hadn't seen my fall, they hadn't seen my exposed granny-pantied ass. Disappointment followed. Feeling my age, I realized that not one single man had noticed me. At least my screen-cracked cell phone still worked.

"Damn. If I'm going to spend this much time on the ground, I need new underwear," I told my non-existent audience.

Or, you could just wear pants, advised my shoulder angel.

From there, my day continued to deteriorate. Down. Down. Down, to the lowest layers of sediment in the sewage depository of my hometown of Maple Hall, it went.

"Patricia." A large man waved his hand in front of my face. The tone coming from the youthful mountain that sat across from me oozed annoyance. It was the same way I addressed my students when they played on their cell phones instead of paying attention to my lessons.

"Patricia, I'll ask you again, what brings you here?"

I sighed and tucked my dilapidated cell phone into my jacket pocket, rendering it inaccessible in the dark hideaway between my car keys and medicinal throat spray.

Since my guardian angel had been on a three-year vacation, it was entirely in line with my luck to get this way-too-young therapist. He didn't look much older than my students. Okay, that's an exaggeration, but he was younger than my baby brother Jimmy Junior, so how could he possibly have enough knowledge or experience to help me? I was in a snit, and I didn't like the doctor, or his age, one single bit!

Greene's office was close to my house, and his name was the first one on the Approved Provider Directory my union attorney had emailed. I should have done more research. Maybe I should have called the second or third, or perhaps the tenth name on the list. I think any number would have been a better choice, but the truth was, I hadn't put much time or effort into my search. In my defense, I had an excellent reason. I hadn't gotten out of bed much since my assault. Besides, I didn't need a therapist. All I required was a heavy narcotics prescription to dull my deluge of distressing emotions.

"What brings you here?" he asked for the third time.

"How old are you? You look too young to be a therapist." The shocking question, paired with my scratchy voice, made a grating combo.

His jaw clenched, and he practically growled, "How old are you?"

I suspect that was his way of letting me know he didn't appreciate my comment. It took every ounce of discipline I had not to stick my elderly tongue out and tell him to kiss my ancient ass. My fall had set me on edge. However, I wouldn't have been the picture of Pollyanna sweetness even if I hadn't exposed my hind end to the neighborhood, mostly because—I did not want to be there!

I leaned forward and narrowed my eyes. "I'm fifty." He wasn't going to intimidate me into confessing that I was having a midlife crisis on top of my other issues. I deflected with, "Did you even look at my paperwork? It took me twenty minutes to fill it out. If you weren't going to read it, why did I bother?"

I'm opinionated, a bit of a smart-ass, and I have issues with my filter, but I tend to have more etiquette than I was displaying at that moment. The problem was, my story was humiliating, and repeating it was emotionally and physically painful, and let me reiterate—I did not want to be there!

"I have your paperwork right here." He tapped the clipboard on his lap. "But, if I'm going to help you, you're going to need to communicate with me. If your throat hurts too much to talk, we can reschedule. If you are being obstinate, then we are finished."

His reprimand struck a chord, and I caved. Greene's blue eyes watched as my internal dam cracked and my mental rubbish spewed.

"My daughter went away to college this fall. My ex-husband has a girlfriend who is half his age. I'm exhausted. I lie in bed, but I can't sleep. A few years ago, I had an unsolicited assignment change. Now I teach at-risk kids in the Alternative Program. Some of my students have severe emotional problems, and a couple of them have police-issued ankle bracelets. Over the past few years, my resources have dwindled to a bare minimum. At the end of last school year, my supervisor slashed my budget again, and I lost my classroom aide." I briefly paused to rest my vocal cords and take a sip of water before blurting out the most dramatic part of my pronouncement. "Two weeks ago, one of my students tried to strangle me. He almost killed me because he wanted popcorn."

Dr. Greene's face was void of emotion. I itched to hand him emoji masks attached to popsicle sticks so that he could hold them in front of his blank expression.

Although I was annoyed by his lack of empathy, I continued with my saga. "I had to go to the school nurse. Then I ended up in the emergency room with heart palpitations. I had to have an EKG and stay overnight in the hospital. My heart is healthy, but I sustained damage to my vocal cords. My voice is just now returning. Although, as I indicated in my paperwork, it still hurts to talk."

I removed the scarf that I had loosely looped around my neck to reveal a thick greenish ring of bruising. Greene's eyes became baseball-sized as he lost his poker face. I replaced my scarf, and his emotionless visage returned.

"My general practitioner, Dr. Long, recommended a medical leave to allow my injuries time to heal. She thought it would also give the school time to deal with the student who attacked me. She insisted I talk to a therapist. I don't want to." I shrugged my shoulders. "But here I am."

Greene twisted his lips and rubbed the side of his nose.

I continued blabbing. "I feel helpless and terrified." I was trying to find the words to articulate what I was going through. My next statement thrust the dagger in my heart, emotionally finishing me off. "I thought all of my students, despite their issues, adored me."

Greene took a few more notes.

I finished my rambling with, "To make things worse, I have probably aged ten years since school started this fall."

"How long ago did you divorce?" Greene asked.

"We separated three years ago and finalized the divorce about two years ago."

He nodded and wrote something down. "Do you currently have a boyfriend?"

"What kind of question is that?" I frowned but answered. "No, and I'll probably never go on a date again."

I stopped my whining because my throat hurt, and I needed to do a mental brain slap. *Dating? WTF, Patti?*

"Patricia, you are an attractive, young-looking woman. I'm sure if you wanted to date—"

I interrupted his sentence with an indignant, "Seriously?"

I had poured my heart out to him, and his response was to bring up my appearance and divorce while I sat in front of him, vulnerable and bruised?

"Does a woman who is old-looking not deserve to date?" I asked.

He frowned and rubbed his temple.

"And why are you bringing up my appearance?"

Being an unhappy, physically assaulted, fifty-year-old school teacher spilling her guts to a thirty-something detached therapist fueled my *Go, girl* attitude. In retrospect, maybe I was trying to forget that either of us had made the humiliating dating reference?

"That isn't what I meant, and you are the one that brought up your appearance, not me," he snapped.

"No. I said I feel old. Besides, I'm the psycho behaving like a histrionic woman. Aren't you supposed to be the professional, calm voice of reason?" I'm unsure if I meant to insult his professionalism aloud, but I thought him a pompous ass, and at least my verbal diarrhea had made my feelings on the matter known.

He frowned, abused his clipboard with his pen, and asked, "Have you requested a transfer back to your original classroom?" Changing the subject alleviated some of the tension in the air.

I spent the next few minutes explaining that my supervisor denied my request to return to my old special education classroom. She responded with, "assaults are a possible risk of the job." I had contacted the police and was pressing charges. This didn't sit well with my boss, and I had landed myself Grand Poobah of the Bad Teacher List.

I felt screwed all around. My only allies were Dr. Mary Long, my union attorney, my friends Missy and Valentina, and my dog. My psychotherapist had fast-tracked himself to my foe list. It now read *P's Enemies: Evil Anne Westbrook, The Ex and his girlfriend Shelly the bimbo, T. Jones, Guardian Angel, and The Shrink.*

"Sometimes, it helps to make a list of things you are grateful for. Tell me something good that happened to you this week?" the green Greene said.

A sixteen-year-old punk had tried to murder me, I had temporarily lost my voice, I was terrified that I might never earn another paycheck, I had just cracked my cell phone, and he wanted to know something good that had happened to me? That would require a heaping dose of optimism because I was anxious about returning to work, I was divorced and lonely, my daughter was away at her freshman year of college, and I missed her so much it hurt. To top it all off, after my attack, I felt like I had aged at warp speed. My life was in the toilet.

After some thought, I responded, "My dog, Zoomie, loves me." The comment sounded uncertain and more like a question.

Then I recalled the moment of joy I felt at discovering my grandfather's memorabilia in the basement. It had been like finding a treasure chest of jewels in the midst of a never-ending turbulent voyage. It was a glimmer of golden light in the darkness that was shrouding my life. Ha! Most importantly, it was something positive I could share with my probing inquisitor. I simply needed to dig deep and find the strength to talk a little longer.

I conjured forth my last bit of energy and shared my cherished discovery with Greene, adding, "My grandfather's story is fascinating. He was a radio operator on a B-17 during World War II."

The doctor's arrogance had slightly subsided, so I took a swig of water, swallowed two squirts of my doctor prescribed Vocal Eze throat spray, and settled into Ms. Moore's Storytelling Mode.

I told him an abbreviated version of the night my grandfather parachuted into enemy territory and his injured spirit wandered home to gather strength from his parents. I searched my doctor's face for signs of emotion. Being a teacher, I prided myself on my ability to tell a captivating tale, and this true story was close to my heart. It had been handed down in family lore for almost eighty years and had fascinated many a listener. By his steady gaze, I could tell I had his rapt attention, but he still showed little sentiment. I'm not sure he even appreciated the effort it had taken for me to ignore my aching throat. I concluded that Dr. Jacob Greene was utterly callous.

Our forty-five minutes of banter had come to an end. My story left him unmoved. I had behaved like a crazy woman, and he had been an impatient jerk. He recommended I journal and breathe, leaving me far from fixed. I remained terrified to return to a classroom in which my assailant would sit across from me, smiling menacingly. I was still angry, lonely, confused, and lost. I was every horrible human emotion rolled into one middle-aged enchilada.

I did the only thing I could. I made an appointment for the following Thursday.

Augh!

Patti

…..…..*…..*

October 17, 2019

Dear Diary,

It is close to midnight, and I can't sleep. So...

After my stressful session with the testy therapist, I needed a drink at my favorite watering hole. I needed the good stuff—hazelnut coffee with extra cream and a low-fat brownie. Maybe because I wanted it to be true, Tina, my best friend and owner of the local coffee shop, convinced me that a low-fat brownie was a guilt-free treat.

Tina's name is Valentina Perez-Smith. She shortened her name to Tina when she moved to the United States from the Dominican Republic. Interestingly, Tina was one of my students almost two decades ago. She had been a fiery, creative, and intelligent teenager. Not much has changed over the years. Tall, beautiful, and curvy, with her long black hair, cocoa-colored skin, and big brown eyes, she had captured the attention of almost every man in town. She chose to marry Cody Smith, the local high school football star who had gone to nursing school. He became a full-time nurse in the cardiac unit at East City Hospital and a part-time handyman/barista at his wife's charming storefront coffee house located a block from my house.

Most days, I find Valentina's Cup to be a godsend. As an awesome perk—ha ha—my dog is always welcome to be my coffee date.

Zoomie is a trained service dog. In the good old days, he visited my classroom on Friday mornings. Two years ago, the school newspaper columnist did a short feature on him in early spring, and by late spring, Evil Anne, in her attempt to bring misery and despair to everything she touched, mandated that he could no longer visit. The students started a Bring Zoomie Back to East City High petition. Although the mini protest made the evening news, it didn't change Westbrook's decision. Unfortunately, it only served to add another slash to her Punish Patti List. Tina has been kind enough to allow Zoomie to keep his social skills sharp, as long as he wears his official purple vest and doesn't enter her kitchen.

Sandwiched between the hardware store and an art studio, the coffee shop showcases a seasonal exhibit in its bay window. The fall display consists of colorful herbs and a cornucopia filled with tiny pumpkins and squash strategically lit by the vintage crystal chandelier. Today's pastry case held chocolate chip muffins, cinnamon scones, Rice Krispies Treats, and the legendary low-fat brownies. The self-serve coffee bar choices of the day were dark roast and hazelnut. Good thing, because at least something went right in my crap-ass day.

My job as best friend to the owner, regular occupant of one of the wingbacks, lover of literature, and resident school teacher is to keep the built-in shelving units stocked with interesting books. I've amassed close to eighty titles over the past few years, and I created a special shelf titled *Ms. M's Picks of the Month.* Since my passion for everything seems to have withered, my prized display reads *August* in mid-October. Therefore, *Of Human Bondage, I Know Why the Caged Bird Sings,* and *A Prayer for Owen Meany* have sat on those shelves for over two months.

My best friend yawned and plopped into the wingback next to Zoomie and me. "How did therapy go?"

"Oh, Tina, I hated it! I hate feeling this weak and scared."

She yawned again, then rubbed at her eyes. "Did he give you any advice? Say anything to help you?"

"Not really. He told me to keep a journal. Anytime I'm feeling anxious, I'm to take deep breaths and write. Hell, I could've told myself that."

"I'm sorry, Patti! I really am. Just give this guy a chance. Okay?" Tina paused to wait for my response. When I didn't say anything, she repeated herself. "Give him a chance. Seriously, si?"

I sighed and then told her what she wanted to hear. "Okay. But he seems too young to be a doctor."

"How old is he?"

I thought for a moment and then replied, "I would guess in his early thirties?"

She scrunched up her nose. "What are you talking about? Thirty isn't too young. Oh, wait a minute." Then came her deep chuckle. "Is he good looking?"

I needed a moment to mull this over. "I don't know. Maybe?"

Chelsea, the klutzy coffee barista, demonstrated perfect timing, rescuing me from further interrogation when she dropped a cup. The contents splattered across the floor, and the cup smashed into a dozen pieces.

"Shit! Not again." When she was angry, my friend's accent crept back into her voice. "¡Maldita tonita," she yelled in Chelsea's direction. Then Tina's frown turned into a smile as she walked away, taunting me with, "Patti's shrink is hot! Patti's shrink is hot!"

I shot Tina a middle finger.

She stopped, turned around, and walked back to me. "Hey, chica. You've always had a 'tude, then a couple of years ago, you got wimpy. Now you are just—" She thought for a moment. "Como una perra." Then she smiled at me, blew me a kiss, and belted out in a sing-songy voice, "Patti's bitchy, and her shrink is hot!"

I protested by sticking my middle-aged tongue out at her. I leaned over to confide in Zoomie. "Mommy needs new friends."

Perhaps what I am most frustrated about is, maybe Greene is attractive, and I'm pretty sure my hormones dried up a few years ago.

Unlucky,
Patti

..........*.....*

The East City High Gazette Spring 2017 Edition
Student of the Month
written by Angelica Diaz

Meet East City High's shortest student, Zoomie. Zoomie is a Shetland Sheepdog who has been attending Ms. Moore's English classes on Fridays for the past four years. He enjoys listening to students read. Ms. Moore says his favorite selection is *Beowulf.* Zoomie is a graduate of the esteemed East Branch Service Dog School. When he isn't in class, he enjoys terrorizing squirrels, running 5ks and 10ks with Ms. Moore, playing catch with his flippy flopper, and napping. Freshman Diamond Washington states, "Zoomie is my bud. After he listens to me read, I give him a belly rub and a treat. Fridays are the best day of the week."

..........*.....*

National Small Town Living Magazine: Fall 2018 Anniversary Issue.
America's Iconic Timepieces
written by Alicia Bender

A symbol of pride, the cast iron timepiece that stands in the center of the community park in Maple Hall, Pennsylvania, is one hundred forty years old and symbolizes the town's nostalgic charm. The magnificent four-faced clock stands almost twenty feet tall, sits on a three-tiered pedestal, and is a Mother-Nature-friendly shade of green. In 1976, during the country's bicentennial birthday, the clock had its insides replaced with electric wiring.

Leonard Writestone, the owner of Writestone's Clock Repair, says that his grandfather built the clock in 1878. Writestone states, "Throughout history, public clocks have been the personality of a community. They provide a place to gather and a sense of commonality. Every day at noon, everyone in town stops and listens to the same chiming bells. What could be more grounding and civic?"

The borough of Maple Hall is home to seven thousand inhabitants and boasts a rich history. In 1735 its Great Road became a public pass open to travelers. A few of the original buildings still exist, impeccably maintained. The borough website opens with the story of a 1775 Revolutionary War general quartering his troops in the fields that are now tree-lined neighborhoods. Ten paces from the clock is a marker that sits between the hot pink spring azaleas and the powder blue summer hydrangeas, indicating this spot was the northernmost point of the Battle of Gettysburg. Union Troops camped where there is now a town square and community park. A second marker, smaller but no less important, indicates that the town was incorporated as a borough in November of 1885. To the south of the grand clock sits an ivory lattice gazebo. The lovely pavilion is the perfect location for a picnic in the park, a picturesque prom photo, or a sweet kiss between lovers.

Except for the newest-model Mercedes and Beamers, Maple Hall's main street looks like a 1950s postcard. Like most small-town main streets in Central Pennsylvania, the vista includes a coffee shop, pizza parlor, hardware store, hair salon, bank, a few small art studios, and that iconic movie theater built in the 1920s.

Many borough residents have a deep connection to the town. Born in Maple Hall, educator Patricia Moore recalls that as a child, she spent lazy summer afternoons reading in the shade the elegant timepiece provided. Patricia's daughter is the fourth generation of her family to both admire the clock and reside in their century-old Colonial. Patricia recalls how her family came to call Cedar Crest home. "The massive bridge that connects my little town to Harrisburg, Pennsylvania's capital city, is a historic landmark. Italian immigrants built the masterpiece at the turn of the twentieth century, and it just so happens that my father's grandfather was one of the masons. In 1959, after teaching middle school English in Western Pennsylvania, my maternal grandfather, a war hero, acquired a job at the local Navy Depot. At this time, my mother's family bought the home where my daughter and I still reside."

Next time you travel through Central Pennsylvania, be sure to check out this quaint town with its proud residents and charming clock.

Chapter 3

"Words mean more than what is set down on paper. It takes the human voice to infuse them with shades of deeper meaning."

Maya Angelou, *I Know Why the Caged Bird Sings*

October 18, 2019

Dear Diary,

Wait until you hear about the mortification I experienced this afternoon. I suppose God didn't think almost dying in front of an entire high school was an embarrassing enough punishment for whatever sins I have accrued in this life. He saw it fit to have a horrifically gory World War III erupt in my underwear today in front of total strangers.

First of all, I would have been content to stay in bed all day, but Tina insisted I "get my shit together and stop feeling sorry for myself." Some friend she is! Then my freaking period appeared out of nowhere. I was drinking a cup of coffee at Valentina's when I got the icky sensation that my running skort was sopping wet. I ran to the restroom to examine myself, and my sad state was revealed. I had heavily bled through my old lady panties and my favorite navy skort.

"You've got to be shitting me?" I berated my aggravating, ancient uterus.

I scrubbed the blood from between my thighs and took a paper towel from under the sink to sop the liquid from the crotch of my skort. Bereft of supplies that might stop the unholy flow, I made a makeshift pad by folding a piece of toilet paper and shoving it into my underwear. I figured it would have to do until I got home.

Taking a deep breath, I made my way back to the scene of the bloodbath, where I ran headfirst into a bespeckled gentleman staring at a Hansel-and-Gretel-style trail of blood leading from my wingback to the bathroom.

"Hey, are you okay? I think you're bleeding," he hollered to Saturn's farthest moon.

Humiliated, I studied the repulsive drips that started at one end of the shop and ended at my crimson-stained ankle. I searched for a way out that didn't involve disclosing perimenopausal horrors to a stranger.

"Um, I cut my ankle," I answered.

"You cut your ankle? On what?" He looked around for the offending object.

"On a sharp table leg," I replied.

I should have known better than to tell a man there was a home improvement project lurking about, because my knight in shining armor scoured the room. "Which table?"

"Um, that one." I pointed at an innocent table that sat close to the start of my sticky trail.

"That needs to be fixed. Those table legs can be dangerous," he declared, having found his life's purpose.

As Sir Galahad the Bespeckled inspected the lethal leg, Cody and an elderly bearded man joined him.

"There's a sharp edge on this table that cut that poor woman. She's bleeding all over the place. It needs fixed right away," announced my protector.

"The problem is, I can't seem to find it," Sir Galahad the Bespeckled confessed to his brave brothers in arms.

The three of them conversed in life-or-death tones. Since they displayed the furrowed brows and hunched shoulders of defeated warriors, I realized they needed assistance in solving their dilemma and saving the damsel in distress.

"It's right there," I accused the perfectly smooth leg.

While they saved the world, I grabbed paper towels and Lysol and tried to mop up my disgrace. Tina watched in horror as The Knights of the Round Table turned her lovely piece of furniture upside down and then slid their hands along its wooden appendages in close examination.

A thrilled Sir Bedivere the Bearded raised his hand into the air in triumph. "I found it."

I grimaced.

Excited, because he was about to dig out his beloved toys, Cody ran to retrieve his ginormous Craftsman toolbox.

I cornered my friend behind the counter. "Tina, I got my period, and I made a mess. I told that man I cut my ankle on the table leg. Obviously, I didn't. The table is fine," I whispered.

Tina leaned on the counter to hold herself upright as guffaws rocketed her body.

"Some friend you are. Wait until you're fifty and get these disgusting heavy periods," I snapped.

She ignored me and continued laughing until tears dripped from her eyes.

Eventually Tina joined her husband, Sir Cody-Gwain, and his new comrades. She dramatically told tales about all of the innocents who had almost lost limbs falling victim to the treacherous table.

Let me say—I did not appreciate her pleasure at my expense.

Finally, proud as peacocks, the three men turned the table upright on all fours.

Sir Galahad the Bespeckled called out, "It's fixed, Miss. It should never give you trouble again."

I uttered, "Thank you," right before I sprinted to the exit so that I could die in private.

I spent the early evening trying to shake off my degradation by returning texts to my daughter and my work friend, Missy McMann. The kids at school refer to Missy as Ms. M&M. She and I started our teaching careers at East City High in 1989. She teaches Algebra and Geometry, and her students love her. She is as round as Henrietta Hippo and as jolly as Old Saint Nick. She has one of those contagious laughs, and I have always been envious of her infinite energy. She never married because she spends twelve hours a day living and breathing school, four hours a week drinking whiskey and line dancing at Charly's Place, and the summers riding her Harley cross country.

I considered sharing my horrific bloody afternoon with Missy, but Valentina's mirth was more than I could handle. Missy's would push me over the edge. Instead, I buried my nose in the Kindle edition of *I Know Why the Caged Bird Sings,* occasionally calling out to the author as if she was sitting in my living room beside me.

My "I feel you, Maya! Girlfriend, it sucks when you can't get your words out" was met with exuberant Sheltie kisses. As usual, my furry sidekick shared my literary enthusiasm.

Maybe Maya would be more sensitive to my period-stained mishaps than my current gal pals. Perhaps she would be my friend. Lord knows I was desperate and lonely and in need of a few.

My humiliation did expose an important universal truth to me. I can say for certain that God is a man, because a female deity would never have played such a cruel, inhumane joke on an already pathetic woman.

One more thing, I'm pretty sure Cassie loves her dad more.

Lonely,
Patti

..........*.....*

October 18th

Missy: Hey, GF. How are u? Been so worried. That kid is nuts!

P: Hi, Missy. I'm hanging in there. My voice isn't 100% yet. Tanner is nuts!

Missy: Let me know if u want to get a cup of coffee or lunch. Love to meet u at the coffee shop near your house.

Cassie: Mom-does it matter if I mix my whites and colors in the washer?

P: Sounds good. I'll keep in touch. Gotta go talk to Cassie about her laundry.

Missy: Take care, GF. I'm here if u need me.

Cassie: Hey, Mom! U there? I need underwear!

P: Was finishing a text to Missy.

Cassie: Tell her I said hi and never mind. Dad said it doesn't matter if you mix laundry.
Cassie: How was your shrink apt? How crazy are you? 😄

P: Insanely crazy! My shrink is an arrogant ass, and your dad doesn't know the first thing about laundry!

Cassie: lol. My roommate stinks! Bad! Do you think I can ask for a new one? Who do I ask?

P: Are you sure it isn't your laundry? 😄 and idk

Cassie: Dad says I should ask. He sent me the number to call.

P: Make sure it isn't his girlfriend's number. He tends to write it down on everything.

Cassie: Ha, Ha, Mom. Bitter much? By the way, my professor loved my family piece about Great Grandpa. Got an A++++

P: Grandma Susan and Uncle Jimmy also loved it.

Cassie: So glad! Please stay safe! Gotta go. I love you! ♥

P: I love you more! ♥♥

Cassie: I love you the most. ♥♥♥

Chapter 4

"If history were taught in the form of stories, it would never be forgotten."

Rudyard Kipling, *In Black and White*

October 19, 2019

Dear Diary,

When my alarm went off this morning, I whimpered and muttered an emphatic, "No!" I was complaining to myself, but Zoomie heard and responded to my moans of laziness. He leaped onto my head and planted a huge, wet kiss on my lips. His eyes, wide with excitement, studied me, then he licked my entire face.

I placed a good morning kiss on the white stripe running through the center of his long nose and said, "It's a good thing I love you, bud, cause you have way too much energy in the morning. Let's stay in bed today?"

Lying in bed has become my favorite pastime. I have accomplished millions of things from under my blankets. I have scratched my annoyed Shetland Sheepdog while telling him walkies, fetch, and squirrels are overrated. I have daydreamed about the punishments I will dole out to adolescents who try to kill me. I have planned cheap meals since I no longer have a paycheck. Ramen noodles three times a day is one of my most ingenious plans ever!

Zoomie was having none of my excuses or my depressed seclusion in bed. He had had enough, and there was no arguing with him. He jumped up and down on my bosom until I separated my ass from my mattress. Then he poked his long nose into the back of my knees, herding me down the stairs.

My smart Sheltie was correct! The warm sun peeking through the living room draperies was life-affirming. Drinking coffee in my flannel PJs and bunny slippers was heavenly. It was way better than staring at the backside of my blanket. Let me back up for a moment. I don't actually have bunny slippers. I own a bedraggled pair of mismatched fuzzy socks, but I've always wanted a pair of bunnies.

As the rays reflected off Zoomie's majestic white mane and dappled his marbled grey, black, and silver coat, my pup and I made our plan for the day. We were going to spend time going through my grandfather's files. I aimed for the lofty additional goals of tidy hair and clean teeth. I didn't need fresh clothes because my PJs were the perfect attire for my seclusion in the basement corner.

While brushing my hair, I unhappily studied my reflection. The deep crevices setting in on my forehead overshadowed my green eyes, and the gray army had begun its march across my temple. I grabbed my can of L'Oreal red root spray and attacked those relentless soldiers. I forced a fake smile for the mirror as I attempted to capture a youthful look. For a split second, I did. If only I could find more to smile about. I tilted my head down, and the sagging skin under my chin disappeared. I considered spending the rest of my life with my head held at that perfect angle. Then my eyes settled on the line of hellish, now yellowish bruises encircling my neck. I sighed. It was one of those moments when I understood why some women reach for Botox or a facelift in their middle years.

The current politically correct craze is body positivity. I struggle to embrace it. But today, I tried. "Darling, you look fabulous for your age," I told my image. Practicing positive affirmations isn't my thing, so embracing and loving my appearance isn't happening anytime soon. I snickered at my attempt and invited Zoomie to head to the basement with me.

I'd been looking forward to digging into the documents and old cassettes. My grandfather had carefully labeled each of the tapes with a date. I no longer owned a cassette player, so while sitting beside my ex in the emergency room, I had sent him a text to ask if he still had one. When I explained why I needed it, he confessed he had found the files years ago. He had meant to tell me but kept forgetting. He also reminded me that my cell phone contained a flashlight, so I didn't have to navigate the house in the dark when I blew the fuse. Lucky for him, I couldn't engage in a verbal takedown without a voice. Instead, seated three feet from me, he received an angrily texted frowny face emoji. At least he loaned me the tape player. He had the device with him the following day when he picked me up from the hospital. I guess he felt guilty about his twenty years of forgetfulness. I suspect it was also his way of looking out for me in my time of need.

Okay. Enough complaining about Mike—for now. On to more positive things, such as my grandparents. I have such warm nostalgic memories of them.

My grandparents met in their small hometown of Burnside in Western Pennsylvania. My grandfather delighted in telling his love-at-first-sight story. He played piano at one of the local clubs and saw my grandmother sitting with her sister, my Great-aunt Dot. He thought Grandma was the most beautiful woman he'd ever seen, so he asked her to dance. She handed him a comb, telling him he needed to fix his hair first. My grandfather was immediately smitten. Soon after the war they married, and he devoted the rest of his life to making my grandmother happy.

He never did gain control over his thick locks. They remained incorrigible and at almost ninety years of age, my handsome grandfather still had a luscious head of hair. I can still see him, standing in front of the mirror, slicking back his hair and loudly singing, "Brylcreem—a little dab'll do ya. Brylcreem—you look so debonair. Brylcreem—the girls will all pursue ya. They love to get their fingers in your hair."

Living in my grandparent's house has kept these memories alive. Forty-year-old images of my grandfather sitting in the living room watching John Wayne movies and Pittsburgh Pirates games are as real as if they happened yesterday. I can see every detail of my tiny grandmother, in her red pants and polka dot shirt, sitting on the front porch behind the stack of newspapers she read from beginning to end. Even though my memories have remained intact, the sound of their voices is much more difficult to recall, making the discovery of my grandfather's tapes all the more emotional.

Zoomie sat beside me as I made myself comfortable beside the cabinet. I considered carrying everything upstairs to the couch but decided against it. Maybe it was impatience, or perhaps I didn't want to move them from the place that my grandfather had left them. I suspect it was a little of both. Plus, for some reason, that particular spot made me feel closer to Pap.

My grandfather's voice, with its slow cadence, raspy from cigarettes, deep and clipped, warmly emanated from the recorder. Occasionally I could hear a "ppht," the sound he made as he spit out the tobacco from his unfiltered Pall Malls. Before he started his entry, he introduced himself with his characteristic greeting, adding a long-drawn-out "o" and then abruptly placing his "p." His hello was never dull.

After weeks of gray days, today I saw brilliant colors. I sat beside my dog, on an uncomfortable floor, in the corner of a dusty furnace room, with an old tape recorder I borrowed from my ex-husband, and once again listened to my grandfather weave tales and paint rainbows.

Touched,
Patti

…..…..*…..*

Recorded by Robert Stauffer I, TSgt on October 17, 1972
Transcribed by Patricia Moore
Helloop Contraption,

Last week when the whistle from the firehouse down the street went off, I drove under the kitchen table like a damnable fool. It took me a minute to collect myself, and I was glad that Marty wasn't in the room. Last time it upset her, and she decided we needed to have soundproof windows installed. It took weeks to convince her that the cheap plastic was a bad idea.

The nightmares have also come back. The Veterans Affairs doc told me that when these things happen, I should find ways to relax. I've been tryin' to listen to the hypnosis tapes that he suggested, but I don't think they do a damn thing other than annoy me. He also told me to write in a journal. That'd be great if I had a right hand to write with. Marty's my scrawling digits these days, and I don't want her exposed to these stories. I did all of those left-handed dexterity exercises after the war, and before I retired, I could type slow but decent on the typewriter. The problem is, I'm gettin' slower and more labored as the arthritis sets in. So, here I am talkin' into this goddamn tape recorder. A doctor tellin' you to listen to hypnosis tapes after you have blown up innocent civilians, and write in a journal when you haven't got a goddamn right hand, isn't worth two hoots and the dime spent on him.

Anywho, I've been ponderin' those years before the war. I knew that Pop and Sarah would be proud if I went to college like my older siblings. Unfortunately, the Depression had temporarily put my dreams of becomin' a teacher on hold.

I still recollect all the job hopping. Times were tough, and I took work wherever I could get it. There was railroad work, pipeline construction, waitin' tables in a restaurant, workin' on an electrical line, and whatever other odd jobs I could find. My last job before I left for the front was with the Civilian Conservation Corps, chef-in' at a lumber camp. I was so desperate for work that when I was told that the only job they had left was as the camp cook, I said, "What luck, I'm a damn fine chef de cuisine!" Nothing teaches you to boil potatoes faster than starvin' loggers that would just soon as eat you than go hungry. Over the months, I grew tired of their incessant bitchin' about what we served. There was a war going on. They were lucky to have any food in their bellies.

Those were tough times, doin' whatever I could for a bite and a bed. I wouldn't trade them, though, because I had my hopes and dreams. I knew that somehow I was gonna save up enough money and get that sheepskin. I also had my piano playin' gigs. I'd play wherever I could and whatever type of music I could. One of the bars I played in had this beautiful old player piano with a stained glass front and a rich cherry lid. The sound wasn't as good as my baby grand, but she was a fine old machine. I miss those days.

Lately, I've been thinkin' about Sarah. She was a damn good mom. I also miss Pop, Abe, William, Elizabeth, Gerti, and Margaret. I really miss Margaret. Since she was the oldest, and the one that helped to take care of me when I was a sickly pup, she has always had a special place in my heart. Her life was too short, too tragic, and too riddled with loss.

Damn, I miss everything! I miss Burnside and being young, and having two damn hands to play the piano with. I even miss the lumber camp, with its tiny living quarters and the endless dishes, and damn if I don't miss cookin' shit on a shingle for the bitchin' lumberjacks.

What I don't miss is being cold and hungry. More than anything, I wish I could forget that damn freezin' cold war. The last time I truly felt warm was a hot sticky night in July of '42 when I met my older brother William by

Burnside's decrepit train station. I asked him to meet me there so we could talk without Pop and Sarah overhearin' us. I wasn't ready to tell them that the thirty-five dollars a month I was sending them wouldn't be coming in. And I surely wasn't prepared to tell them I was goin' overseas. *Hell,* I told myself, maybe they'd understand. I could just tell them it might be safer to be in Germany than servin' shitty grub to large, angry loggers. The camp was closin' anyway cause most of the men were bein' drafted to go overseas. Good brother that he was, William promised to help break the news to the family and look out for Marty.

There was a popular saying around town, "If you want three square meals a day, and a bed, join the Air Force." The infantry was associated with mud and sleepin' in tents. I wanted to do my part for my country, and I wanted to fly, so I decided to enlist. A kid at the camp was only sixteen, and he'd forged his records so that he could do his part. If a young pup like him could face his fears and bravely fight, so could I. I got word soon after I returned—I guess that was about the summer of '46—that the kid didn't make it. Broke my heart. Damn nice kid. He never bitched about what I served him.

There, Doc, I talked into this contraption, and I don't feel one iota better. And, for the record, the Nazi bastards were way worse than hungry loggers.

Yada, yada, yada.

Chapter 5

"I define manhood simply: men should be tough, fair, and courageous, never petty, never looking for a fight, but never backing down from one either."

John Wayne

October 20, 2019

Dear Diary,

Yesterday, after listening to Pap's tapes, I became lost in memories of a double date Mike and I had gone on with my grandparents. We had ventured to the local dinner theatre to see a matinee of *Damn Yankees*. I remember how excited Pap was when Grandma came down the staircase wearing a pretty cream-colored blouse. Perfect pin curls adorned her head, and a glamorous shade of red lipstick coated her lips. As soon as she reached the landing, my six-foot pap leaned over and smooched my five-foot, two-inch grandma on the cheek.

Mike and I also told her how gorgeous she looked.

"Still the prettiest filly in the room," said my infatuated grandfather.

As a child, I had never understood John Wayne's appeal, but Pap idolized The Duke. He had watched and read his fill of old Westerns, and the expressions filtered through his speech, along with an occasional British accent—just because Pap liked the Cockney sound—Western Pennsylvanian colloquialisms, and mountain man sayings.

The unique combination, along with his quick wit, were the qualities that made my grandfather such a captivating storyteller.

My seventy-year-old grandmother waved her hand, shooing him away. "For Christ's sake, Bob! Show some restraint in front of the kids."

That made me smile. Mike and I were in our late twenties and hardly kids anymore.

My quiet reverie was disturbed when Zoomie ran toward the stairs barking. I jumped, and a sharp thumping sensation in my chest made it difficult to catch my breath. I reminded myself that my recent emergency room visit had indicated my heart was healthy. I needed to fight both my anxiety attacks and my hypochondriac tendencies. Once I was calm, I realized my doorbell was ringing.

"Shhh, Zoomie. Mommy has become way too jumpy. You don't want to give me a heart attack, do you?" Zoomie ignored me and continued his job as my barking security system

By the time I reached the front door, I was panting. At first, I didn't recognize the police officer assigned to my case because instead of wearing his uniform, he wore jeans and a tan sweater.

He studied his sneakered feet before his eyes traveled to take in my striped lime-blue right foot and my neon orange and pink polka-dotted left foot, then slowly shifted upward to settle on my face. After an awkward silence, he greeted me. "Hi, Ms. Moore."

My panicky feeling from moments before returned as terrifying things went through my mind. *Is something wrong? Are the police going to side with my crazy Student Services Supervisor and not allow me to press charges?*

"Hi, Officer Harris. Is everything okay with my case?" I asked.

"Yeah," he said. "You should get a letter from the magistrate about the hearing soon."

I studied the awkwardly shuffling officer, wondering why he was standing at my front door.

"Well, Patricia," his "Ms. Moore" had morphed into "Patricia," so I knew something was up. Nervously stuttering, he continued, "I was wondering, would you want to go grab a cup of coffee with me? There is a coffee shop down the street. Seems like you've been through a pretty tough time, and I thought we could maybe talk or something. If you want?"

I was a fifty-year-old divorcee attired in flannel PJs and threadbare socks that I pretended were bunny slippers, and the cop assigned to my case had just asked me out on a date. I wondered if there was some sort of law against cops and civilians dating. I considered that he might be one of those corrupt officers that took drugs and money out of the evidence locker right before asking out unsuspecting assault victims. I spent quite a bit of brainpower trying to decide what to do. He was attractive in that I'm-almost-a-middle-aged-dad kind of way. He had soft blue eyes behind his glasses, and he had a sweet smile. I confess, his nervous blush made him endearing. Besides, I liked that he was younger than me, maybe in his early forties—and my ex was dating—and my therapist was arrogant, and I didn't have anything better to do, so I answered him.

"Sure, Officer Harris. A cup of coffee sounds great, but I'm in the middle of something right now. How about tomorrow afternoon? And how about we go to a bakery over in the city?"

No way am I going to Valentina's Cup. The last thing I need is Tina in my business, asking me questions about this. The bakery is about twenty minutes away, so, hopefully, I won't see anyone I know.

Holy shit! I have a date!

Patti

…..…..*…..*

October 21st

P: Hi, kiddo! Guess what? Your mom has a date

Cassie: OMG! Who? The Shrink? My mom is dating her shrink??

P: The Shrink? What? No!!!! Why would you mention the shrink? The cop on my case.

Cassie: A donut eater? 🍩 So, the shrink is hot?
Cassie: BTW, I think it's great you have a date with the cop. Where are you going?

P: Why would you think my shrink is hot? Deckers, in the city, for a cup of coffee and dessert.

Cassie: You just answered my question. What are you wearing? Please don't wear that old blue sweater!

P: Why? What's wrong with the blue sweater? It's pretty.

Cassie: Mom, you always wear that. It isn't sexy. Wear the green blouse. Leave the top button undone. It shows off your boobs better.

P: 😳

Cassie: Have fun, Mom! ♥ Don't do anything I wouldn't do.

P: The doorbell just rang. Help!!!!

Cassie: Woohoo!

Chapter 6

"But, what is the black spot, captain?"

Robert Louis Stevenson, *Treasure Island*

October 22, 2019

Dear Diary,

Attire the grim reaper in a designer suit, plop a blond bob on his bare skull, then coat with layers of red lipstick, and you will know my horror. Dr. Anne Westbrook slashes budgets, programs, staff, and the human will with the flick of her bony wrist. I had considered asking my real doctor, or my shrink doctor, to get me out of the meeting. I knew it would be confrontational and consequently detrimental to my delicate emotional state. In the end, though, I decided to be brave and face my vicious enemy head-on.

Today I waited in the Wicked Witch's office. She was late—as usual. I watched the clock, sent a text to my daughter, then typed my short grocery list into my decrepit phone. I itched to check Mike's social media feed, chock-full of smiling workout selfies with contracted biceps. Somehow, I found the strength to boycott my childish whim.

It was not the first time I had sat in that office, waiting for Anne Westbrook. Three years ago, when she first arrived in Harrisburg, I made a social call to introduce myself and welcome her to the East City School District family. I went out of my way, even taking her a cup of coffee and a muffin from Valentina's. She had turned green, then stared at my offering with all of the graciousness of a hungover sorority girl eyeballing a shrimp cocktail. It was coffee and a muffin, for crying out loud, not a raw crustacean. I politely ignored her displeasure and explained that as one of the senior teachers at the high school, I was at her service. She told me she was busy and practically threw me out of her space. One week later, she sentenced me to the basement of the school. When I tried to stand up for myself, I found myself drowning in paperwork. After that, every communication with her resulted in another punishment. From there, my professional life had deteriorated. Jump forward a few years, and I had gained a few wrinkles, pounds, and gray hairs. I had lost a husband and my zest for life. And, according to Valentina, I had become wimpy, then bitchy. One thing had stayed the same: my supervisor still ran absurdly late. How was it that Westbrook, with her important title, refused to adhere to a schedule?

Restless and bored, I became increasingly fidgety. The next thing I knew, I had knocked my water bottle over. It sputtered and spat onto the massive, disorganized desk at the same moment that I felt an evil presence. Dr. Anne Westbrook had arrived.

There she stood, her fake blond hair, and her perfectly tailored suit, and her bitchy expression. Today she wore a disturbing shade of blood on her lips and smelled like cheap fermented body spray.

She held out her hand. "Hi, Patricia. Thank you for meeting me." She hadn't yet noticed my mini mess.

Thank you, my ass, you icy incompetent bitch! is what I was thinking. "Hello, Dr. Westbrook," is what I said as I tried to wipe away the rogue water droplets that threatened the haphazard piles of papers.

Taking notice of my spill, she scowled. She rummaged through the folders on her desk. Finally, she found the one she was looking for and held up a copy of my doctor's note. "I see that Dr. Mary Long has requested a six-week leave." She shuffled through what appeared to be my personnel file. "And, at the end of that time, she will reevaluate you to see if you are ready to return to work."

Westbrook's intense glower distorted and elongated her already harsh features. I wondered if she practiced her grimaces in the mirror. Picturing her daily scowls, growls, and evil-eye pantomime, I had to stifle a laugh. Of course, she would need some extra practice to counteract the effects of too many Botox injections. A giggle escaped, and I covered my mouth.

She sent another fiendish look my way. "I understand you had a nervous breakdown at work. This is most unfortunate. You know, we don't have anyone to teach that class while you're out. Right now, there is a different substitute every day. Inconsistency isn't good for at-risk students."

My desire to giggle flung itself out the window, and I struggled to take in air. I wanted to ask, *If they're so important to you, why have you relegated them to a basement with no services?* Since it was not the time to have one of my Freudian slips, I summoned my smart-ass filter and composed myself. "You were misinformed. I didn't have a nervous breakdown. As the school nurse explained, I went to the emergency room to have my heart checked, and I had significant damage to my vocal cords from being strangled." My voice remained raspy, and it was apparent I still struggled to talk. "I'm sorry for the inconvenience, but it's what my doctor thinks is best. After all, a student physically assaulted me, and you ignored it." I emphasized the word *you* and added, "And I suppose it's impossible to keep a substitute in that crazy classroom."

My overtaxed filter had failed.

Oh, well.

"You are a teacher and dealing with students with mental health issues is part of your job." She stopped and gave me a predatory snarl before continuing. "It's my understanding that you plan to press charges against a sixteen-year-old. You know this is against the school's recommendation and violates our confidentiality policy?"

The absurdity was, if the school had handled the discipline issue, I wouldn't have had to go to the police for protection. Even more absurd, if Tanner had been receiving the mental health services he required, the incident might never have happened. Crazier still, if my classroom assistant hadn't been an Anne-casualty, an additional adult in the classroom might have defused the incident before it kaboomed. Besides, it in no way violated confidentiality as long as I didn't bring up the specifics of his IEP.

I liked it better when I had found her nastiness humorous. Anger boiled in the pit of my stomach. Fury reached my cheeks and threatened to explode from the top of my head. I held my tongue and changed the subject. "Have you received my request to be reinstated in my previous assignment? I haven't been trained for the Alternative Education Classroom, and I never requested to be transferred to it. To make matters worse, you have cut services so that I can no longer provide the students with what they need."

Anne dismissed me with her arrogant tone and her demoralizing assessment. "A true professional finds a way to make whatever they have at their disposal work. You don't need to have resources to be a good teacher."

Overcrowding at-risk students in a tiny, understaffed room and cutting all of their services was in no way acceptable, but I let her continue, knowing nothing I said would persuade her otherwise.

"And I have considered your request. It isn't possible. I've placed another teacher in your previous classroom. I won't discuss personnel decisions with you."

So, that was that, the final word. What else could I say? The old Patricia would have continued to stand up for herself and her students. Tina was right. The aging Patricia was wimpy. I simply stood, pulled my shoulders straight, turned my back to her, and walked out the door. What a powerful exit it would have been, had I not returned to the bowels of hell to retrieve my traitorous water bottle.

After my horrific meeting, I needed a drink. I stopped at home, attired Zoomie in his service vest, and the two of us shuffled into Valentina's. Chelsea, the barista, was in rare form. Not only was she euphoric from her new facial piercings, and having added a fresh coat of purple to her already blue and red hair, I think she had also forgotten to take her ADHD meds and downed a pot of her own brew. She was colorfully vibrating a frequency that could channel Mars.

"Hey, Patti, I hear you had a date with my Uncle Neil!" she yelled across the coffee shop. She flashed me a big toothy grin and gave me a thumbs-up.

It took me a second to recover from my embarrassment and grasp the meaning. Neil, the cop, is the coffee girl's uncle? "Damn incestuous small town," I whispered to my furry one-and-only friend.

Tina was no longer my friend because she leaned her head through the kitchen door and added to my humiliation. "Yeah, about that. Thanks for telling me you had a date, chica." Then she popped back into the kitchen, calling out, "Un momento. Baking cookies."

I cringed at the profane utterances made in her native tongue that alerted the faint of heart to stay away. The master was at work in her kitchen.

I had hoped to decompress with Tina, but the truth is, these days, I avoid her when she's baking. Anxiety from my morning meeting made me so desperate for a confidante that I considered telling Chelsea my woes. I was on my way to place my order and maybe entrust in rainbow-girl when my phone rang. I had forgotten Mike was getting off work early to come over and change my furnace filter. He still insists on doing my home maintenance chores.

"Gotta go, talk to you later," I yelled to Tina.

"Do you like my Uncle?" Chelsea had a Cheshire cat-ish grin plastered across her face.

"I gotta go. I forgot I have an appointment," I told the odd latte artist.

"Uncle Neil likes you a lot," she called after me. Next came the cringe-worthy holler of the decade. "Patti, maybe you'll be my aunt!"

I returned home to find Mike's black Mustang convertible parked in front of my house. Within weeks of our separation, he had a new car and a new wardrobe. Within months of our separation, he had new muscles, and within weeks of our divorce, a young girlfriend. Over the years, his brown hair, russet eyes, and pink complexion had grayed. Since our divorce, his youthful colors had returned. He had also regained his chiseled jawline and sinewy biceps. I hated to admit that marriage with me had dulled him, and divorce suited him.

Realizing his old buddy was in the house, my pup went wild with excitement. "Go see Daddy, you big traitor." I opened the basement door so that Zoomie could zoom down the stairs.

"Hey, Mike. I'm home," I called after my furry Benedict Arnold. Then I listened to them squeal with joy at the sight of each other.

Assuming that Mike would join me for a cup, as he often did after his maintenance chores, I busied myself making tea. I took a quick look in the mirror and attempted to un-muss my hair. Then I dabbed at a spot of mascara that had smeared.

Soon, Mike and Zoomie ascended from the basement. I greeted them at the top of the stairs with tea— the way Mike liked it—and a doggy biscuit for my pup, who I needed to remind that Lassie was faithful and didn't get all googly-eyed over Timmy's exes.

"Hey, Pat. What's the deal with the pillow, blankets, and flashlight in the furnace room? Are you sitting down there on the floor, going through your grandfather's stuff?" Mike asked.

He knew me too well. Since I had spent the morning with a heinous scowl master, I had caught her contagious Bitchy-itis. I puffed up my chest. "Zoomie and I like it there."

"Okay." Mike chuckled. "As long as you're comfortable, but isn't it cold?"

For some reason, I was annoyed that he knew what I was up to, so I was not about to admit that the basement floor was hard and icy. When I didn't respond, Mike continued, "You now have a fresh furnace filter."

"Thank you. I think the faucet upstairs is leaking, and there's a spot on the front door that needs sanding. It tore my skirt a couple of weeks ago." The truth is I can fix the faucet, the door, and the filters myself, so I have no idea why I allow Mike to continue his landlord duties.

"Okay, I'll take care of it." Mike shot me a stunning smile. "Could I take Zoomie to the park this weekend?"

Zoomie, traitor that he was, even after a treat from me, remained glued to Mike's leg.

"I don't know. Is Miss Big Boobs going?" I asked.

Mike sputtered a "pfft," before responding, "Again with that crap, Pat? When are you going to let it go? Her name is Shelly. Besides, look who's talking, Miss I Had A Date Yesterday!"

Cassie had ratted me out. Perfect, I had hoped she would.

"Yes. I did. With the cop assigned to my case, and he was a gentleman."

"Gentleman? You mean boring?" A self-satisfied laugh accompanied Mike's insult.

I deflected but didn't deny. "I'm going out with him again Friday."

"Since you won't be home on Friday, I'll come over and hang out with Zoomie—and, no, Shelly won't be with me. She's going out with her girlfriends."

We stared at each other as I wondered why Mike appeared baffled. I'm not sure how I felt about my ex dog-sitting while I was on a date.

He changed the subject. "Cassie has a boyfriend."

"What? No, she doesn't! Why didn't she tell me? Who? How long? Why didn't she tell me?" Heartbroken that she hadn't confided in me, I repeated myself.

Mike walked over to the kitchen table, put his teacup down, and sat in the same seat he had sat in for decades. Zoomie and I joined him.

"Look, Pat, she wants to tell you, but you've been under a lot of stress. Besides, you get all goofy about these things. You would have asked her a million questions, really grilled her, bugging about when you were going to meet the guy. You know how you are?"

I plopped into the seat beside him. "What do you mean? No, I wouldn't have!" There was no use in defending myself further. I knew that I would have been as annoying as father and daughter predicted.

"I think she's planning on telling you soon. So, be cool. Don't go overboard. Are you listening to me?"

"I'm her mom. I need to ask some questions."

"Make sure you let her talk, and you listen. She isn't one of your kids at school."

I have always hated Mike's lectures!

He changed the subject again. "Did you talk to Dr. Westbrook today?"

I filled him in on my unsuccessful meeting.

"Pat, you didn't have the UniServ representative with you?"

As usual, Mike's judgmental attitude made me feel like a child. I wanted to prove that I was still strong. I hated how much I had allowed life to beat on me since my transfer, divorce, and assault.

"Mike, I wanted to try to stand up for myself first."

His brow furrowed. I didn't think he was angry; he appeared more contemplative.

"Don't worry. I won't do it again. Next time I'll have Leigh Ann with me," I assured him. Mike was the last person in the world to whom I wanted to confess defeat.

Once again, we studied each other. Thirty years ago, we had looked at each other with lust in our eyes. Twenty years ago, it was love; two years ago, hatred; today it was sadness and confusion. He stood and leaned over to pat me on the shoulder.

"Pat, I worry about you. You seem to be losing your fire. Years ago, you never would have gone into a meeting without a solid plan, and you would never have let that woman walk all over you."

That was the worst thing he could say to me. Why didn't he understand how he crushed me when he saw me as weak? I opened my mouth to defend myself, but no words came out.

"Bye, Pat. Please call me if you need anything." He bent down to scratch Zoomie's ears. "Bye, bud. See you Friday night."

I didn't walk Mike to the front door because I didn't want him to see the tear I wiped from my eye.

Fire-less,
Patti

Recorded by Robert Stauffer I, TSgt on November 10, 1972
Transcribed by Patricia Moore
Helloop Contraption,

Other than having some heart problems and spendin' a few days in the hospital, retirement seems to be treating me well. I'm glad that I'm home now because I missed seein' my mini Big Red.

Doc says I gotta keep talking out my feelings. So anywho, I was assigned to the 728th Squadron of the 452nd Bomb squad of the US Army Corps. My first mission was on October 9, 1944. My recollections of this mission are probably the clearest. After that, the memories of my next twenty-one flights mingle together. On that particular day, our target was one of the major railroad marshaling yards in Mainz, Germany. Devastatin' hits to this particular target would impede the German front line.

The day started with a three a.m. flashlight in my face. The potbelly stove in our sleeping quarters didn't give off much heat, so I was always tryin' to innovate ways to keep warm. Something that helped was keepin' my socks and knickers under my blankets with me while I slept. My body heat kept them toasty, and I could get dressed under the covers. Breakfast was bland SOS and dried eggs. This was a good omen for a B17 crew because the shittier the breakfast, the less dangerous a mission you had in front of you. Marty and the kids bug me to make them that creamed shit-on-a-shingle, but these days I can't stand the smell of it.

Anywho, the radio room was between the bomb bay and the waist section. If both doors were closed, the radio room was the warmest spot on the plane, not that forty degrees below zero was warm, but it was warmer than the fifty to sixty degrees below zero of the cockpit. It's hard to find the words to articulate how damn cold that war was. It's been over two decades, and my body hasn't warmed. I'm still haunted by the ice that formed in my oxygen mask on those long flights.

Unfortunately, the small room was also a bit claustrophobic. I made my minuscule desk in the center of the *Sky Queen* as comfortable as I could. I taped a picture of Marty wearing her monogrammed blouse below the escape hatch. My gun was mounted on the roof, and somehow looking into Marty's eyes and seein' her smile brought me comfort and gave me strength. Although I never developed a taste for firing a weapon, I knew what I needed to do if I ever wanted to see her again. I kept a copy of my Kipling poems on my desk so that I could memorize them on the long flights. Somethin' I learned in those lean Depression years was that a good book could make the most intolerable, endurable.

The mission started successfully. We had dropped our load on the target and still had seventy-five percent of our fuel. Our jubilation only lasted for a few moments because we were surprised by enemy fire. Our number two engine was hit and started leakin' fuel. Then the number three engine started to shake. We were able to make it out of the flak before our number four engine started to twitch. We made it past enemy lines but were still a long way from our home base in England, so our pilot decided to land in an emergency airfield in Brussels.

Several other B17s that had run into trouble had also landed at the base. As soon as we were on the ground, soldiers boarded and confiscated our ammunition and non-mounted machine guns. Although we were warned that this would happen, the silence of our visitors collecting the weapons was unnervin'.

We were assigned filthy, cold, and uninhabitable livin' quarters for the night. German newspapers littered the floor, and Nazi graffiti decorated the walls. At least we were alive. Although I never felt safe knowing that Nazi sympathizers were hiding in the hills surroundin' us.

Some of the guys left the cover of our pigsty quarters to travel into town. At first, I didn't want to go. Since I could no longer tell the difference between friends and enemies, I felt safer staying put. Eventually, my buddy Ralph, our tail gunner, convinced me that vittles and a drink would do me good. The crowded streets made the walk into town disconcerting because there was something nightmarish about the hordes of well-dressed people heading to night clubs in a bombed-out city as the war waged around us.

Ralph and I followed a couple of British soldiers into one of the decrepit buildings to order food. I'm not sure what we ate, and I wasn't about to ask. For all I know, it was rat in cream sauce. I was just happy to have food in me belly. The waiter overcharged us for a couple of shots of whiskey, and a few fancy Belgian women asked us if we'd like some company. We declined, figurein' they were ladies of the evening, and headed back to our quarters.

It was a long, cold night, and the bonnie dawn did not come fast enough. The next morning, we learned that it would take a few days to fix our *Sky Queen*, so we traveled back to England by Air Transport Command.

Once we were safely in England, the Captain produced a couple of bottles of cognac that he had purchased from a nightclub in Brussels. We celebrated all night long. Best damn cognac I ever tasted!

Take er' easy!

Chapter 7

"You're short on ears and long on mouth."

John Wayne

October 24, 2019

Dear Diary,

It was hard to get out of bed this morning. I tossed and turned most of the night, trying to decide what to do about my work situation. I hate to admit it, but yesterday I only got out of bed to take care of Zoomie. I didn't even brush my hair or teeth.

It was Grandma who came to me last night in my brief moments of sleep. "Patti, get dressed. You have to take care of yourself. Even though your grandfather is a major braggart, you should get up and listen to his stories," she said as she waggled her finger.

A word of advice: if you don't want your dead relatives nagging you, don't live in their house.

Ashamed at having become so pathetic that I required ghosts visiting my dreams to get my ass in gear, I forced myself to crawl out of bed, then guzzled half a pot of coffee.

Prior to my divorce, I ran 10ks with fervor. As the stress of life increased, I ran less often. This school year has been so awful that I haven't run since August; consequently, my pants are getting tight. Today I laced up my ASICS Gels, shoved my body into my leggings, hooked Zoomie to his harness, and we trotted and smiled. My blood pumped, and my ponytail bounced up and down. Since it's been a while, we only ran the circuit around the borough. Still, it was glorious. Why have I allowed piles of paperwork to force me to give up my passion?

My calves already hurt, and I suspect my entire body will ache tomorrow. I don't mind; I welcome it!

Panting, sore, and happy,

Patti

…..…..*…..*

TO: PAMoore@gmail
FROM: Cassfldhock@gmail
SUBJECT: Hi
DATE: October 24, 2019
Hi Mom,

Are you taking care of yourself? Have you had any more dates with the cop? And give me the scoop on the hot shrink! Lol. I am anxious to learn more about Great-Grandpa Stauffer. We are studying World War II right now, and it is fascinating. I'm thinking of changing my major to World History. What do you think?

I love you!

Cassie

TO: Cassfldhock@gmail
FROM: PAMoore@gmail
SUBJECT: Re: Hi
DATE: October 24, 2019
Hi Cassie,

I love hearing from you. Guess what? Zoomie and I went for a run around the neighborhood earlier today. It felt great. I think I'd like to start training again. I'll start small. Maybe a 5K race with Zoomie, then work back into 10Ks.

Neil, the police officer, is taking me to dinner Friday night. Why in the world do you think my psychotherapist is hot?

I'm transcribing your great-grandfather's tapes into a journal so that you can read them the next time you come home. He mentions me in them. Isn't that cool? His nickname for me was Big Red. At the time he recorded the tapes, I was his only grandchild, although I'm pretty sure my cousins Chrissy and Clarke were on the way.

I can see you earning your PhD in History and teaching at a college. Keep in touch.

I love you more!

Mom

…..…..*…..*

October 24, 2019

Dear Diary,

Being taunted by my daughter and best friend bothered me. What made them think that Dr. Greene was hot and I was attracted to him? I hadn't given them any indication that I was interested in him. I wasn't even sure of what he looked like. All I knew was he was young, massive, had blue eyes, and was unbearably pompous.

Sitting across from him on our second meeting, I knew I had to take a peek to see if he was indeed all that.

Jacob Greene was broad-shouldered and stood over six feet tall. Long golden lashes edged his sapphire-colored eyes, and his blond hair was a sun-kissed honey shade rarely seen in anyone over the age of twelve. His wavy locks weren't overly moussed but carefully held into place. His chiseled jawline and proud nose gave him the profile of a Roman statue. His tie hung over the back of his chair, and he had unbuttoned the neck of his tailored shirt. The kicker was he smelled of an expensive citrusy and pine musk.

Crap!

They were correct.

My shrink is crazy sexy. How had they known? Had I subconsciously noticed and given off some kind of tell?

Since he was spectacular, it's no wonder I behaved like an insane fool at our first session. Looking at him made me self-conscious and ashamed of the creases that decorated my forehead.

"Hi, Patricia. How did your week go?" he asked.

I had a tough decision. Should I tell the magnificent specimen across from me about the humiliation I had endured the past week, or should I conceal it and keep all of the horrible moments to myself? I decided to travel the embarrassment path—minus the bloodbath—because if I wasn't forthcoming, he couldn't help me. If he thought I was mentally healthy, he might send me back into the alternative education jungle, and I wasn't ready. I wasn't sure I'd ever be ready.

"It was tough, Dr. Greene." My cheeks turned into spicy cinnamon hearts.

He nodded and wrote something on the notebook sitting in his lap. "Have you been sleeping better?"

I sighed. "I'm not sleeping well at all." I chose my words carefully. "Although I'm spending a lot of time in bed."

His disinterested expression indicated I bored him. Abashed, I continued, "Some days I only get out of bed to feed my dog."

"At least you're still taking care of your dog?" Although his face appeared dispassionate, to his credit, he was attempting to find something redeeming in my pitiable life.

"I have horrible nightmares when I finally fall asleep."

He looked up from his note-taking as if to say, *Well, this is pointless, but go on and tell me about them.*

"I have a recurring dream that I'm in my classroom, and there are so many students that there aren't enough desks. I'm trying to teach, and kids keep walking into the room. They are talking over me, and nobody's paying attention. I talk louder and louder, trying to explain why it's important to learn to read, and more kids walk through the door, and then they all start fighting. Blood is dripping from their eyes and mouths, and I can't make any of it stop. I try to yell to get their attention, but I don't have a voice, and they keep coming in, and fighting, and bleeding." I took a breath. "I wake up with a sore throat, and I feel like someone has strangled me all over again."

The doctor set his pen down and launched into a new topic. "A couple of days ago, I watched a news report that made me think of you. There is a nationwide crisis because teachers are being scratched, kicked, bitten, and punched at work."

"Don't forget strangled," I chimed in.

"Well, they didn't mention that, but it would fit into the same category. The problem is, the assaults are going unreported. These teachers are terrified to talk about it and aren't pressing charges. In fact, according to the reporter, nothing is being done."

"Of course they aren't talking about it," I replied. "Teachers aren't permitted to talk about it or press charges, and they have to stay in classrooms with the kids that are attacking them. In fact, I met with my supervisor, the evil Dr. Westbrook, earlier this week—"

He interrupted me. "Wait. Who?"

I hesitated before answering. "Anne Westbrook."

His eyes snapped wide. I wondered if he was interested, concerned, or confused?

"Do you know her?" I asked.

That indecipherable emotion in his beautiful eyes disappeared. Once again he wore his haughty, indifferent countenance. "I thought I recognized the name from somewhere. But maybe not. Go ahead, continue."

"Well, this crazy kid, Tanner Jones."

He picked up his pen and scribbled away.

"Dr. Greene, do you know Tanner?"

"No, I don't know him. I'm just taking notes, and I think you are brave for standing up for yourself." A smile replaced his indifference.

Damn!

His smile was beautiful, and his teeth were perfect. Plus, he thought I was brave. I put extreme effort into gathering my wits and focusing my attention back on my story, away from his bright eyes and golden hair.

"What was I saying? So, anyway, they plan to make me stay in the same classroom with Tanner. He didn't receive a punishment or consequences. Dr. Westbrook won't budge. I think she might try to force me or guilt me into returning to work, but I'm not ready."

"You aren't," Dr. Greene said.

Was that sincerity, sarcasm, or an insult about my mental fortitude? If Mike had said the same statement, it probably would have been some type of commentary on my inadequacies. I couldn't read this enigma of a man who smelled like sex in the woods.

"You can't return to work until Dr. Long and I agree, and right now, I don't think you're ready."

I knew I wasn't ready to return, and I didn't want my psychotherapist to send me back, but I also didn't want him to think I was weak. I found myself in a lose-lose situation.

He tackled a new issue. "Tell me, did you talk to your daughter this week? It seems as though you miss her."

I filled him in on our messages and how she and her father had kept her new boyfriend from me. He surprised me by taking my side.

"It seems as though your ex-husband should be encouraging her to tell you."

"Exactly!"

Maybe this guy wasn't so bad. He had graced me with a smile, and he thought Mike was wrong.

He rested the tip of his pen on his face. When he lifted it, it left a small blue line on his chin. "What seems to be an acceptable timeline for her to tell you before you confront her and tell her you know?"

"Three days," I responded. I have no idea why I picked that number, but it seemed reasonable.

I think he made a checkmark in his notebook.

"Have you been studying your grandfather's records?"

My spirits instantly lifted as I told him about my discoveries. The crazy part being, he listened. He didn't even take a note—or accidently draw on himself—for an entire five minutes.

In fact, his eyes lit up. "Your grandparents sound amazing. And your grandfather had his arm amputated and was a teacher after the war? Tap into his strength right now. What would he have done?"

"Yes. His students called him Professor Stump. He went to college under the GI Bill, and we have the same alma mater." I responded with one of my pap's favorite sayings. "He would have threatened to beat Tanner Jones 'about the face and eyes'." I half laughed, half sighed. "But we can't beat kids these days. And the truth is he wouldn't have laid a hand on Tanner. He was a gentle soul."

Dr. Greene grinned. "From the stories you've told me, I suspect Professor Stump would have had other tools up his sleeve."

"Up his sleeve, with his stump." I smiled at my imagery.

While Dr. Greene stared into space, I fought my desire to lick my thumb and wipe the ink from his chin. Eventually his voice interrupted my daydream.

"That stump of his seems to have a personality of its own. It's a symbol of his mental and physical fortitude. I suspect you'll find strength and insight in your grandfather's stories. That is your assignment for the week: listen to his tapes, keep journaling, and stay StumpStrong."

"StumpStrong! I love it." I smiled then repeated the word again, a bit louder.

"Also, honestly confront your daughter and ex-husband. One more thing, I think we need more intensive sessions until you are sleeping at night and getting out of bed in the morning. Please see Mrs. Stewart on your way out. Have her schedule two appointments for next week."

I decided that two appointments a week wouldn't be too torturous since Greene thought I was brave and Mike was wrong.

"Thank you, Dr. Greene. By the way, I had a date with the officer on my case," I preened.

I didn't want a man who smelled like bright sunlight, fresh forests, and lustful kisses to think I was too pathetic.

Strong,
Patti

…..…..*…..*

The Error
December 18, 1951
written by Robert Stauffer

A splintering crash broke the still of the night;
I jumped from my warm bed and turned on the light.
At the end of the back yard in wild disarray
Was old Santa, eight reindeer, and one up-turned sleigh!
Toys scattered about on the new-fallen snow,
reindeer draped o'er the roof peak with Santa below
lying prone on the ground a jumbled red haze—
he'd been klonked on his knot and was in a mild daze!
As he regained his senses, took stock of the score,
He saw a half-moon had been carved from the door.

"Dammit, Rudolph, you goofed it, you stupid young louse,

I told you that this stop would be the 'Schmidt house!'"

..........*.....*

Alex Davis
123 Oakwood Lane
State College, Pa.
December 20, 1971
Robert Stauffer
15 South 24th Street
Maple Hall, Pennsylvania
Dear Professor Stump,

I am not sure if you will remember me, but I was one of your students at the Indiana Normal School in 1951. I am Alex Davis. I was the chubby blond-haired kid that sat in the back of your last period English class. I am the one that never shut up and consequently spent a lot of time with you in after school detention.

Lately, I have been thinking about those detentions and how much I enjoyed them. I think they were supposed to be punishments, but after a while, I would purposely get into trouble so I would have to stay after school. You made me clean the chalkboard and erasers first, but then you would give me a piece of candy and talk to me. You told the best stories and gave the best advice. You read passages from books to me. I remember sitting in that classroom, watching the snow outside fall, listening to you read *Treasure Island*. That spring, you read me *The Jungle Book*.

I remember the world globe on the pedestal like it was yesterday. I would spin it and then stop it with my finger. Whatever country it landed on would become our project of the day. We used the *Encyclopedia Britannica* you kept on the shelf to find out about the country. You encouraged me to make up exciting adventures and stories. I remember the disappointment I felt if my finger landed on a body of water, but the disappointment only lasted for a second because then I would spin the globe again.

I haven't forgotten that when my dad was injured and lost his job at the lumber mill, you and your wife made sure I had a winter coat and gloves, and you sent my mom a card and money so we could have a Christmas dinner. I kept the card and the hilarious Christmas poem you wrote to cheer me up. I still laugh whenever I read the lines about the half-moon and the "Schmidt house." Just the other day, I explained Western Pennsylvania outhouses to my citified wife.

I thought you should know that you inspired me to become an English teacher. I remember the lessons you taught, the poetry you recited to the class, and the kind way you treated us all. We thought the world of you, and I often tell my students and my two sons the stories of my favorite teacher, the war hero who flew in aB17, stood up to the Nazis, and had to start his arm amputation.

I hope you and Mrs. Stauffer are well and you have a wonderful holiday. Thank you both for everything you did for that poor incorrigible young boy who sat in the back of your class. Professor Stump, may I be half the teacher and man you are.

      Fondly,
      Your Student,
      Alex Davis

Chapter 8

"...I deny your right to put words into my mouth."

Robert Louis Stevenson, *Treasure Island*

October 25th

Cassie: Hi, Mom. I have a friend I want you to meet tomorrow. Please don't embarrass him by asking a ton of questions. I'll be home around 4, and then we're all going to Grandma Susan's and Pappap's for dinner.

P: ~~It's about time you told me.~~
P: ~~I don't ask too many questions.~~
P: ~~All good moms ask questions.~~
P: ~~You mean your new boyfriend?~~
P: Hi Cassie. Sure, but what if your grandparents have plans?

Cassie: I already asked Grandma Susan, and she said yes. She said you found the recipe for Great-grandpap's lasagna. I can't wait to taste it. I told Pappap not to tease my friend too much. 😂

P: ~~You told your grandparents before you told me?~~
P: What is his name?

Cassie: Farez

P: Okay. See you tomorrow. Do you want to spend the night? Please! I could fix up the guest room for Farez.

Cassie: I'll ask him. Bye. Love you 🖤

P: Love you more 🖤🖤

Cassie: Love you the most 🖤🖤🖤

…..…..*…..*

October 25, 2019
Dear Diary,

"All daughters tell their mothers about dinner parties after they've invited everyone else in the family," I explained to Zoomie.

Zoomie thought it seemed reasonable.

Unconvinced, I dialed my parents' number. My dad answered the phone.

I plopped myself at the kitchen table and said, "Hi, Dad."

"Hi, kiddo. How's it going? How come you never call your dear old dad anymore?"

My father had latched onto the word "kiddo" two decades ago and thought it still suited me even though I was half a century old.

"I'm okay, Dad, and I called you last week."

"Yeah, that was last week. I am gettin' old. I could have the big one any day."

My father had been threatening to have the "big one" since watching Red Fox warn his son of the same impending doom in the 1972 *Sanford and Son* pilot.

"Dad, you're healthy. You aren't going to croak off anytime soon," I insisted.

The truth was, I worried about my parents' aging. Occasionally it turned into anxiety about what I would do when they were gone. Of course, lately, almost every thought I had turned into anxiety, if not a full-fledged panic attack.

"You don't know that. Larry Wilkins was healthy and fishing one day. The next day he had a triple bypass. A goddamn triple bypass and his insurance skyrocketed." My dad sighed. "Are you back at work yet?"

"No, Dad. I'm off work for at least six weeks. Remember, I told you last time we talked?"

"I couldn't understand a damn thing you said with your voice all messed up. So, what are you gonna do for food? You won't lose your job, will you? Do you wanna stay with your mom and me? You can have Junior's room." He sounded out each syllable of his laugh. "Ha, ha, ha."

I drew roses on my message notepad as I explained. "I'll be okay, and I can't go back to work yet. I have to heal a little longer, and the kid is still in my class."

I didn't know if I could pay my bills long term, but I didn't want to worry my dad. I didn't want him to actually have the "big one."

"What the hell? He oughta' be locked in jail. What's happenin' to this world? Damn crazy people are runnin' around all over the place. No discipline in schools. The world is goin' to hell!"

"I'll be okay, Dad," I reassured him again. Although perhaps I was trying to convince myself.

"You oughta' get a lawyer. Do you need a lawyer? I can ask Peter Monaco who he's using. He's suing that guy who keeps drivin' through his yard and runnin' over his azalea bushes."

For the past two decades, I'd been of the opinion that Peter Monaco was a paranoid nutball, but he was my dad's lodge buddy, so I kept my distaste to myself. Still, under no circumstance did I want to share an attorney with the old man because anyone willing to encourage Crazy Monaco's delusions needed their head examined.

"I have a union attorney. She is working on my grievance. It's just moving slowly. All types of laws protect the kid, and my supervisor is trying to cover up the incident."

"What about the laws to protect you? The whole damn country is goin' to hell!"

Since I wasn't sure if there were laws to protect me. I needed to change the subject. "Hey, can I talk to Mom?"

"Yeah. Your mother is acting like a crazy woman, cleaning and getting ready for Cassie and her boyfriend."

I held the phone away from my ear to prepare for what I knew came next.

It was perfect timing because a millisecond later, my father screamed, "Susan! Patti's on the phone!"

My parents had not grasped the concept of holding their hand over the receiver as they called for each other. They also spoke to each other in a volume that could break crockery.

Although he had called for my mother, my father hadn't finished talking. "You want me to go over to the school and teach that little punk a lesson? I could give him a knuckle sandwich."

As antiquated and clueless as my father could be, he was my Daddy, he protected me, and he made me laugh.

I chuckled. "No. I don't want you to go to jail."

My mom picked up the other line. "Hi, Patti," she said, her voice puffing out in little bursts. My mom spent her life panting because she ran around, cleaning up after my dad and my adult brother, who still went by his childhood name, Jimmy Junior.

"I'm gonna drive over there and give him a knuckle sandwich. Nobody goes to jail for anything anymore. The country is pure chaos. Everything is goin' to hell in a handbasket!"

"For Christ's sake, hang up, James," my mother scolded.

My dad chuckled and hung up.

"Hi, Mom. I'm sorry about Cassie's last-minute dinner request. I hope it isn't causing you too much stress."

"I had a week to get ready. That would have been plenty of time if your dad had helped me. Instead, he made a mess. He just tracked mud on the carpet, and he won't eat his pretzels over a plate. He spent the last few mornings at breakfast with the old retired guys. I wish I could go to breakfast every morning."

There was no reason my mother couldn't go to breakfast whenever she wanted, but I didn't address that at the moment because I had just received a sucker punch to the gut.

"What? A week?" I asked.

"Now Patti, don't get mad. Cassie wanted to tell you, but since that kid murdered you, she didn't want to add any additional stress, so she asked me to take care of everything."

"What the hell?" First of all, I was still alive. Secondly, I was never too stressed to talk to my daughter. Seeing Cassie was one of the few things that cheered me up during challenging times.

"Um. Don't be upset. And please, try to stay calm," my mother hem-hawed. "Um, Mike is coming."

My family kept my daughter's visit and boyfriend from me, and the thing my mom thought would upset me was Mike coming to dinner?

Absurd!

"Please try to be nice to Shelly. I know she's a bit of a dingbat."

"Wait! Mom? Is Shelly coming? What the hell? You invited Shelly?"

Fucking absurd!

With this revelation, I said goodbye and hung up.

Had my entire family lost it? How could they justify treating me so horribly? Did Tina know? Did Zoomie know? Did Chelsea, the klutzy coffee barista, know? Was the entire world in on my family's deception? Why in God's name did they think I would be upset that my daughter had a new boyfriend? I was thrilled, and I wanted to be a part of it. Although inviting my ex-husband's girlfriend was unacceptable.

The farce must be Mike's doing. One of the reasons we divorced was that he had treated me like I was fragile in the last year of our marriage. Now that something horrible had happened, he felt justified. I've forgotten some of the other reasons we split up, but his propensity for being over-protective had left me with a toxic bitterness.

I was psycho angry by the time Mike showed up at my house with a new ball for Zoomie. The idea of slamming the door in his face tempted me, but I decided it might be more satisfying to let him into my house, then tell him exactly what I thought of him.

"Why didn't you tell me Cassie was coming home? How could my entire family be plotting a visit behind my back? My parents? How did you convince them to leave me out of this? And Shelly knew? Are you seriously taking your girlfriend to my parents' house? They are my parents, Mike!"

His usually confident shoulders caved forward. "Pat, you were under so much stress. We wanted to protect you. Cassie's coming home to see you, but she didn't want you to take over the dinner and get overwhelmed."

"You didn't think that keeping things from me would stress me more? Cut me a break. Stop making my decisions for me. Stop telling me how I feel, and stop telling everyone around me to protect me. Mike, I'm a big girl. I can protect myself."

"I'm sorry. I worry about you. I still want to take care of you," Mike confessed.

I had the last word on the subject. "It isn't your job. You aren't my husband anymore."

It was impossible to tell which of us hurt more at that moment. Heartbreak laced the air between us.

I broke the heavy silence. "Now look. You made my mascara run." I took off up the stairs. I needed to wipe away the salt water that threatened to spoil my carefully applied make-up. Mike tried to follow, but I flashed a palm to stop him.

"I think your mom accidentally invited Shelly. You know how nervous she gets about etiquette with these things," he yelled to my retreating back.

"Fuck him," I confided to the wall.

I was studying my reflection in the mirror when the doorbell rang. Since there was no way I could get to the door faster than my ex-husband, I took my time. I wiped away the tears, reapplied my mascara, and took a few deep breaths before heading downstairs to face my troublesome situation.

A confused-looking Neil sat on the loveseat across from a relaxed-looking Mike. His Royal Presumptuous had comfortably arranged himself on his usurped throne. He was smugly scratching Zoomie's temple.

"Hi, Neil. How are you?" I forced a smile.

Mike interrupted before Neil could respond. "I just asked Officer Harris how the investigation into your assault is going. He was about to answer."

The scene was Webster's definition of awkward, and I needed to get away from Mike.

"We better go, Neil." I grabbed his hand.

"Bye, Zoomie. I love you, be a good boy," I said sweetly. Then I growled a very sarcastic, "Thanks a lot," to Mike.

Sitting across from me at an intimate Italian restaurant, I think Neil attempted to understand why he felt out of place when he arrived at my house.

"So, that was your ex-husband, and he is babysitting your dog?" he asked.

"That about sums it up," I said right before shoving a breadstick into my mouth.

Triple sighs,
Patti

Chapter 9

"If you care about something you have to protect it. If you're lucky enough to find a way of life you love, you have to find the courage to live it."

John Irving, *A Prayer for Owen Meany*

October 26, 2019

Dear Diary,

I spent an hour with Cassie before we had to head to my parents' for dinner. Hearing her call out, "Hello, Mom. I'm home," when she entered the front hallway was medicine for my soul. I embraced her so tightly that she let out a soft squeak. Zoomie ran circles around her, wagging his tail, joyfully barking his hello. I was relieved that she carried a suitcase and a pillowcase of dirty laundry, sure signs she was spending the night. She had twisted her strawberry blonde hair into a loose French braid, and she wore a feminine flannel shirt, high-heeled ankle boots, and pink lipstick. My blue-eyed, rosy-cheeked daughter was beyond beautiful!

Her boyfriend stood one arm hanging at his side, the other extending a box of chocolates as he declared, "Your house could be in a British novel."

I accepted the candy with a squinted eye. However, two seconds later I was beaming at the prospect of chocolate-covered cherries.

I can't take credit for my home's elegance. It remains as it had been when my grandmother was the matron and decorator. She had chosen lush draperies and richly textured wallpapers for each room of the house, and she had arranged ornately patterned oriental rugs on the hardwood floors. Greek revival columns announce the entrance to the grand living room. Wooden beams embellish the ceilings, and most of the rooms boast a crystal chandelier as the aesthetic focal point. I could see why it might remind him of a British country cottage.

Despite Farez's charm, I remained paranoid. I stared into his big brown eyes wondering if he was involved in the grand Don't-Tell-Patti Conspiracy. Since he appeared virtuous, and he bore treats, I decided he was innocent.

Zoomie sat at Cassie's feet as we drank tea and engaged in stories of college life. I intently listened as I learned that Cassie and Farez met in their History class. They talked of study dates in the library and weekly competitive racquetball games in which they jovially trash-talked each other. Cassie had found a new roommate who didn't have an offensive stench. My bitter feelings about being left out faded as I listened to her talk about how happy she was and how much she loved school.

At a quarter till six, Cassie announced it was time to head to her grandparents'. My heart sank. I didn't want to share my daughter with anyone, especially Mike's girlfriend.

Luckily, dinner at my parents turned out to be Shelly-free. Mike explained that she wasn't feeling well.

"Thank you, God. You don't totally hate me," I accidentally said aloud following his announcement. At least I hadn't shared all my prayers aloud. I confess, I secretly hoped Shelly had the plague.

My mother set a beautiful table. The polished silver shined, the pink rose Royal Albert china was expertly arranged, and her crystal candelabra sat atop a lace table runner. Upon first glance, one might be under the impression that the Easterling family dinner was a classy affair. They would be grossly mistaken.

Things went downhill the second Jimmy Junior called out, "Hey, Dad. Pass the salad."

My dad ignored Jimmy and continued to shove large bites of pasta into his mouth.

"James, you need your ears checked. Jimmy asked you to pass the lasagna," my mom nagged.

"What?" asked my dear old dad.

"Pass the goddamn lasagna," snapped my mom.

"You don't have to be so damn mean. I heard you the first time," he quipped back.

My mom placed her hand firmly on the table and stared my dad down. "What the hell are you over there bitching about?"

Since he was the live-in child, Jimmy's full-time job had become refereeing my parent's constant battles. "He told you not to be so damn mean. And I asked for the salad, not the lasagna. You are both deaf."

My mother stiffened. "I can hear just fine. Your dad is the one that needs to get his goddamn ears checked. He probably destroyed his eardrums because he turns the TV volume too loud, and I knew you wanted the salad, but maybe Mike wants more lasagna."

"That's it, Mom. The TV destroyed his damn ears. It has nothing to do with the fact he's as old as time itself." Jimmy took a swig from his crystal wine glass.

My dad ignored Jimmy, and my mother looked like her favorite child had broken her heart. My ex made a valiant effort to hide his smile behind his napkin. Mike thought his demure family boring, and he put up no pretenses about equating quiet sophistication with blandness. He had always gotten a kick out of my obnoxious family.

Unfortunately, the situation continued to deteriorate.

"Susan, pass me the salt," my dad bellowed.

My mom scowled. Before handing anything to my dad, she felt the need to lecture him. "Taste it first. You use too much salt. It's not good for you." Then she begrudgingly handed him a small china dish from the center of the table. God forbid my mother use a normal salt and pepper shaker. I suppose that would be too gauche.

My dad ignored her, dumping the substance onto his pasta. He took a huge bite and hissed. "Goddammit, Susan. That's the sugar. Where in the hell are your glasses? Or were you trying to ruin my dinner?"

"Go to hell, James," my mom hollered.

Mike could no longer hide his amusement. He let out a low chuckle.

My mother forced a smile for Farez. "We don't always fight like this. It's just Cassie's grandfather can be stubborn."

"The hell you don't," Jimmy added. "All you two do is fight. Twenty-four hours a day of your nonstop nonsense. Don't lie to the company."

"That's because your mother is blind as a bat and mean as cat piss." My dad took a ginormous bite of lasagna, rolled it around in his mouth, and swallowed. "Actually, this tastes pretty good, like a big old lasagna cake. Anyone want a bite?" He held up his fork and sugar-encrusted pasta glittered under the chandelier's glow.

No one took my dear old dad up on his offer. Six noses wrinkled in horror as he shoveled "lasagna cake" into his mouth.

"If you two don't settle down, I'm going to put you both in an old folks home and then turn the house into a strip club," threatened my baby brother before shaking his head in horror. "Damn, Dad! That's disgusting. Would you just get a new piece?"

I'm not sure if my dad ignored Jimmy's request because he was deaf, passive-aggressive, a member of the swine family, or actually enjoyed his sweet pasta, but he was hell-bent on finishing his ruined meal.

Finally, Dad spoke. "Ha, ha, ha, Franklin. We're just joking. My wife may be blind and mean, but she can cook, she's beautiful, and she's a good kisser."

Mike choked, then belly-laughed. He knew my mother well enough to know that my dad had won this battle, his weapon of choice the mention of an appalling, scandalous kiss.

"Christ, James. Shut the hell up," my mother growled, then conceded the battle by joining Mike in a good-humored laugh.

"It's Farez, Pappap. His name is Farez, not Franklin," Cassie reminded her grandfather.

"That's what I said, Fred." My dad winked at Farez.

"My Pappap is silly," Cassie declared as she smiled at her well-mannered boyfriend. "Pappap, Farez's grandpa is a goofball too, so you can't scare him. I already warned him you were a teaser." She winked back at her grandfather.

My father pushed his chair away from the table and rubbed his full tummy. "I got more room in there, Fred." He reached for the top button of his jeans.

"James!" my mother screeched.

He grinned. "Hey, Fred, maybe your grandparents can come over for dinner sometime. I just hope your grandma isn't as mean as Cassie's grandma. If she is, I better have a beer for the poor man."

My mother was a master at clenching her teeth while she played hostess. Sweet as the sugar on my father's pasta, she asked, "Farez, would you like more lasagna?"

"Yes, Mrs. Easterling. Lasagna is my favorite," declared Farez.

Despite their atrocious manners, my family behaved while he told the story of his grandparents' immigration to the United States from Lebanon. Then Farez again complimented my mother on her cooking, reiterating that lasagna was his "favorite" dinner. My mother explained that the recipe had been her father's and I had recently found his cookbook. This led to the second time everyone quieted to listen to a story. My story. I enthusiastically elaborated on the treasure chest of memories I had found.

"Mom, Pap mentions me in the tapes. I think Aunt Lynn and Uncle Bob were expecting at the time, but I was the only grandchild who had been born. Do you know why he called me Big Red when I was such a tiny kid?" I asked.

My mother furrowed her brow.

"He used to like to drink some old-fashioned cream soda called Big Red," my dad said.

"Nah. It was because of some cinnamon gum he liked to chew," said my brother.

I shook my head. "Pap never chewed gum."

Jimmy thought this over and shrugged.

"Anyone need more bread?" my mother asked.

"Me," Mike, Dad, and Jimmy said in unison.

My mom passed the bread to Mike. "There was this Irish Setter named Big Red in a movie that your grandfather loved. I think that's where he got the name."

"I bet it was because you had a big mouth, red hair, and you never shut up," Jimmy theorized.

"Yeah. That was it," my dad said. "Now pass me the bread."

Tucking his stomach under the table, he piled bread onto his plate while I considered tossing a chunk of salad onion at my brother.

I studied a chortling Mike before cutting my eyes to my mother. "Mom, do you know why Pap referred to his mother by her name?"

The room quieted as Mom looked to the ceiling. "I'm not sure. I know he loved her and they were close. I think it was because he saw her as being larger than life."

I took a sip of wine and thought about this. "Hmm," I finally muttered.

Jimmy had chugged a few glasses of wine and went into master storyteller mode. "Hey, do you remember the time I zippered myself in the suitcase and got spanked with the stump?"

Dad chortled, Mom giggled, and I held my hand to my mouth to stop my food from falling onto the table.

"I don't remember hearing that one," Mike said.

Jimmy held up a finger, wet his whistle, then cleared his throat. "I was about five or six, and I got this brilliant idea to play hide and seek with Pap. The problem is, he didn't know he was playing because he was busy making a pot of vegetable soup. I hid in a suitcase inside his bedroom closet. I zippered myself in and realized I had forgotten to ask him to find me."

My baby brother had never been accused of being a genius.

"After a while, I panicked and started yelling." Jimmy cupped his hand to his mouth to form a megaphone. "'Pap! Help me. Please, help me!' Pap ran all over the house, trying to find me."

I jumped in, telling the best part. "Pap looked in the closet and could hear Jimmy but couldn't see him. Then he saw a little finger sticking out of the zipper closure, waving back and forth!" I waggled my index finger in the air.

"Pap spanked me so hard. Damn, it hurt," moaned Jimmy.

"That stump was lethal!" I added.

The truth was, our grandfather spanked with the palm of his left hand, not his stump, but over the years, the legend of the stump had grown. We adored our grandfather and had an unwavering respect for that rounded limb. He had bravely earned the battle scar, and it made Pap stronger than the average man. Ask any of Professor Stump's grandchildren. There was no way that stump, could in any way, be weak— it was the amazing instrument that taught us to mind our manners and behave, and we, because of that, were the luckiest grandchildren in the world.

"Patti only got spanked once. She was Pap's favorite, and the girls got off easier," Jimmy whined.

"I was a perfect little angel, and you were a hyperactive monkey." My hands formed a prayer pose as I looked into the heavens at my halo.

Jimmy rolled his eyes and sputtered out a "Pft," before continuing. "Oh, and at sleepovers, the girls got to sleep with Grandma. The boys had to sleep with Pap. He had night terrors and would accidentally bean you with the stump in the middle of the night. Damn, that hurt."

We all knew that although getting a "bonk on the noggin" in the middle of the night was a risk of being one of Professor Stump's grandsons, none of them would have traded it for anything.

"Patti, do you remember the time Grandma decided that we should have a real coconut, and she sent Pap to the commissary for one coconut?" Jimmy asked.

Mike joined in on the family nostalgia, saying, "I can see Martha doing that."

"What happened?" asked Cassie.

I answered with so much enthusiasm that my waving arm almost knocked over my wine glass. I steadied the dishes before continuing. "Pap had no idea how to cut open a coconut. He tried a knife, a hammer, a chisel. Finally, he went and got a saw." I laughed so hard, I snorted, and my rib-splitting quivering made it difficult to finish the story.

"I didn't think it was that hard to open a coconut," Farez said.

My brother took over narrating while I gained control of my guffaws. "Yeah. Well, he was trying to hold the coconut in place with his stump and saw it in half with his left hand. The coconut would fall onto the floor and then roll across the kitchen. I'd pick it up and carry it back to him." Jimmy wrapped his arms around a pretend coconut and rocked his body back and forth. "Then Pap would try again. Grandma was holding the *C* volume of the encyclopedia and kept yelling, 'You damn one-armed fool, you can't even open a coconut!'"

The image of Grandma yelling at Pap as he tried to saw a coconut in half on the kitchen table had us all in stitches. Mike's deep chuckle stood out amongst the joyous, celebratory sounds. Since our divorce, his smiles had become like burning pokers to my heart. Tonight, they made me feel—I don't know—happy and warm?

Farez's brow furrowed.

"My great-grandfather only had one hand," Cassie explained. "He lost his arm in the war. It was amputated right under his elbow. But he was still amazing! He could play the piano, cook, drive a car, write poetry, and play badminton."

"Climb a ladder carrying the electric hedge trimmer," added my dad.

My mother leveled a terrifying squinty-eyed scowl on him and shook her head. "You don't know what you are talking about, James."

"Hell. He only fell out of the tree twice," Dad said.

"Three times," my mother insisted. "And you know I didn't like it when Mom made him trim those branches. So, I don't know why you would even bring it up."

My dad dismissed her like he was swatting at a fly. She shot him dead with venomous eye darts.

Jimmy took a swig. "Anyway, Pap could pretty much do everything but stay on a ladder and open a damn coconut."

"I figured he had lost his arm in the war, but wasn't sure," said Farez. "My great uncle died in Operation Exporter." The conversation halted until he added, "The entire planet hurt during that war." He placed a hand on Cassie's. "I think your grandfather sounds wonderful."

I suppose my father still had a millimeter left from his waistband to his belly because he called out, "Are we ready for cake?"

My mother prepared a special dessert using Pap's famous pistachio cake recipe. She passed out thick slices topped with vanilla ice cream. We remained seated, talking and laughing long after our plates were empty. Eventually, Cassie and I helped my mom clear the table. Desperately needing girl time, we encouraged the four men to retire to the living room.

Mom grasped my daughter's hand in hers. "Cassie, I like your boyfriend."

Cassie beamed. "Isn't he awesome?"

"Yes, and he's very handsome," I added.

My mother placed her hand on my forearm. "It was good to see you laughing tonight."

I took a deep, cleansing breath. "Oh, Mom. It felt good to have fun."

Even with their appalling behavior, having my family together was the happiest I'd felt in years. Perhaps I'm not a lonely loser, and maybe my life isn't so bad.

Content,
Patti

..........*.....*

October 27th
Dear Diary,

This morning I awoke to my doggy tongue alarm clock. Thank goodness for Zoomie because I overslept. I wanted to get up early to prepare a traditional Moore family breakfast for Cassie before she left for school. I was also determined to have her laundry washed and folded. I desperately needed a chance to play Super Mom.

Before racing down the stairs to begin my chores, I checked my phone messages. Mike had texted in the middle of the night to tell me that dinner was fun, my parents looked great, Farez seemed like a good guy, and our daughter was beautiful.

I had too much to do to take time to respond. By the time Cassie and Farez bounded down the stairs, I had breakfast made and her laundry folded. The kitchen felt warm and cozy, and the smell of the baking muffins and brewing coffee created a wistful nostalgia.

Cassie eyed the spread. "Mom, cinnamon muffins and Mexican omelets? Just like Sunday breakfasts when I was little!" She gave a hop, accompanied by a clap, and then turned to her boyfriend. "Farez, these muffins are to die for. Wait until you taste them. Every Sunday, my mom would bake, and my dad would make omelets. Then we'd spend the morning reading. It was my favorite day of the week."

Farez took his seat at the table. "My family did the same thing, except we had tea, pita, and jam. My dad read to my brothers and me, and then we would listen to his favorite music."

"That sounds fun. Don't you think, Mom?" Cassie asked as she sat beside him.

"Sounds amazing," I agreed.

"Ms. Moore, you'd love my father's music. Someday I'll play it for you—Umm Kulthum, George Wassouf, Fairuz—there are so many amazing Arabic musicians. My parents' generation has a lot of pride in their rich culture. My father sings, and my mother is a beautiful dancer."

I thought it sounded like a wonderful way to pass the time, and I was flattered that Farez wanted to share his family traditions with me.

Farez studied the fare, and his eyes lit up. "Bacon." He licked his lips. "Bacon's my favorite." He piled the crispy meat onto his plate until he had created a tower.

Cassie giggled. "Mom, Farez really likes bacon."

I took a sip of coffee and smiled. "I can tell."

Farez expertly destroyed his meat sculpture in record time, then built and decimated another.

Breakfast was leisurely and fabulous. I'll never give Mike the satisfaction of knowing that I took his advice, but as the kids chattered away, I listened, hanging on their every word.

After breakfast, Cassie and Farez packed their bags and met me at the door.

"You'll be home for Thanksgiving, right?" I asked Cassie. "And Christmas?" Then I addressed Farez. "I can fix up the guest room for you, and I'll make you bacon every day, and we can listen to your parents' favorite songs." I would have promised him the world to have Cassie home.

"Thanks, Ms. Moore, I'd like that," Farez said.

"Please call me, Patti," I requested as I hugged the wonderful young man.

"Yes. I'll be home," Cassie promised. She held me tight. "Mom, take care of yourself. Please, don't go back into that terrible classroom. And keep listening to Great-grandpap's tapes. I want to hear more next time I'm home."

With those parting words, my sunshine walked out the door, leaving Zoomie to deal with my torrential tears.

Still Crying,
Patti

Bob's Lasagne

Ingredients:

1 pound box of noodles
2x 15-ounce cans of tomato sauce
1x 16-ounce can of tomato paste
Chopped onion
1 medium clove of garlic
5 or 6 fennel seeds
1 ½ tablespoons oregano
2 tablespoons sugar
1 tablespoon salt
½ tablespoons pepper
1 tablespoon of basil
1 ½ pounds of hamburger
16 ounces container ricotta cheese
8 ounces sharp shredded cheese
8 ounces grated parmesan and provolone mixed

Preparation:

1. Brown and drain hamburger.
2. Add spices and tomatoes.
3. Simmer for two hours.
4. While the sauce is cooking (30 minutes before it is finished), prepare a pack of lasagna noodles. Do not wash.
5. In a large baking dish, melt 1 tablespoon of butter to grease the pan.
6. Put a small amount of sauce on the bottom of the pan. Alternate noodles and cheese (sauce, noodles, cheese, salt, etc.).
7. Bake in a 375° oven for 30 minutes until cheese is melted.

Bob's Pistachio Cake

Ingredients:
Box of white cake mix
3 eggs
1 box of instant pistachio pudding
1 cup of vegetable oil
1 cup of ginger ale
½ cup of flaked coconut
½ chopped pecans
½ cup of pecans

Cake
1. Heat oven to 350°.
2. Grease and flour 2 round cake tins.
3. Combine cake mix, eggs, 1 pack of pudding mix, 1 cup of vegetable oil, and ginger ale.
4. Fold in ½ cup of chopped pecans and ½ cup of coconut.
5. Pour batter into baking pans.
6. Bake for 30 minutes.
7. Cool on rack.

Icing Ingredients:
1 box of instant pistachio pudding
1 envelope of Dream Whip
1 ¼ cup of milk
(extra coconut and pecans to taste)
Combine:
1. 1 box of instant pistachio
2. 1 envelope Dream Whip
3. 1 ¼ cup of milk
4. Beat
5. Add up to ½ cup of coconut and pecans to taste
6. Let cake cook.
7. Ice and enjoy your mouth waterin' vittles

Chapter 10

"You think you have a memory; but it has you!"

John Irving, *A Prayer for Owen Meany*

RAF Deopham Green
England
December 28, 1944

Dear Pop and Sarah,

Today I received the Christmas package you sent. It arrived in good order. The warm socks are needed, and the can of sardines and jar of pickled pigs feet were enjoyed. I am glad to hear that Margaret is better. I can't imagine the pain she must feel at losing her sweet babe. Please give her my love. Marty said that she was able to visit last week and that you both looked well.

Twenty-two missions, five this week already, and I am exhausted but feeling surprisingly chipper. The radio I purchased for the barracks brings my crew much comfort. We hear news from home, and tonight Nat King Cole, Perry Como, Bing Crosby, and Dinah Shore are being broadcast into our room.

In answer to your question, Pop, the camp cooks prepared a wonderful Christmas dinner of turkey, gravy, sweet potatoes, cranberry sauce, celery, mincemeat pie, and coffee. The enlisted men were invited to the Officers' Club for Christmas carols. There is an old upright piano in the club, so I played along, accompanying the singing. The evening ended with cigars all around. We all know how much everyone back home is looking out for us. Like I always say, "Every little bit helps, said the old lady who peed in the sea."

Please give everyone my love, and let them know that I am happy and army life is treating me well.

Your Loving Son,
Robert

..........*.....*

The Clearfield Progress
January 6, 1945
Sergeant Robert Stauffer Missing, Germany
written by Warren Fox

Mr. And Mrs. Horace P. Stauffer of Burnside have received word that their son, T/Sgt Robert S. Stauffer, was reported missing in action over Germany on December 31st.

Robert enlisted in the Air Corps in July 1942 and was assigned to radio aerial gunner school, receiving his basic training in Tampa, Florida, and completing his training at Gulfport Field, Mississippi.

He, with the members of his crew, flew their ship, the *Sky Queen*, across the ocean, landing in England in September 1944. Robert has been awarded the air medal, two Oak Leaf Clusters, and several other citations.

In his last letter to his parents dated December 28th, he said army life was treating him well.

..........*.....*

Recorded by Robert Stauffer I, TSgt on November 11, 1972
Transcribed by Patricia Moore
Helloop Contraption,

I had those damnable nightmares again last night. They're so real—like I'm relivin' the worst parts of the war. Last night's incubus was about New Year's Eve day, 1944.

It was a cold and dreary three a.m. when the Sergeant stuck that unwelcome flashlight in my face. We had already flown five missions that week, and even though they had all been somewhat easy milk runs, I was exhausted. Our four a.m. breakfast was once again bland dried eggs, so we were convinced our day consisted of another long, but safe mission. The briefin' at five a.m. seemed to confirm this. We were to bomb the oil facilities in Hamburg. Take off would be at six a.m.

The flight to and from the North Sea was predicted to be anti-aircraft free. P-51s were to meet us at the North Sea before we entered Germany and then protect us until we were back over water. We'd be under complete cloud cover over the target, so it would permit the aluminum chaff I dispersed to create false radar echoes that would hide us from the enemy. In less than ten hours, we'd be safely back at our base in England.

I guess the first clue that we were about to look death in his soulless eyes was that we weren't assigned to our beloved *Sky Queen*. Instead, we were given *That's All Jack*. We had flown her once before, and she was a fine machine, but we felt safer in our *Queen* because, like a mother, she lovingly protected us.

The sky was an ominous black when our squadron took off at twenty-second intervals, flashing colored flares. Over three hundred planes were gettin' into formation, and the colorful splotches were lightin' the sky up like a Christmas tree.

My feelings of unease were growing, and soon I knew why. Wayne, our navigator, announced that our inexperienced group leader had arrived at the target eight minutes early. This meant we had to circle back around to line up, makin' us eight minutes late. Because we were now running behind, the P-51s turned back, and we no longer had our protective escort.

When we reached the target, instead of having cloud cover, it was completely clear. This meant that the German anti-aircraft gunners could see us. I'd prepared to release the radar-blocking chaff, but now it was a pointless endeavor. Yuppers, it was provin' to be one hell of a morning. By the time we started our ten-minute bomb run, the squadron below us was taking an immense number of hits, and black puffs filled the sky. The flak was so damn thick it looked as if you could walk across the sky on it.

We remained on course as bursts pounded on our mighty fortress. We took our first significant hit to the number two engine. Oil instantly started to leak, leavin' a four-foot streak in the air. A chorus of utterances, not fit for a drunken sailor, rang out when Wayne announced that the number three engine had also been hit. We were only in the first few minutes of the bomb run and things were not lookin' good.

The next hit was to the throttle column, which meant the captain couldn't control the plane. We had sustained so much damage we had to drop back. Once we were out of formation, several German FW fighters started firing at us. I got on the intercom to let the captain know that we no longer had cables runnin' from the rudder to the elevator. Then the fatal blow occurred, and gasoline leaked out of the holes openin' up in the left wing.

The plane was violently shaking when our captain called out, "We're still over twenty-two thousand feet, so when you disconnect your oxygen supply, get out fast so you don't pass out." The last thing I heard him say was, "Bail out fast, and good luck!"

The next few events happened so damn fast.

I think most of the crew parachuted immediately, but I was still in the radio room completin' my final task. Each day our top-secret radio codes were written on a flimsy piece of rice paper. Part of my job was to keep these from getting into enemy hands. I placed the paper into the side of my mouth. Since my mouth was dry from fear, it took forever to swallow it. Then I grabbed my security blankets—my volume of Kipling and the picture of Marty—and shoved them inside my coveralls. I zipped my jacket, checked my parachute harness, and was reachin' for the door to the waist section when shrapnel hit me.

Later I discovered that there was a four-inch-long piece of flak, pointed like an arrowhead, lodged in my forearm. At that moment, all I knew was I hurt, my arm couldn't move and blood was seepin' through my layers of clothing. Ralph, our waist gunner, was frantically calling for me to jump.

I didn't think I could pull my ripcord with a paralyzed arm. If I couldn't release the chute at twenty-two thousand feet, I was dead. Hangin' onto the door, thinking *I can't!*, I resigned myself to a cowardly death.

Luckily, I snapped out of it when I heard Ralph calling to me over our *Jack's* loud wheezing and bangin'. I followed his voice to the hatch, still unsure if I would be able to pull my ripcord with my injuries. The last thing I remember him sayin' was, "I waited for you. So, damn it, Robert, you better jump!"

The cold may have numbed the pain in my arm, but those unworldly temperatures didn't numb my terror. Every airman knew that he only had a twenty-five percent chance of completing twenty-five missions. Up until this time, I had seen myself as joining the ranks of the successful. Now, I was facing the realization that I was to join the unlucky seventy-five out of one hundred.

The knowledge that Ralph had risked his life forced me to find my nerve, because I wasn't about to let my crewman down. I prepared to jump as our dying fortress rolled to her side. In one last-ditch effort to protect her crew, just moments before exploding, she threw me out the hatch.

I don't remember pulling my ripcord. I also don't remember the fall. What I recollect was the pain from the bullet that hit me in the forehead. The pain of being shot in my arm was nothing compared to that of the searing burn that consumed my brain. The blackness of my temporary blindness followed.

Unable to see, I crash-landed in the middle of a field, shattering my hip. I tried to stand, but ended up dragging my body with my one good arm. Unfortunately, I had no idea where I was headed.

I think it was only a few minutes later that I heard voices. At that time, I didn't know who I was begging to help me. It ended up being a German man and woman. They half-dragged, half-carried me into a barn, where I hid under a pile of hay until dark.

My nightmare had begun.

Radio to Contraption, Over and Out!

…..…..*…..*

October 28, 2019
Dear Diary,

This afternoon I had a scare as I stood in the cereal aisle at Giant, contemplating what granola bars to buy. One of my pet peeves is how narrow the aisles are. Grocery store designers must be on the low end of the IQ scale, because how intelligent do you have to be to know that the lanes should be three cart-widths across? A cart should fit on either side, and there should still be room for people to travel down the center. If that were the case, I could have avoided today's embarrassing scene.

"Chocolate-cherry or blueberry-oats?" I asked myself right before I felt someone behind me. Fear took over, and I panicked.

He's too close. I can't breathe. What if he grabs me?

I whirled around and pushed the unsuspecting shopper as hard as I could.

The incident didn't end there. I ended up outside, seated on the curb, my head between my thighs, gasping for air. My victim, along with the store manager, eventually tracked me down. The large man I pushed was uninjured. He apologized for intruding into my space and startling me, explaining that he thought I had been asking him a question. Humiliated, I also apologized, confessing that I sometimes talked to myself. I ended up granola-less, so filling my cupboards will have to wait for another day.

Pap and I both started our mornings with what should've been a piece-of-cake, easy-peasy "milk run." The difference being, I hyperventilated in a grocery store parking lot while purchasing processed oat products, and Pap survived a twenty-two-thousand-foot plunge into Nazi Germany.

I'm so pathetic!

Wimpy teacher, Over and Out!

Patti

Chapter 11

October 29, 2019

Dear Diary,

Dr. Greene was absent when I arrived at my appointment today. His receptionist, the sweet blue-haired Mrs. Stewart, gave me a brownie, ushered me into his office, then told me he would be with me in a few moments because he was busy researching something.

My time alone allowed me to take in Jacob Greene's space. I suspect that in the past, I'd been busy taking in the doctor, because I felt like I was seeing everything for the first time. His office is one half of a restored turn-of-the-century duplex. Writestone's Clock Repair resides in the other half. I know the shop well since the elderly Mr. Writestone, the proprietor, was an old friend of my grandparents and an esteemed member of the borough Council. When I was younger, I had often visited Writestone's with my grandparents.

Delores Stewart's desk is in the small but pleasantly furnished waiting area. Dr. Greene's office has a masculine scholarly feel, the exact opposite of the country living floral motif of Mrs. Stewart's feminine room.

Greene's office is warm shades of beige, cream, and brown. A richly carved chair rail runs above wooden wainscoting paneling, and lavish crown molding frames the edge of the ceiling. Matching Arts and Crafts style lamps give the room a rugged elegance, and ornately carved frames showcase his numerous diplomas. The doctor's tidy mahogany desk, swivel chair, and matching file cabinet take up one side of the room. Today, an old-school office phone, a single file, and a laptop computer sat neatly arranged on the shiny surface of his workspace. A heavy roman shade covers the bay window behind his desk, serving double duty. Not only does it keep out the afternoon sun, it also protects the privacy of his patients.

Distinct from his private area is the therapy space where the healing takes place. It contains his leather chair, an end table, and the luxuriously upholstered settee I use. I would like to point out that offices like his don't have loveseats; they have settees.

"Pretentious. He needs some plants," I complained to the walls.

"What did you say? Who are you talking to?" the doctor asked as he entered the room.

His voice startled me, and I jumped. Embarrassed, that I was skittish, and talking to myself, I responded with, "Nice of you to show up, and I was taking notice that this room is in desperate need of a few plants."

My rudeness caused the usual arrogance to creep back into his voice. "What's wrong with my office?"

My mouth said, "I guess plants would be messy and ruin your macho brown theme?" Although the comment was not my fault. The yellow-eyed creature sitting on my left shoulder had said it. Most of me thought it was a nice office, perfectly suited to a cozy blanket, a hot cup of tea, and a volume of Sherlock Holmes.

He frowned, walked over to his desk, and looked at the lone file with contempt. Then he eyeballed me with a disconcerting I'm-staring-deep-into-your-psyche stare. He sighed, picked up the file, and delivered it to the mahogany cabinet in the corner. Either my impertinence had ruined his day, Mrs. Stewart had forgotten to do a filing chore, or he hadn't been laid in a while. He was, for sure, in a major snit. Seeing as how he looked like he looked and smelled like he smelled, I assumed it was not the latter.

Unable to look away, I watched as he reached for his tie, undid it, set it on the back of his desk chair, and unbuttoned the top button of his shirt. My left shoulder companion—the wound-up misbehaving one that has scary eyes and dresses in devil red—whispered, *Keep going. You have more buttons.*

Since both his theatrics and my fantasies were quite entertaining, I clamped my lips together, firming up my filter. I had embarrassed myself enough for one day, and it would take ten million lifetimes to recover from begging my psychotherapist to disrobe. Something became apparent as he stiffly walked across the room and sat in his leather chair. His suit and tie were strangling the life out of him.

Interesting!

Maybe we do have something in common.

"Hey, take it easy on Mrs. Stewart. All those files look the same. I'm sure she didn't mean to grab the wrong one," I said.

"Did you look at it?" he asked.

I pulled my chin back, looked at him, and huffed out an indignant, "Seriously? Why would I do that?"

If he scrunched up his face any more, his sinus cavities were going to implode. "Are you insinuating that I'm upset because Mrs. Stewart set out the wrong file?"

I shrugged. "Well, something has you in a mood. There's a big dark cloud over your head, and I'm supposed to be the depressed, anxiety-filled one. Have you considered your designer ties are strangling you and making you grumpy?"

His jaw tensed. Then he shook his head and laughed. It was a low chuckle emanating from deep inside his bench-press advertisement of a chest.

Dang!

"Patricia, let's start over. Are you sleeping any better?"

For once, I had good news. "I slept great Saturday night."

He looked up from his note-taking. "Why do you think that was?"

"My daughter came home for a visit and brought her boyfriend." I proceeded to fill him in on our happy family gathering.

He listened, made a few notes, and then brought up Mike. "The relationship you have with your ex-husband seems complicated. You still seem to be attached, despite having divorced two years ago."

I cringed. Mike and I probably had a dysfunctional relationship, and it was more complicated than I felt like dealing with at that moment.

Being the queen of deflection, I changed the subject. "What are you researching? Mrs. Stewart said that you were late because you were engaged in research."

His brain seemed to struggle with switching gears. I think he had already forgotten his project. It was a long moment before he responded. "I was researching something I think might interest you. Have you ever heard of epigenetics?"

"Epigenetics? No. Is it some sort of DNA-enhanced robot?" I asked.

This time I felt his low laugh vibrate and tingle the length of my body. What was wrong with me? I reacted to him like I was a horny college girl. Hadn't my hormones recently taken up residence in the Sahara Desert?

"Epigenetics is the study of how trauma can affect DNA. Many scientists believe that trauma can influence and change the genetic code for at least three generations."

"Why would that interest me?" I asked.

"From what you tell me of your grandfather, he struggled with post traumatic stress disorder. It's not uncommon for soldiers who have experienced combat to struggle with this. Interestingly, their children, grandchildren, and perhaps even great-grandchildren are at a higher risk of experiencing PTSD. For a long time, experts believed that it was environmental and that soldiers were instilling this propensity for PTSD in the way they raised their families. Now, through research, scientists are finding an actual change in the DNA. Therefore, the way you're reacting to your stressful situation may be due to changes in your family's genetic code."

I contemplated whether I should pretend like I understood what he was talking about or admit my confusion. He saved me the trouble when he continued his explanation.

"You experienced something terrifying, your work conditions are stressful, you are obsessed with aging, and you are genetically at risk for developing PTSD. It was wise of Dr. Long to suggest a medical leave and send you to me."

Mary Long hadn't sent me to him specifically. His name was the first on a list and popped up quickly on Google, but that seemed like an insignificant detail. The significant details were that a punk-ass kid had assaulted me, I was having a midlife crisis, and I had messed-up genetics.

I struggled to take in a breath as Ms. Angel and Mr. Devil hopped about on my shoulders and chanted in unison. *Yikes, there is a lot wrong with you! You are pathetic and don't stand a chance!* Then I thought about the grocery store incident, and my heart and brain raced each other in an all-out pant-producing sprint. I didn't have a smart-ass response because I knew Dr. Greene was correct. Getting out of bed was difficult, and it took every bit of strength I had not to crawl under my covers and hide from the world.

"I don't want to overwhelm you with that information. It's just something I find fascinating," he explained.

I didn't find it fascinating in the least, and he had failed miserably at not overwhelming me.

"I think you should look at it positively. If your grandfather could survive a hellish war, so can you! Not only do you share his DNA, but you also share his fortitude." Then he added, "StumpStrong!" I guess it was his way of being motivational.

I glared at him like he had two heads coming out of his perfect body. He frowned and looked at his notebook. It seemed to hurt his feelings that I didn't find his research fascinating. I continued to make distorted facial expressions until he rolled his eyes and bobbed his head. I suppose he was shaking off my negativity.

He changed tactics. "Tell me your favorite story about your grandfather, not a war story, a family story."

Good!

I wasn't into the entire Patti-is-a-loser-for-a-million-reasons discussion, and I had so many stories.

"My grandfather encouraged us to memorize poetry for fun. I can still recite 'Jabberwocky' and 'Gunga Din,' by heart, if you ever want to listen to me?" I teased.

Unfortunately, nobody had wanted to listen to me recite poetry since the advent of Netflix and the internet offering twenty-four-hour-a-day access to YouTube videos.

He laughed. "I love poetry. Maybe later."

Dr. Greene loves poetry?

Was he screwing with me?

I filed the comment away and told my tales. "My grandfather had a penchant for handicapping the ponies. He would sit at the kitchen table with his racing form, a cup of coffee, and cigarettes. Much to my grandma's disdain, he was always certain he was going to 'hit it big.' Grandma would occasionally throw his forms away, but within a week, he would be back, sitting at the kitchen table, 'kallating the odds.'"

I loved the way the doctor's smile started at the corners of his mouth, growing outward until it consumed his face.

I dove in, embracing storytelling mode. "When I was about twelve, he took me and my cousins Bobbie and Danielle to the racetrack. He gave us each ten dollars and let us place our own bets."

"Place your own bets? Weren't you too young for that?" Greene asked.

"My grandfather was so charming. He had a way with people. He sweet-talked this lady who worked at one of the betting booths, and she let us. I came home with twenty-two dollars. It was crazy fun! Plus, life was different in the seventies. Things weren't quite so..." I searched for my word, settling on "uptight." Then I smiled as I recalled the end of my first and only experience with gambling.

"When we got home and told Grandma how much fun it was and that the nice lady at the window had let us place our own bets, she went ballistic. Pap got grounded from his racing form for a couple of weeks."

Greene leaned back in his chair and chuckled. "Professor Stump sounds like a character."

Since Dr. Greene finally seemed to enjoy my stories, I continued.

"My pap drove around this boat-sized Cadillac. I think it was pink when I was a child and then beige when I was older. He was a regular taxi service, driving his grandchildren and his grandchildren's friends all over the place. My friends adored my grandparents. In fact, instead of going to beer parties on the weekends, we went to parties at my grandparents' house. They made us dinner, got us snacks, played games with us, told us stories, and rented movies to watch on their VCR. Having a VCR was a luxury back then."

At first, I doubted that my young doctor had any idea what a videocassette recorder was or that he would understand the significance of a teenager's life in the 1980s. However, he seemed to get it.

His sapphire eyes twinkled. "I think your grandparents and your childhood sound amazing. Your stories make me think about my family."

I loved reminiscing with the doctor, and he had told me I had fortitude like Pap. Perhaps he didn't think I was as pathetic and weak as I felt. The problem was, I had dismissed his theories on post traumatic stress disorder, probably because he had hit too close to home—and I still hadn't told him about my experience in the grocery store.

Sitting here trying to unwind from my day, I wish that I had filled Doctor Jacob in. I think he would have understood. How far gone am I?

Hopeless,
Patti

..........*.....*

Recorded November 13, 1972, by Robert Stauffer I, TSgt
Transcribed by Patricia Moore
Helloop Contraption,

Last time I talked into you, I was explaining how I had parachuted out of the *That's All Jack*, had taken shrapnel to my arm and a bullet to my brain, and had smashed up my hip. I was hiding out in that barn, waitin'. I was waitin' for the farmer to come back for me, waitin' for food and water, and waitin' to die.

I know my family takes pride in me pluck, but I didn't feel brave lying there. I was terrified and crying. I remember calling to my mother from that cold, damp barn. I thought for sure I was dying, and the thing I wanted most in the world was to say goodbye to her. I knew that somehow she'd hear me.

I had lost all concept of time and whatnot. I still had my photo and book inside my jacket, and that brought me some comfort. Talking to my mother over the miles was another source of solace.

When I finally heard the barn door open, I held my breath and tried not to make any noise in case it was the Gestapo. I made out three voices, a male, a female, and a young boy. Although I wasn't an expert at speaking it, I had gained quite an understanding of the German language from my pop speaking Pennsylvania German, my four years of high school German, and the language classes I had taken in basic training. I deduced they were a family of farmers discussin' what to do with me. The man was contemplatin' helping me get to the underground, his wife thought I was too injured for them to care for, and the young boy wanted to turn me over to the Gestapo for a reward.

Wondering what I could do to convince them to help me, I remembered the chocolate ration in my pocket. I got their attention by calling softly, and in slow, broken German, I begged them to clean up my wounds and protect me. Then I offered them the candy as payment.

The woman, kind and gentle, held a cup of water to my lips. She sang as she warshed my head and face. As she cleaned the dried blood from my eyes, and I relaxed, my vision returned. The doc explained to me that there are stories of soldiers temporarily losing sight from shock. Who knows? I had just sailed through the air like a wingless bird while having foreign objects inserted into my cranium. Terrified, but feelin' there was no other choice, I allowed her to take off my jacket and shirt. All three of them gasped because my forearm was ghastly. The woman broke the news that I was seriously injured by saying "bad, over and over again. However, she continued to comfort me and warsh my wounds. Her husband and boy left, and when they returned, the farmer had a knife in one hand and a bottle in the other. This time the liquid held to my lips was a strong schnapps-like beverage.

"Must get that out," the woman told me in broken English.

The farmer continued to force-feed me something akin to panner piss. His fingers pressed on my forearm. "Here, cut here," he said. He placed the knife, not much sharper than a butter knife, in my hand.

I think they were tellin' me I had to operate on myself because they couldn't help an American. I tried to cut out the shrapnel but failed. Eventually, the farmer took pity on me and lent assistance.

Terrified, feverish, cold, and drunk, I fell asleep listening to them discuss what they should do with the "Kaugummifresser," who might not live through the night.

I awoke the next morning with the shrapnel still in my arm. I was alive, hungover, gangrenous, and facin' a full-on Gestapo interrogation. That traitorous bastard of a Hitler youth turned me in, then absconded with my candy.

Over and Out!

..........*.....*

October 30, 2019
Dear Diary,

I had graphic life-like nightmares again last night. What started with Zoomie and I locked out of the house turned into my grandfather running through a field dragging a parachute behind him. I awoke right before a faceless person in a barn cut off my arm.

It took me an hour to convince myself to open my eyes and get out of bed. Having none of my pathetic pity party, Zoomie eventually jumped on my head and licked me until I had no choice but to get up if I wanted to wash his slobber from my face. Once I was coffeed up, I decided that I was in the mood for a run.

When Cassie was little, I loved to watch her create her artwork. I can still see her tiny fingers holding a fat blue crayon as she sketched fluffy clouds. Next, she would draw a yellow circle in the right-hand corner, then orange lines radiating from it. In the bottom left corner of the paper, she would plant her tree. It would reach high on the paper, sprouting thick, misshapen branches. Her tongue hung out the side of her mouth as she concentrated on creating a small circle in the center of the massive trunk. Inside the ring, she precisely set a four-limbed creature with a fluffy squirrel tail. She created tree leaves by forming a green amorphous shape at the top of her trunk. Finally, she would spatter pink and purple lollipop-looking flowers and V-shaped birds anywhere that the paper remained white.

I bring this up because it is precisely what my hometown looks like.

While I warmed up, Zoomie stood by the front door and howled a, *Hurry up, Mom.* It was a gorgeous day, warm enough to get away with leggings and a sweatshirt, and cool enough to cleanse and refresh the lungs. Mirroring Cassie's masterpiece, the sun was bright, its warm beams casting a golden glow on everything they touched, and fluffy white clouds were juxtaposed against the clear blue sky. The feel of the crisp air in my lungs was invigorating, and with every step we took, there was the satisfaction of hearing leaves crunch underfoot.

Massive ancient oaks lined our route and provided a shady canopy for most of the run. Zoomie knows what comes with oaks—acorns! He also knows what comes with acorns— squirrels! Thousands of chunky, spoiled squirrels live in our Central Pennsylvania version of Pleasantville, and they torment our furry children with a vengeance. Weeping cherry trees, hemlock evergreens that reach into the clouds, sweet red-leafed maples, towering elms, and flowering dogwood intersperse with the majestic white oaks.

The architectural hodgepodge of our neighborhood resembles a picturesque toy train Christmas village. We jogged past the gabled dormers of cozy Cape Cods and the symmetrical brick masonry of massive Georgian colonials. We viewed a bright blue Victorian Lady adorned with red and green gingerbread trim next to a timber and stucco fairytale-ish English Tutor. Every yard was perfectly manicured, and most had a porch of some sort. Quaint porch furniture and pots of planted flowers are the barometer of worth in my neighborhood.

Zoomie yipped at the young children on bikes, and I smiled at the retired folk tending to their late fall roses. Neighborhood etiquette requires we wave and say hello to everyone. My pup and I fervently obey this rule.

Zoomie, long-legged and athletic, strutted along with a graceful gait that rivaled a prize Peruvian racehorse. He called out to his buddies as he sashayed by. Tito, the snippy Chihuahua, seemed to think he was superior to Zoomie, although this didn't faze my self-assured Sheltie in the least. Leroy, the black Lab, joyfully raced us as we passed by his fence. Zoomie insisted on calling out a happy hello to Dexter, the massive snarling dog who smashed his body full force into his front window. Finally, we passed by our favorite English bulldog. We ran along his pine privacy fence with its cut out window booth and blue shutters. A painted name plate above the doggy height window read *Buster*. I tugged on Buster's cast iron visitor bell and waved as we chugged on by.

The last half mile of our run took us along the main street, past the town center, the great clock, and Valentina's Cup.

At first, I felt great following our three and a half miles. Unfortunately, after sitting at the coffee shop for fifteen minutes, my furry companion and I limped home. I recall the days that I could run forever pain-free. Today, every inch of me ached. I could feel arthritis in my hips, and my knees felt as though I needed to borrow the Tin Man's oil can. I had to remind myself that I was back at it and still putting in the miles at fifty. I stretched and took two Ibuprofen. Zoomie cuddled up beside me, and I read him some John Irving.

I crawled into bed early. Although my day wasn't productive, I did my best. With Zoomie's assistance, a tale from Pap, and an afternoon spent in my hometown with Mother Nature, I'd gotten out of bed and sweated my butt off. Although only a small victory, I feel StumpStrong. I defeated my demons today.

Fighting,
Patti

Chapter 12

"I suddenly realized what small towns are. They are places where you grow up with the peculiar—you live next to the strange and the unlikely for so long that everything and everyone becomes commonplace."

John Irving, *A Prayer for Owen Meany*

Halloween, October 31, 2019

Dear Diary,

When I showed up for my therapy session this afternoon, Mrs. Stewart was attired in a *Little House on the Prairie* dress and matching bonnet. Her costume suited her naturally old-fashioned look, and the plate of iced pumpkin cookies sitting in the waiting area added to the bygone ambiance she created. Mr. Writestone, the scrappy white-haired clockmaker from next door, sat beside her in his Stetson cowboy hat.

"Hello, Patricia. Happy Halloween! Have one of my homemade cookies," Mrs. Stewart insisted.

Since delayed calories are easier on the waistline, I decided to wait for forty-five minutes and responded with, "I'll grab one on the way out. They look delicious."

"This is Leonard Writestone. He owns the shop next door," she said.

I greeted him with a warm smile. Then I addressed Mrs. Stewart. "Actually, we know each other. He was a friend of my grandparents."

"Hi, Patricia," he said. "So good to see you." He turned to Mrs. Stewart. "Patricia's grandfather was a war hero. One of the bravest men I've ever met. Boy, could he tell a story. He was an amazing cook, played the piano, handicapped the horses, and wrote many a witty limerick. He was one of the greatest of the great generation, and her grandmother, Marty, was a beautiful woman—a real firecracker!"

I never tire of hearing how wonderful my grandparents were. My chest expanded to the moon as it filled with pride. "Thank you. I miss them."

"Delores, you would have loved Marty and Bob. They prepared a full course dinner every night. They were both amazing cooks. They invited everyone who showed up at their door to the meal, and the expectation was you ate until your belly hurt. They'd pull up chairs and squeeze everyone around the table. Of course, they insisted you stay for coffee, dessert, and stories."

I recalled seeing a much younger, dark-haired Mr. Writestone at the dinner table. Grandma and Pap had been fond of him.

"After living through the Depression and wartime famine, my grandparents had a rule. Nobody would go hungry during their watch." I smiled at my sweet memory. "Grandma used to call after-dinner time 'Coke with Kipling.'"

Mr. Writestone thought for a moment; then, his face lit up. "I remember that."

I filled Mrs. Stewart in. "The family across the street did Tea with Shakespeare. Grandma thought it pretentious, so we drank soda and listened to Kipling."

Mrs. Stewart had a youthful giggle. "Sounds delightful. I wish life were still like that."

Although I loved the nostalgia of my childhood, and my grandparents were the best, I knew life hadn't been perfect pre-Civil Rights. However, that was not the present discussion, so for once, I swallowed my opinion.

"They would have approved of your baked goods, Delores." Mr. Writestone winked at Mrs. Stewart.

I chuckled at the charming geriatric flirtation.

"How are your parents? Your mother was a beauty too. Took after your grandmother." Mr. Writestone paused for a moment, focused his eyes on me, and added, "My goodness, Patricia, you look more and more like Marty each passing year."

At that point, ignoring the cookie plate took most of my focus. I managed to get out, "Thank you. My parents are doing well. They haven't killed each other yet."

Mr. Writestone's knee slap signified he found my statement amusing.

Mrs. Stewart watched him for a moment before reaching for the phone. "I'll let Dr. Greene know you're here."

I couldn't help but smile, watching Laura Ingalls buzz her boss.

A few moments later, Dr. Greene greeted me. He had forgone a Halloween costume to sport his uncomfortably-dressed-sexy-psychotherapist attire.

Our session began with his usual questions. Was I sleeping at night? Was I getting out of bed during the day? What was I doing to manage my stress? Was I journaling? Was my daughter contacting me? Were Zoomie and I running? Was I standing up to my boss? And finally, was I listening to my grandfather's stories? Since it had only been forty-eight hours since my last appointment, not much had changed, except today I sat there in my low-cut green blouse instead of the pretty—or was it mangy?—blue sweater I had worn to Tuesday's session.

Finally, he asked me an unexpected question. "Are you doing anything fun for Halloween?"

After weeks of hard questions, I gave a sigh of relief over this easy one. "Tonight is trick or treat, so Zoomie and I will hand out candy. Zoomie has a Super Dog costume. He looks adorable, and the neighborhood kids love when he dresses up."

There was a gleam in his eyes when he nodded.

"Tomorrow night, I'm going to a holiday party at the police station with Neil Harris, the cop on my case."

I was a bit nervous about the date and uncertain if I wanted to go, but I didn't feel like exploring it with my therapist, so I decided not to mention my doubts.

"Saturday is the Harvest Walk. Have you ever been to it?" I asked.

Doctor Jacob raised an eyebrow. "No, I've only lived in the area for a little over two years, but I've seen signs around town. Tell me about it."

As of late, I may have had the energy of a frying slug on a hot patio, but the fall festival still got me excited.

"It's so much fun. The small businesses on Main Street all open for the evening and host a big party. My best friend owns Valentina's Cup. It takes her all day to set things up, so I lend a hand. This year's theme is Yo Ho, a Pirate's Life For Me, and pirate skeletons and tiki torches will line the street. There will be a bonfire, and the hardware shop is building a full-sized ship mast and plank. We're decorating the coffee shop to look like an old tavern. Most people come in costume. Most of the adults will probably dress like pirates, and the kids wear whatever costume they want. Last year's theme was the Roaring Twenties. Fun for the entire family for only ten dollars a person," I said in my best salesperson voice and giggled like a fool before finishing my pitch. "You purchase a wristband at the borough building, and then you can wander around town, eat great food, play games, and listen to the bands."

"Sounds very quaint." Greene scribbled something in his notebook.

I bristled, wondering if "quaint" was an insult. Since my handsome doctor was an outsider, I hoped he wasn't making fun of my hometown.

Whatever!

As a teacher, it was my job to focus on others. I'm not great at embracing change, so forty-five minutes dedicated to my shortcomings still made a hard pill to swallow. Hoping to change to an offensive position I asked him a question. "Do you have any fun plans?"

Doctor Jacob jerked his attention from his note-taking to stare at me like I had sprouted a third eye. He appeared to contemplate something profound before answering, "No. None at all."

The weeks of staring at his tense muscles, the obsessively neat office, and rare smiles indicated to me that he needed some enjoyment. After all, I was a teacher; the world was my classroom, and everyone required my pedagogical advice. "You should do something fun. What would make you happy?"

His eyes lost their earlier sparkle, and his lips straightened. "Let's get back to you."

I had touched a nerve. I silently diagnosed my psychotherapist with a severe case of Uptightis Avoidancitis.

I blurted out, "You should check out the Harvest Walk and be sure to stop by my friend's shop."

I have no idea what got into me. Perhaps cookie deprivation had addled my brain. Why else would I have invited my therapist to my haven?

He scribbled again. I hope that it wasn't *the crazy red-haired lady hit on me,* because inviting him was an accident. I certainly wasn't hitting on him. I simply thought he required a dose of fun. Well, that and the sugar withdrawal thingy I was experiencing.

I sighed in relief at a quarter before four, when the session timer on his cell phone beeped and he promptly ended our session with, "Have fun handing out candy. Enjoy your date, and have a blast at your Pirate Party." I was almost out the door when he added, "Hey, Patricia. That green blouse is pretty, and it matches your eyes."

Holy Crap!

Patti

..........*.....*

October 31st

P: Hi, Cassie. Happy Halloween! 🎃 Are you doing anything fun tonight?

Cassie: No! I Have a big paper due Monday.
Cassie: Did you get a lot of trick-or-treaters? Did Zoomie dress up and help hand out candy?

P: Zoomie was Super Dog. Lots of kids! Missed having you help me.

Cassie: I wish I could come home this weekend.

P: Why don't you? Please! Should be fun. I'm helping Tina make the coffee shop look like a Pirate tavern.

Cassie: I really want to, but I need the campus library to finish my paper.

P: Your dad showed up tonight to sand the front door. He was trying to fix it while the kids were ringing the bell??? 😳

Cassie: Sounds like Dad. He probably wanted to see the trick-or-treaters. He doesn't get any at his apartment. 😄

P: I have a date with Neil tomorrow. He's taking me to a Halloween party at the police station.

Cassie: Cool! Have a blast!
Cassie: Love you, Mom. Gotta go. Take pictures this weekend for me.

P: Love you the most! 🖤
Friday, November 1st

Cassie: Hey, Mom. How was your date? Did you wear a costume or that mangy sweater? 😄

P: Well, aren't you funny? I just got home. I wore my slinky witch costume! Happy?

Cassie: Awesome! That a girl! What was Neil? Did you have fun?

P: He wore surgical scrubs. I think he borrowed them from Cody Smith. I didn't want to go, but I'm glad I did because it was fun. Neil is nice, and he makes me feel pretty.

Cassie: Mom! You are pretty!!! Don't you notice everyone staring at you? I know you think it's because you have Medusa-hair, but it's because you are beautiful.

P: 🖤

Cassie: Gotta go. I need sleep. Remember, send pics tomorrow.

Cassie: Love you the most! 🖤🖤

P: I love you more than the most!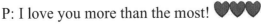

Chapter 13

"This is a handy cove, and a pleasant sittyated grog-shop. Much company, mate?"

Robert Louis Stevenson, *Treasure Island*

November 2, 2019

Dear Diary,

Arrr! It was one hell of a night!

It's been so long since I've felt pretty. I have become obsessed with the smattering of gray hairs creeping in around my ears, the creases on my forehead, and the strange Miss Prissy-like thingy going on under my chin. Recently, I've had to deal with the ugly bruising on my neck and an unappealing raspy voice from injured vocal cords. Since my divorce and unsolicited teaching transfer, I have felt exhausted, bitter, and lonely. Since my violent assault, I've added "panicky" to the list. Perhaps it was my daughter's text yesterday, or the way Neil stared at me, or the jealousy apparent in Shelly's comments, or the way Jacob Greene's eyes followed me as I danced, but tonight I felt vibrant and beautiful! Unfortunately, the way Mike and I reacted to each other threw me into a tailspin.

I suppose the tight corset, false eyelashes, and red-ribboned Lady Morgana stiletto boots had done their job. I didn't look hideous. Upon seeing me, Tina yelled an obnoxiously flattering, "Caliente!" She looked voluptuous in a tight-laced purple corset that enhanced her already plentiful cleavage.

Let me start at the beginning.

Tina, Chelsea, and I spent the morning at Connie's Day Spa. Connie's is more of an old-fashioned neighborhood beauty parlor than a day spa. Most of the women in town between the ages of nine and ninety patronize it before special occasions. Although Connie's daughter is now the proprietress and every decade it has received a fresh coat of paint, and every few years a new shampoo girl, little else has changed since 1952 when it opened its doors. I didn't have the heart to tell my friends that my shoestring budget, with me being on leave from work, no longer allows luxuries such as hair and nails. I scraped together fifteen dollars for a basic polish. Chelsea and Tina ordered *The Works,* and I chose a vibrant red lacquer and listened to the latest gossip. Apparently, Kalee and Mitch Johnson are getting a divorce because of the scandalous Stacy Lebowitz. I wonder if people talked about Mike and me when we divorced? Perhaps they had, since Mike has always been popular, and I am Robert Stauffer's oldest granddaughter, with hair the color of fire. I suspect that even if the crowd at Connie's hasn't gossiped about the Moores before, we'll surely be next week's topic of conversation following our behavior at the pirate party.

By late morning the girls and I were back at Valentina's Cup. With Cody's assistance, we had turned the coffee shop into a pirate tavern called Ye Olde Jolly Mug. There were barrels of grog a'plenty, a festooned Jolly Roger Flag above the coffee bar, and black and red striped fabric covered the tables. We had placed eye patches and tricorn hats on the skeletons scattered around the room. Below the bookshelf sat a large treasure chest full of Dollar Store pirate booty.

Tina had decorated cookies to look like pirate faces, and she had carved a watermelon into a ship and filled it with fresh fruit. There were also cheese and crackers speared with hors d'oeuvres swords, a plate of fresh veggies, and a four-layer chocolate cake decorated to look like an overflowing chest of gold coins and colorful jewels. Tina had outdone herself in true Cake Boss Style. In addition to the grog, we had refreshed the coffee bar, and a keg of beer was available for those over twenty-one.

The crisp sixty-degree evening meant perfect conditions for harvest visitors to stroll along the main street and enjoy the festivities. A bonfire in the town center would keep everyone warm if the temperatures dipped too low when the sun went down.

Although the festival hadn't officially started, Zoomie and I took a stroll along the street earlier in the afternoon to enjoy the fall air and snap selfies for Cassie. We walked the plank at Miller's Hardware, decorated a pumpkin at the Main Street Art Studio, and peeked at Davy Jones' Locker housed at Toni's Original Pizza. Tiki torches and skeletons dressed in pirate garb lined the main street and then encircled the town square. The charming old clock and the lattice gazebo formed the backdrop for the make-shift stage where the bands were to play. A performance by the high school jazz band was to kick off the show at seven p.m. A twelve-piece old-school funk band was to take the stage at nine. By one minute after ten, our quiet little town would be back to normal, but from six to ten, it was slated to be a raucous pirate party.

By five forty-five, Zoomie was at home napping on the couch. By six, I was back at Valentina's. Chelsea contributed by operating the coffee counter and serving snacks. I considered explaining that a pirate wench wouldn't wear neon arm sleeves and large glitter hair flowers, but what was the point? Chelsea's style sense, although offensive to the eyes, was hardly hurting anyone. With Cody, our beloved local football celebrity's assistance, I greeted the marauding sea-rovers at the entrance. Tina sprinted around on her stiletto heels, tending to everything else.

Our borough council had borrowed a couple of city police officers to help with crowd control. As I expected, Neil, dressed in his uniform, stopped in the shop to say hello. He took in my costume, grinned, and said, "You were a sexy witch and are an even sexier pirate." He greeted his niece before grabbing cookies and coffee, and then he was off to protect our celebrating town.

His responsibilities for the evening might consist of reuniting a lost child with a parent or discouraging a few seventeen-year-olds from hanging out near the kegs. Mostly he would reroute cars as they tried to drive down the closed-off main street. I doubted it would be as exciting as his typical Saturday nights in the city, busting pimps and breaking up bar fights.

When Neil exited Ye Jolly Old Mug, Valentina, Chelsea, and Cody pointed at his retreating back and winked. I need to gently break it to my cheer squad that although Neil is a great guy, the relationship isn't going anywhere. I'm too old for him.

I also expected to see Mike. As annoyed as it made me, this is his hometown too. I had hoped he would pass my station by, but he didn't. Instead, he and Shelly strolled right in and sat down at one of the tables. Every business on the street had a place for them to be, and they were going to camp out in my sphere? So be it, but I didn't intend to be friendly or wait on them.

I hate to admit it, but Mike looked healthier than he had in decades. His once gray hair was the chocolate brown shade it had been during our college days. His eye patch added a rugged touch that suited him. He had tucked his breeches into leather captain's boots adorned with brass buckles. A crimson velveteen waistcoat accentuated his newly muscular physique, and he had stashed a fake dagger into the silk sash tied around his thinned-out midsection. His costume must have cost a fortune.

Shelly, on the other hand, looked absurd. She had more cleavage, bigger hair, higher heels, and wore more make-up than—well, more than me. What a wench!

Tina sashayed to me. "Should I send Chelsea over to the table? Maybe she'll spill coffee and beer all over them."

"Shhh," I whispered. I didn't want to appear as immature and mean-girl as I felt. Although, in my defense, they had come into my haven, and when one's ex-husband starts to date a brainless twit half his age, one should be entitled to feel a tiny bit mean-girl. Right?

What I didn't expect was for Doctor Jacob, attired in a baggy white shirt unbuttoned to reveal his spectacular athletic chest, to walk into the pirate tavern. But he did, at precisely six twenty-seven, with a beautiful blond girl dressed as a French countess. Layers of blue chiffon ruffles formed her costume—that was even more expensive than Mike's—and she looked classy among the scantily dressed pirate strumpets.

The doctor held out his hand in greeting. He had rolled up his sleeves revealing his muscular forearms.

Perhaps scribbling builds sinew?

I took his extended palm in mine, but immediately pulled back because his touch caused an unsettling ripple of heat to travel the length of my body.

He ignored my absurdly awkward withdrawal and introduced me to the smiling girl beside him. "Patricia, this is my fiancée Claire. Clair, this is Patricia."

I helped Claire fix a cup of coffee while the doctor busied himself at the keg. Then I left them at their table and resumed my greeting post.

Tina pranced my way. "Who are they?"

"You're so nosey," I chided. Although occasionally annoying, Tina's curiosity was also one of her endearing attributes.

"If you must know, that is my psychotherapist, Dr. Greene, and his fiancée."

She fanned herself in jest. "Muy guapo!"

Since I thought he might be watching, I hushed her and used my body to conceal my slaps to her fingers. Tina, not one to be told what to do, continued pretending to cool herself off as she flitted away to talk to the other visitors.

Concentrating on my hostess duties became increasingly difficult. I felt oddly conspicuous, and as though every eye in the place was watching me. "Paranoid much?" I muttered under my breath.

Yes, it has occurred to me that given everyone in my gossipy town probably knows that I'm seeing a therapist, I should stop talking to myself in public. Unfortunately, that is much easier said than done.

I felt Mike and Shelly's stares and knew they were talking about me. Shelly wore an energy-sucking grimace and Mike a frown. Since I wanted to know what they were saying, and Mike's cup was empty, I took him another.

"Ahoy, ye scurvy dog, I see ye need more grog?" I placed my booted foot on a chair and plopped a fresh beer on the table. "That-a-be all your doubloons, unless ye wantin' to be turned into shark bait."

Mike threw his head back and laughed. "Thank ye, wench."

"He is capable of getting his own beer," Shelly declared.

Given my luck, I figured I was showing crotch, so I placed both feet on the ground. Then, ignoring her annoyance, I continued to run a rig. "Aye, aye, landlubber. Shiver me timbers. I see ye doth surely have two legs and no pegs." I dramatically peeked under the table at Mike's boots.

He continued to play along. "A smart lass ye be. Fetch yerself a cup and rest a spell."

I guess Shelly wasn't well versed in pirate lingo or appreciative of our jokes, because her body stiffened and she spat, "I hear a kid at school tried to kill you. Did you tell him a bad pirate pun too?"

For a dumb girl, Shelly sure knew how to stop a conversation she wasn't enjoying.

Mike gasped. It had been such a wonderful day that I had forgotten all about my tragic incident. The mention of it felt like a slap across the face.

"Mike, they don't have anything here I want to eat or anything I want to see. Let's go!" Shelly stood and stomped off.

"I'm sorry, Pat. I shouldn't have told her I thought—"

"Come on, Mike. Now!" she called.

"Sorry," he said again.

Without finishing his sentence, leaving me desperate to know what he had told her, he followed Shelly out the door like an obedient puppy. My heart ached to see that he allowed her to treat him so poorly.

"Was I so bad that you traded me in for that?" I whispered as he disappeared into the night.

So much for not talking to myself.

Dr. Greene and Claire sat wide-eyed. I think they had witnessed the entire scene. I took a deep breath, walked to their table, my heels clicking on the cafe floor indicating a confidence I didn't feel.

There was no pirate talk this time. It had lost its charm. "Are you enjoying yourselves?" I asked.

Claire swallowed. "Yes. This cake is delicious."

"We couldn't help but notice those people seemed upset. Were they giving you a rough time?" the doctor asked.

I figured the truth was the least embarrassing explanation. "That was my ex-husband and his girlfriend. She doesn't like me very much."

"Oh." He nodded. "I can see why."

I bristled. "What do you mean by that?"

Why would anyone not like me? Besides the obvious reasons. I was anxiety-filled, paranoid, opinionated, and had a rather porous filter.

Still, what a rude thing for him to say.

"All I meant was, well, he is your ex-husband. You have a lot of history."

Since he was hem-hawing, I didn't think that was at all what he had meant. This conversation was far from over, but it would have to continue at another time. I had no intention of having more guests walk out of the party I was helping to hostess.

"Patricia, I noticed the bookshelves." Greene pointed to my project. "The one shelf says *Ms. M's picks*. Is that you?"

I eyed my shelf. "Yes. I need to update my choices."

He squinted to make out the titles from his seat.

I filled him in. "*Of Human Bondage* by Somerset Maugham, *I Know Why the Caged Bird Sings* by Maya Angelou, and *A Prayer for Owen Meany* by John Irving."

"Interesting choices." Dr. Greene tapped his fingers on the rim of his empty cup. "Well, we're going to walk around and check out the rest of the activities. Thank you for inviting us." He stood.

I had accidentally asked him, and I hadn't invited the pretty young girl on his arm. But I didn't think it polite to articulate it. And what had he meant by "interesting choices"?

"I want to walk the plank." Claire stood and extended her hand. "Thank you, Patricia. Jacob tells me all about you, so I'm glad we had a chance to meet."

It seems to me that a psychotherapist telling his girlfriend about his nutty-ass middle-aged patient might be against the Hippocratic Oath. I'm pretty sure that even if it isn't illegal, it's invasive and odd. Although, what do I know?

Dr. Greene grimaced. "Come on, Claire." He grabbed her hand to escort her out before she divulged any more of his secrets. When he gave me a look of protest and shook his head, I guess it was his way of saying, *No! I didn't tell my girlfriend about you, crazy lady!*

"Don't miss the bands at eight," I called after them.

"Maybe we'll see you there," he called back.

Chelsea walked toward me.

"Humiliating!" I told the psychedelic pirate before fleeing to seek protection behind a locked restroom door.

I was almost fifteen minutes late for the concert because it took me that long to settle my breathing and pull myself together. The high school band had just finished when I approached. Hundreds of people of all ages gathered around the makeshift stage and roaring bonfire. I think most of the town had turned out. Middle school boys tossed around a football. High school cheerleaders wound up the crowd. Boys in monster masks terrorized little girls in princess costumes. Pirates carrying plastic cups of grog roamed the town square. I snapped a photo of the happy fête to send to Cassie.

After a barbershop quartet entertained us, a country band took the stage. First, they got everyone up honky-tonkin', and then they played a slow song so that happy couples could pair up and hold each other tight. I giggled when I noticed that Mrs. Stewart and Mr. Writestone had paired off. I didn't laugh watching the doctor take his partner in his arms. Seeing his hand on the small of her back as he turned her in an intimate circle, I felt a pang of jealousy. When his eyes met mine, I broke contact to find a waving Neil.

The band played another slow song, and more dreamy couples joined the dance floor. A pig-tailed girl being twirled around in her father's arms reminded me of Mike and Cassie.

Mike's voice interrupted my moment of nostalgia. "Come on, Pat. Let's dance."

I protested for a moment, but he pushed me to the center of the action. He had discarded the eye patch that I found alluring. At least now I could see his thick black lashes and heavy eyebrows. I had loved those lashes and brows and had always been envious because my fair features required daily coloring.

"What about Shelly?" I didn't particularly care, but I asked anyway.

He leaned close to tell me, "I took her home. She wasn't having fun. I wanted to come back and listen to the bands."

Being with Mike was comfortable. We had danced together hundreds of times, so there was no awkwardness in our embrace. Although he's much taller, I had on my ribboned heels, and I could rest my head on his shoulder. I clung to him as he held me tightly and sang with the band.

Mike captured my heart the first time he whispered sweet lyrics to me at his fraternity formal in 1989. He had sealed the deal with the slow dance at our wedding in 1992. Tonight, the sound of his velvety voice crooning softly in my ear left me confused and aching.

When the song ended, we remained glued together. The feel of his breath warmed me to the core. In our younger days, he had lost himself in the scent of my gardenia and rose shampoo. Tonight, Mike stood in the middle of our town square, inhaling my scent, as I desperately held on to him. It was the first time I've felt safe since Tanner Jones asked me for popcorn, and it was the first time I haven't felt lonely in years.

Minutes after the band picked up the pace, Mike and I separated. I'm fairly certain the entire town witnessed us clinging to each other long after the slow song ended. Tina scowled at me. Mr. Writestone winked at me. Dr. Greene peeked out from around his girlfriend to stare. I searched the crowd for a police uniform, but I couldn't find Neil.

"Oh, Mike!" I whimpered.

Since there was slim to no chance that the earth might open beneath me and swallow me whole, I contemplated sprinting from the town center to hide my flushed face under my blankets.

Mike cleared his throat. "I'm going to get a beer. Do you want one?"

"God, yes!" I answered.

As he walked away, Tina made her way through the crowd to scold me. "¿Que rayos fue eso?" Over the years, I learned this meant, *What in the hell was that?*

"I don't know, Tina. I guess it's been a long time since Mike and I have danced."

"Be careful," she said. "He hurt you."

I wanted to defend him and tell her that it wasn't all his fault, that I shared the blame. Instead, I stood there, feeling the fool. Finally, Mike returned with my beer, which I promptly chugged.

As soon as the funk band started to play, Tina grabbed my hand and pulled me onto the dance floor, where we remained for the rest of the evening.

"You know," she said, yelling into my ear so that I could hear her over the music, "Neil is crazy about you, and he's a nice guy."

I spun around. "I know."

She bumped her hip into mine. "You know, your sexy shrink wants you, bad!"

"What?" I yelled into her ear. "What makes you say that?"

She turned her other hip to me and bumped. "He hasn't taken his eyes off of you all night. His pretty little girlfriend can't get his attention no matter what she does."

"Hmpff," I snorted. "I'm almost old enough to be his mother."

"Knock it off, Patti. Stop being ridiculous. You are not, and you look like you're the same age as me."

Relaxed by the beer that I had chugged, I busted out some Shakira-style hip moves while loudly singing, "She's a brick house!"

Again my best friend was beside me, yelling secrets. "I think Mike is still in love with you, and I think even though you protest, you're still in love with him."

That had to be the most absurd statement she had hollered at me all night.

At ten sharp, the spell broke, the coachmen turned into dirty dishes at the coffee shop, my glass slippers turned into two mismatched socks, and Prince Charming turned into my perplexing ex-husband with a bitchy girlfriend.

Arrr,
Patti

..........*.....*

November 3, 2019
Dear Diary,

Early this morning, Mike showed up at my door. I didn't let him in because I was afraid he would say that dancing with me had been a mistake. Or he would tell me that I looked too provocative with my big hair, false eyelashes, and push-up bra. Or, my worst fear, he would insist that I shouldn't have clung to him while we danced.

At first, I kept the screen door between us.

Mike kept his hand on the handle and his eyes on mine. "Come on, Pat. Let me in. Let's talk."

Not breaking eye contact, I responded, "Mike, go away. It's early."

"Just give me a few minutes. Please?" He shifted his weight back and forth.

"No. I'm tired, and I'm not dressed." I closed the heavy wooden door.

He opened the screen and plopped onto his knees to call to me through the mail slot. "I don't care. I've seen you naked. Hell, I've seen you with puke in your hair, and I've seen you push a bloody baby out of your body."

I closed my eyes and begged. "Mike, please go away."

"Can I at least say hi to Zoomie?"

Hearing his name, my dog was all tail wags, butt wiggles, and Sheltie smiles.

"Zoomie doesn't want to see you either."

Taking offense at my lie, Zoomie barked in protest and stared at me with pleading puppy eyes.

"Don't look at me like that," I whispered to my traitorous pup.

Mike pushed his hand into the slot to hold it open. "Are you talking to yourself again?"

I considered slapping his hand away, then nailing the slit closed. "No, I'm talking to Zoomie."

Mike's russet eye peered up at me. "You know I have a key, right?"

"Thanks for reminding me. I'm going to get the lock changed."

Mike remained calm. "No, you aren't. Come on, let me in. Do you want the neighbors to hear us?"

He was correct: I wasn't going to change the lock, and I didn't want the neighbors to hear us. But I did need the final word. "Mike, go away. Go bug Shelly."

That was the end of our thirty-year relationship to a T. Me getting in the last word. Mike walking away. Me crying. Mike finding solace in another woman.

Patti Pity Party time was a go. I was a fifty-year-old divorcée whose daughter was away at college. I was currently on medical leave and paycheck-less. I was going to die old and alone because even my dog preferred someone else's company.

After about ten minutes of tears, I decided to call Neil and apologize for my indiscriminate dance debacle. But first, I wanted to hear my grandfather's voice.

Patti, the crybaby

…..…..*…..*

Recorded by Robert S. Stauffer I, TSgt on November 20, 1972

Transcribed by Patricia Moore

Helloop Contraption,

I've been sufferin' with excruciating headaches again. Doc says they're a severe type of migraine called cluster headaches. This one lasted a week. It felt like someone was tryin' to burrow behind my eye with a Craftsman drill. I was bedridden most of the time. Big Red came to visit, but I couldn't leave my bedroom. I tried a shot of whiskey to dull the pain, but that exasperated it. The kids got me a tape of *Riders of the Purple Sage* to listen to. I hope they know I appreciated it, but it also made the throbbing worse. Doc doesn't know what is causin' the pain. I wonder if it was the bullet I took to my noggin? It seems to be affecting the same side of my face.

Anywho, my last story ended with me wakin' with the damn Gestapo in my face. The bastard who seemed to be in charge rammed a long rifle in my chest. His English was surprisingly good. He demanded to know my name and what I was doin' there. I told him my name, rank, and serial number and then answered everything else as instructed: "I am sorry, sir, I do not know."

I think I may have been in bad enough shape that he went easy on me. I suspect my interrogators decided that I wasn't long for this world or of much use to them, because a couple of uniformed men scooped me up and tossed me into a dirty wheelbarrow. I was carted out of the barn, across a field, through the streets of a bombed-out town, to a building where I stayed overnight.

I think the trek in that filthy cart changed me. Up until that moment, the Germans soured me milk. I wanted them all dead and had no qualms about droppin' those bombs. Seeing the acres of scorched farms, and the silhouettes of the sickly looking mothers holdin' the hands of grimy children, was gut-wrenching. I witnessed the scraps of what must have once been beautiful buildings and cozy homes. One German mother, a small mite of a babe in her arms, smiled at me and presented me with a shiny apple. A man who thinks he's about to die ponders his decisions, so doubt was settin' in. I wondered if I deserved to have my mangled body transported like a pile of shit in a grubby barrow?

I never saw the farmer or his wife again, and I often wonder what happened to them. Did their little bastard of a Nazi son get them killed?

Make no mistake, the Nazis and the German people were two different beings. The first were hideous evil demons, and the second were innocents trapped in a horrible nightmare of warshin' wounds and handing apples to the enemy.

That's all she wrote. For today, anyway.

Chapter 14

"Older than me, but my first un—
more like a mother she were—
showed me the way to promotion an' pay,
an' I learned about women from 'er!"

Rudyard Kipling, *The Ladies*

November 4, 2019

Dear Diary,

Since I spent most of yesterday feeling sorry for myself, I refocused in an attempt to make today more productive. After our run, Zoomie and I stopped by Valentina's for breakfast. I also needed to update my book picks for November.

It was unusual for the coffee shop to be empty on a Monday morning, but since it was, Tina asked me if I would keep an eye on things while she ran a few errands. She had given Chelsea the morning off, so I was alone. I prepared coffee and a pumpkin scone for myself, and water and one of Tina's homemade peanut butter doggy biscuits for the Zoom-monster.

Zoomie, dressed in his purple service vest, curled up beside the bookshelf and watched with sleepy eyes as I busied myself alphabetizing its contents. I had decided that Ms. M's November Picks would honor my grandfather, so the shelf now contained Stevenson's *Treasure Island,* Rudyard Kipling's illustrated edition of *The Jungle Book*, and *Riders of the Purple Sage* by Zane Grey.

I proudly studied my shelf before declaring, "Pap would be happy."

"A tribute to your grandfather?" a voice behind me said.

Startled, I jumped and whirled around, shoving an unsuspecting Dr. Greene out of my space.

"I'm sorry." I grasped at my chest as I panted out, "You scared me. Did I hurt you?"

Dr. Greene's eyes were narrow but soft. "No. I'm fine, and I'm sorry I startled you. Although you seem a bit jumpy. Does this happen to you often?"

I concluded that I needed to come clean to my therapist even though we weren't in a session. "Yes. It's been happening to me lately. The other day I pushed a man that came up behind me in the grocery store."

I suspected Dr. Greene knew as well as I did that my jumpiness was a byproduct of the unfortunate strangling incident. However, it didn't feel like it was the appropriate time or place to address it.

"I'm sorry. I didn't mean to scare you," he reiterated. "This must be Zoomie."

Upon hearing his name, my pup's tipped black ears popped to alertness. Regal and handsome, Zoomie proudly posed like a supermodel. He barked a greeting and pranced a few steps to bask in the doctor's attention.

"What a gorgeous dog!" Doctor Jacob punctuated some scratches with a couple of head pats.

"Did you lose something the other night? There's a lost and found behind the counter." I assumed there could be no other reason for his visit.

"No. I thought I would come in and have a cup of coffee and read one of Ms. M's picks, but I don't see the book now."

"Which one do you want?"

"*Of Human Bondage.*"

"Great choice. I just alphabetized the shelves by author. Here." I pulled the volume from its spot between *Lolita* and *Paradise Lost* and handed it to him.

"Thanks." He tapped the book. "I have the morning off, so I'm going to hang out and read."

Since his indecipherable comment from the harvest festival still bothered me, I blurted out, "Dr. Greene, what did you mean when you said my books were interesting choices?"

Nope. I'm not paranoid in the least.

His puffed-up chest seemed to indicate he found himself quite perceptive. "A book about a woman finding her voice, another about feeling you are fated to a life of bondage, and a third about friendship."

"Don't flatter yourself or over analyze my choices. I like every book on these shelves." I used a dramatic Vanna White-inspired gesture to show off my collection. Then I gave him a wry smile to let him know I found humor in his silly psychoanalysis.

He shrugged. "I don't know the real themes, I was just guessing. Even though I love to read, I haven't read all three. I liked Owen Meany, though. I'm teasing you since you're intent on knowing my meaning. What I was thinking was, it doesn't surprise me that you're well read. You're full of surprises."

His mouth turned up on one side.

"Surprises? Like what?" I asked.

"Besides being well read, sometimes you're kind of funny. You're a runner, and boy, can you dance."

I rolled my eyes. "You mean for an old lady I can move?"

He huffed out an exasperated sigh. "You need to stop the self-deprecating talk, and yes, you owned the dance floor the other night."

"I like funk music" seemed to be an appropriate response.

He followed me to the counter.

"What can I get you? Coffee and…" I let my question trail off, then added, "I'm manning the counter while Valentina runs errands."

"Pirate lass, funk dancer, and barista. Even more surprises." The grin that followed sent a shiver up the nape of my neck.

For a split second, I thought he might be flirting with me. I wondered what he would do if I reached over and played with one of his sexy blond waves. Would he slap my hand away? Would he laugh at me? Would he let me?

Danger! Back away from the testosterone, my shoulder angel advised. *Your doctor is a player.*

Soft hair! Touch, Patti! Just do it! Touch! my little devil taunted.

You are an idiot, Patricia Moore. Why would he flirt with you? the halo-wearer asked.

It hurt when Mr. Devil slammed his pitchfork into my shoulder. He pointed his spindly finger at his sister in white. *One minute she thinks he's a player, the next, she doesn't think he is interested at all. She's clueless. Listen to me and touch him!*

Freud would have a heyday analyzing my mind to bits because, as usual, Dr. Greene's presence caused me to behave like an insane imbecile. The solution to the cacophony in my brain was to sigh and act like his comment was offensive and annoying.

I flicked my wrist and faked a disgusted tone. "I'm busy. Hurry up. What do you want?"

His chin snapped back in what I assume was wounded pride. "Just coffee, and I take it back. I guess barista isn't one of your skills."

My shoulder devil continued his feisty taunts. *You should reach over and touch his hair to spite him. It would serve him right to have some old lady playing with his pretty young hair. Oh, even better! Touch his cheek.*

I cracked. "Anyone ever told you that you look more like a surfer than a psychotherapist?"

I'm reasonably certain that I hadn't meant to say it out loud. Unfortunately, it was a no-take-back kind of statement.

I expected him to lash out at me with a response such as *Anyone ever tell you that you look more like a horse's ass than a teacher?* Instead, he winked and said, "All the time."

I shivered.

Although he remained calm and collected, I continued poking the bear. "Why'd you say you weren't surprised that my ex-husband's girlfriend doesn't like me? And don't tell me it's because of our history. I think you meant something else."

Hey, Patti? Psycho question! said my right shoulder companion.

Dr. Greene looked me in the eyes. "Are you going to get all huffy when I answer you this time? Because if so, I plead the fifth."

He had me feeling off-balance, but I desperately needed to know, so I conceded. "Yes, I promise I'll behave."

He leaned across the counter, placing his nose inches from mine. "Patricia, no girlfriend is going to like an ex-wife. That's just the way it is, and it's even worse if the ex-wife happens to be beautiful."

He put an end to the fight I'd been trying to pick—all because of his unsettling effect on my hormones—by telling me I was beautiful. A sucker for a compliment, especially one from an Adonis, I made a peace offering of coffee and a blueberry muffin. He accepted it, then sat at a table, engrossed in the book.

He was still reading when Tina returned. She made googly eyes behind his back and mouthed, "Caliente," as she fanned herself.

I gave her my *I'm going to kill* you look and mouthed, "That's original." Then I ignored her pantomime until she got bored and ceased.

Two hours later, the doctor placed the book back on the shelf, gave Tina a few bills, and told her to keep the change. "See you tomorrow," he called over his shoulder to me. Then his broad-shouldered, narrow-hipped physique disappeared out the door.

"¿Qué rayos fue eso?" Tina exploded. I knew she had held that comment in for two hours. She wasn't done. "What in the hell was that?" I think it made her feel better to express her confusion in two languages.

I wasn't trying to be cryptic when I shrugged. I had no clue what had just happened.

Before Zoomie and I left for home, I confiscated my copy of *Of Human Bondage* from the shelf. I have no idea why, since I've already read it—twice.

WTF? and ¿Qué rayos fue eso?

Patti

…..…..*…..*

Recorded by Robert Stauffer I, TSgt on November 21, 1972
Transcribed by Patricia Moore
Helloop Contraption,

It's a fine mornin' to pick up where I left off with my tale. I had plummeted into a farmer's field, taken a beating from shrapnel, and had been captured by the Gestapo.

The putrid smell of my rottin' flesh made me wanna vomit. I'd lay a wager that the Japanese could smell me from the other side of the war. The red streaks runnin' up my arm had mixed with a greenish-black color, and I found myself sprawled out on a flimsy wooden palanquin. I think it had been constructed from pieces of old farm crates, but it was hard to tell since I was the prince stuck on top of it. My royal carriage also became my bed on that lonely night.

The next morning, the Germans crammed about a half dozen injured men into the back of a truck. Three of us were on various forms of makeshift stretchers. We didn't have food or water. Good thing, since even without it, I vomited twice on the journey. One poor bastard, with a cantaloupe-sized hole in his gut, didn't make it. I think those four hours in that truck are what Hell is like—terrified men cryin' in their own piss, blood, and vomit.

I had the advantage of being older than the soldiers around me, so, surrounded by those younger men, I tried to impart words of wisdom and comfort. I attempted to distract them by reciting poems, some Kipling, some Tennyson, and some my own. This was where I first met Joseph Reynolds. He was only eighteen years old, was missin' a chunk of his ankle, and had a crutch made from an old fence post. He sat beside me, teary-eyed from the pain. Still a virgin, he lamented that he had never had a girl and figured now he never would, since he was sure to lose his foot, die, or both. I thought it the perfect time to recite "The Ladies" by Kipling. The coherent men laughed until their bellies ached. Since I had a trapped audience, I also belted out the ballad of "Gunga Din." I have always found that beautiful words provide comfort to a terrified soul. I told young Reynolds that when we got ourselves out of this mess—which we surely would—I'd buy him a beer. Then I watched the pain and fear disappear from his face as I recited my poem:

> An amber liquid rises in the glass,
> a whitish froth surmounts a surface clear.
> Minute and dancing bubbles crowd
> to pass each other as they fill the coming cheer.
> At last, the glass is full; a white arm slides a frosty
> morsel toward me down the bar.
> I reach! And grasp!
> The tingling thrill that glides through my being
> indicates afar; pleasure that surpasses all I knew
> as I gulp down that cooling glass of brew.

As we rode toward our impending doom, we talked about the thrills found in a woman's warm arms and the joy of cold ale.

Four hours later, we arrived at Stalag IX-C. Obermassfield, once a prep school for boys, had been converted into an overcrowded, septic hospital for British and American POWS. Two British orderlies carried me into a brightly lit interrogation room that was bare except for a desk and a few chairs. A tall, well-scrubbed man stood behind the desk. My escorts placed my chariot on the ground in front of him and helped me to sit up.

The pink man greeted me. "Hello, Robert Stauffer. I am Commandant Staufer. You are quite sick. Ja? Are you hungry?"

Christ, what a kick in the ass. We had the same name.

"My goddamn arm is infected, and I'm gonna die if I don't get medicine," I told him.

"Ja, Robert Stauffer. I will get you food and medicine, and we will talk."

I was onto those SS bastards. He planned to play with me and bribe me with food. I felt too nauseous to be hungry, but damn, what I wouldn't have done for a glass of water, a cigarette, and some medicine.

He beckoned, and one of the orderlies placed a cup of water, a slice of bread, and a piece of cheese in front of me. I drank heartily and since I hadn't had anything to eat or drink since the barley-bree the farmer had given me, I started in on the bread. I knew it might be my only opportunity to get somethin' in me belly.

"The medicine will come soon," the commandant promised. "You will sit beside me, and we will talk. Ja?"

"Said the actress to the bishop."

My response with innuendo must have angered him because spittle flew as he hollered, "Where is the rest of your crew?"

I told him my name, rank, and serial number.

The stupid bastard practically screamed, "I will ask you again. Where is the rest of your crew?"

I told him the truth. "I'm sorry, sir. I do not know."

He was gettin' angrier by the minute. "What was your mission?"

That I did know the answer to, but I repeated the same thing. "I'm sorry, sir. I do not know."

"Are there other survivors?" His face had become so red I thought he might blow.

"I'm sorry, sir. I do not know."

He turned his back to me, calmed himself down, then faced me again. That bastard was moodier than a raccoon in heat.

"You disappoint me, Robert Stauffer. That is a good German name, my name. You are on the wrong side of this war with a name like that." He took the plate of food from my stretcher. I hadn't touched the cheese.

I knew there was no point in asking, but I tried again. "I'm gonna die unless my arm is treated."

"Ja, such a shame for a fine German soldier. You could join us in the New World Order since you are one of us."

I didn't think it a good time to mention my Scottish mother. So instead, I told him to go to hell. Probably not one of my smarter moves, because he had me carried to a large room filled with hundreds of men. The orderlies placed my stretcher on the ground between two cots and left me there.

No more food.

No water.

No medicine.

My pain was excruciating, and I vomited up the bread that I had eaten. Yuppers, like a pelican, me eyes can hold more than me belly can.

"Could someone please treat my arm?" I called. Nobody came to help me because at that moment, there was no one available to help anyone. There were just hundreds of injured men as far as the eye could see. That, and a pair of overworked British orderlies.

War is a God-damn crime.

Chapter 15

"It's getting to be ri-goddamn-diculous."

John Wayne

November 5, 2019

Dear Diary,

I didn't sleep much last night. After I finished listening to Pap, I realized there was a message on my landline. I rarely check it anymore since everyone I want to talk to has my cell number.

I listened to the message three times.

"Hi, Patricia. It's Alan Anderson. I hope you're feeling better. I hate to do this to you, but you need to complete some paperwork. We need Devon Walker's Individualized Education Plan updated. Dr. Westbrook said that you need to email it to her before school tomorrow." He paused. "I'm sorry. Do you remember the advice I gave you in the nurse's office?" Another pause. "Please don't resign. Good night."

I prayed for a flaming meteorite to smash into my house and end my misery. Anderson had made the call earlier in the evening, but it was now almost midnight. It would take at least four hours to write an IEP. I wasn't sure I could complete it even if I wanted to because all of Devon's academic testing was in my classroom. My monkey brain set in. *Can they require me to do paperwork on a medical leave?*

Is Anne Westbrook out to destroy me? What will happen if I refuse to write it?

Of course, I remember Anderson's advice. He told me to get checked out at the hospital, write everything down, and contact my union. I couldn't call my attorney in the middle of the night, and messing with an IEP due date is handled like a life or death situation. I'm not in a mental place where I can take a disciplinary write-up, and IEP mistakes often result in due process hearings. Unfortunately, even perfect IEPs are sometimes the focus of a lawsuit. Then there is the worst offense of all for a paperwork error—everyone considers you completely incompetent.

I may be loca en la cabeza, and I may be anxiety-filled and depressed, but I am not incompetent!

He must have known how much the message from Westbrook would upset me, and although I felt like resigning, I had to feed myself, so it was out of the question. I tried to calm down and focus. I liked Devon, and he had a tough life. I decided to stay up as late as it took to complete the paperwork.

I made myself a pot of coffee, got onto my laptop, and did the best I could with the information I had. Three and a half hours later, I emailed an almost adequate document to Westbrook. Then I took screenshots of the message I had sent and texted them to my friend, Missy. I asked her to file them away for safekeeping. I felt paranoid, especially after Anderson's warning. Well, that and because paranoid has become my middle name. My crazy crap aside, things are very wrong with my work situation.

After I closed my computer, I bonked my head lightly on the table in an attempt to stop my racing thoughts. *Why did he bring it up? Did Westbrook pull this little stunt to encourage me to resign? Should I resign?*

Note to future self—smacking your head into a hard surface does nothing to stop unwanted thoughts. However, it does cause a wicked headache.

Between the brief moments of sleep and the disturbing nightmares, I tossed and turned. I awoke late morning with my heart racing and vivid memories of zombies chasing me across the bridge into the city as Westbrook screeched, "Where is that IEP?"

I had a late morning appointment with Dr. Greene, but I couldn't face him. I was too tired, depressed, and overwhelmed to talk to a therapist. I decided I was going to stay in bed for the rest of the day. Maybe I could call Mike— scratch that, I wasn't talking to Mike. Perhaps I could call Tina or my dad and ask them to take care of Zoomie.

I pulled up Mrs. Stewart's office number and called to tell her I was too sick—because I probably had the flu— and I needed to cancel my appointment. Then I crawled into bed. It was late afternoon when a buzz from my cell phone woke me. Because I was out of it from my long nap, I didn't check the caller ID before answering. I wasn't expecting the voice that greeted me from the other end.

"Hello, Patricia. I was calling to check on you since you canceled your appointment," said Dr. Greene.

I strained my voice in an attempt to sound as sick as possible. "I think I have a really, really bad case of the flu." Since I was planning to sleep the rest of my life away, the "really, really bad case" gave me a long-term excuse for my absence from civilization.

"You seemed fine yesterday."

"How would you know?" I asked. "You aren't a physician." Who in the hell was he to insinuate I wasn't sick?

He grunted before saying, "I think you're avoiding your issues. You need to deal with them. If you cancel on Thursday, you will still need to pay for your appointment."

I was speechless. He could effortlessly switch from arrogant to understanding and from flirtatious to horse's ass in a moment.

"Bye, Patricia. I'll see you Thursday."

While I was still trying to form my response, he disconnected.

"Oh Zoomie, what's wrong with me? Why does he make me crazy?"

Zoomie comforted me by allowing me to rub his belly.

Moments later, my phone rang, and once again—this time, because I was distracted by my chipped red nail polish—I didn't check the caller ID. I answered, preparing to lambaste Greene. Yes, I know I had started our venomous battle. What can I say? Since he was beautiful, I deserved to have the last word.

"Hi, kiddo. How come you haven't called your dear old dad?"

My body relaxed. "Hi, Dad. I talked to you a couple of days ago," I reminded him.

"Yeah. That was a couple of days ago. What if I had had the big one yesterday?"

"Dad," I moaned in exasperation.

"Ha, ha, ha. Are you back at work yet?"

"No, Dad. I keep telling you, I'm off for six weeks."

My father isn't senile. He's simply a creature of habit. He called me every day of college and asked me the same five questions in the same order: "How are you? Are you studying? You aren't partying, are you? Did you make a new friend today? Do you miss your dear old dad?" Every day for four years, I answered the questions the same way: "Fine. Yes. No. Yes. Yes."

"Your mom and I are worried. How are you paying your bills?"

I sighed. I didn't want to admit that I would have to choose between the mortgage payment and food if I didn't return to work in the next month.

"Wanna come out for dinner? Your mom is making those good stuffed chicken breasts."

I considered it. "Did you ask Mom if it's okay?"

My dad has a habit of inviting people for dinner without telling my mother. He hadn't learned a single self-preservation lesson in fifty-one years of marriage.

"She won't care," he insisted.

"You better ask," I warned him.

I had learned my lesson when I was in the third grade and invited the Rakowski twins for spaghetti without asking her permission.

"Susan!" he bellowed.

He didn't hear me say, "Dad, put your hand over the receiver," because he was engaged in his hollerin' contest with my mom.

"Can Patti come for dinner?" His inflection was that of a child asking his mother if he could play with a friend, rather than an elderly man asking his wife if his middle-aged daughter could come for a meal.

"I only have three chicken breasts," my mom yelled back.

"Did you hear that? It's okay. You can come over."

I knew my dad well enough to know that he had interpreted her comment to suit his desires.

"Dad, that isn't what she said. She said she only has three breasts."

What followed was an elementary school math lesson in which I tried to explain to my father that if he ate one breast, and Jimmy ate one breast, and my mom ate a breast, that made three. Adding me to the equation meant four cuts of meat, which was one more than three. Hence, we had hopped onto the negative side of the number line.

He huffed. "Hell, your mother never eats hers. She just bitches about how bland it is and ends up eating a Lebanon bologna sandwich."

I found his statement truthful and pretty funny.

Still, I had to protest, "Dad, I'm not going to come out and eat Mom's dinner."

"I'll share mine with you. How's that? You can share dinner with your dear old dad. So, it's settled. You're coming for dinner. And I'll make lumpy mashed potatoes, just the way you like them."

There was no use arguing. I had inherited my stubborn streak from my dear old dad, and he was better at it than me, so I gave in. "Okay, Dad. I'll come over."

"Good. Bring that nice Zoo-y."

Zoomie was eight years old, and my dad knew his name with uncertainty.

"His name is Zoomie," I said.

"Yeah, Zoo-y. He's a good dog. We'll feed him your mom's chicken when she decides she's eating a Lebanon bologna sandwich."

I belly laughed, then temporarily relinquished my beloved pet's name to my insistent father. "Okay, Dad. Zoo-y and I will be there for chicken breasts and mashed potatoes."

"And green beans. I like green beans. Be here at six."

I confirmed the plan. "Zoo-y and I will see you at six for chicken breasts, green beans, and lumpy mashed potatoes."

I hung up chuckling.

How is it that my dad always knows when I need to be cheered up? I guess I'll have to finish my Patti pity party another day.

Hungry,
Patti

…..…..*…..*

November 6, 2019
Dear Diary,

This morning I received my annoying monthly post-divorce text from Mike stating, *Remember, the mortgage payment is due by the end of the week.*

Even though I had managed the payment for the last three decades, Mike has no faith in my ability to care for myself. I no longer respond to his reminders, but it doesn't dissuade him. Like clockwork, he continued his nagging.

Even more annoying was the text he sent twenty minutes later, in which he offered to help pay my bills until I returned to work. All I had to do was give him a call.

No way will I call to grovel for money or help.

The thing is, I am terrified. What if I'm beyond hope and too gun-shy to ever return to work? What if my nightmares continue? What if every time someone gets in my personal space, I knock them over? What if I never receive another paycheck? What if eventually I can't pay my mortgage, and I lose my grandparents' home to foreclosure? What if I can't feed myself or help my daughter with her tuition? What if I turn into a little old lady who has no one to love, nowhere to go, and nowhere to live?

What if...?

You know, it isn't out of the realm of possibilities. If it happens, Mike would have the last word and say something like *I told you so. You should have let me help pay the mortgage.* There he would be with his apartment and young girlfriend, knowing I had failed. I've devoted my entire life to working myself to the bone in a public high school, and now the possibility of being an old woman living alone in poverty seems so real.

His texts weren't the worst part of my day—not even close! Because that honor would be given to The Wicked Witch terrorizing Valentina's.

Yep! No lie.

Zoomie and I happily reposed in our favorite spot. I was drinking a cup of coffee and was engrossed in *Treasure Island* when Zoomie growled. His ears popped into the air, and fangs appeared between his curled lips. My sweet Sheltie resembled a rabid wolf.

I felt her evil presence before I heard her high-pitched squeal. Her voice could simultaneously break glass and boil eggs. "Do they allow dogs in here? It is unsanitary and against the law. I should call and report this to the local health inspector."

Horrified, I blurted out, "Christ! What are you doing here?"

Westbrook's lips formed words, but Zoomie's barks drowned them out. His tail stood in the air as he maneuvered himself between us. Customers sat with wide eyes and open mouths.

Tina came out from behind the counter with a dog biscuit in her hand. She bent low and put her face inches from his. "Zoomie, no! Tranquilo."

Zoomie, ordinarily gentle and friendly, looked as though he could guard the gates of hell.

A red-faced Westbrook backed away, pointed her finger at my dog, then me, and left the establishment.

"Patricia? Zoomie? That customer just walked out!" said my unhappy friend.

I stared at the door, praying the she-devil didn't come back. After waiting a long moment, I said, "That wasn't a customer. That was Anne Westbrook."

Once the news registered, Tina apologized to my pup. "Sorry. You are a good boy." She patted him on the head and handed him his biscuit.

Zoomie let the biscuit fall to the ground because his eyes remained focused on the door.

"What was she doing here? Doesn't she live in the city?" a confused Tina asked.

I picked up the discarded dog treat. "Yes. I'm certain she was spying on me."

That evil woman had to have been standing there staring at me. There could be no other reason for Zoomie's behavior. Unless he knew that she was responsible for halting his visits to read with my students. Of course, I wouldn't put it past her to brandish some sort of medieval weapon of torture under her designer suit coat. Zoomie would, for sure, object to the removal of my head.

I waited until I was confident Westbrook was no longer in the vicinity. Then Zoomie and I sprinted home and down the basement stairs to Pap.

I walked into the furnace room, flicked the light switch, and the room lit up as though a flood lamp had been installed. Someone had exchanged the old dim bulb for a bright one that illuminated my newly decorated space. The only thing that remained on the floor was a maroon doggy bed. My blanket sat on a green lawn chair. My notebooks, pens, an LL Bean camp lantern, the tape recorder, and a package of unopened batteries had been arranged on a card table.

Zoomie sniffed his new bed, looked at me, then plopped onto it. I dropped his biscuit beside him. He licked it and then set his chin on top of it. I think his encounter with the Antichrist had exhausted him.

"Mike, when did you do this?" I whispered to the air.

Teary-eyed, I pressed play, wrapped myself in my blanket, and sat in my new chair.

Touched,
Patti

..........*.....*

Recorded by Robert Stauffer I, TSgt on November 22, 1972
Transcribed by Patricia Moore
Helloop Contraption,

The last time I talked into you, I was in and out of consciousness and surrounded by hundreds of injured men. When I came to, I was being carted out of the room by the two British orderlies. They explained that Commandant Staufer had ordered me moved to a surgery room in a different part of the complex. I made sure that they knew I was no relation to the bastard, and we spelled our names differently. They assured me they knew I was a loyal American soldier. I learned a lot on our trek through the massive, derelict building.

A couple of British doctors and six orderlies staffed the hospital. The bastard commandant oversaw a small staff of German goons, a few German nuns, and the scanty British medical personnel. Once a month, a skilled German surgeon visited the hospital for a few days and then left to make his rounds at other camps. The hospital was acutely understaffed. A month before, it had housed a few injured members of the Royal Air Force. Since then, it had been overwhelmed with American prisoners. It was short on vittles and medicine, ripe with sepsis, and the Red Cross packages were scarce.

The orderlies assisted me from my royal carriage to an actual hospital bed. Assuring me that a surgeon would be back to check on my arm, they left me alone. My health was deterioratin' by the moment. The pain of my hip and head wound were unbearable. I no longer felt my arm, and I was in and out of consciousness from fever. The smell of my rottin' flesh would have made me vomit if I had any vittles in me belly.

Sometime after the orderlies left, the woman that was to save my life visited. Sister Margarette, of the Saint Marienthal Abbey, was about forty years old, had large blue eyes and a soft pink face. Her voice was angelic; she spoke and sang in German, English, Latin, and French, and could alternate between them with ease. The Nazi's had taken these women from their quiet spiritual lives and thrust them into the hell of war when he sent them to the POW hospitals to care for the prisoners. Many of the nuns in Obermassfield were tired, severe women, but not Sister Margarette. She would sit by my bed telling me stories and readin' me whatever she could get her hands on. I told her stories of Marty and my family. She loved to hear of my football days and especially loved my stories about playing piano in the

American clubs. Occasionally we would sing a little ditty together. Each mornin', she smuggled in raw eggs and dandelion tea. She was even able to sneak me a cigarette here and there, but it was the razor she left by my bed that saved me.

That mornin', one of the British doctors reset my hip and stitched up my face. Without anesthesia, both were hellishly painful. I begged him to amputate my arm because I was now on my third day of havin' a gangrenous limb. He told me that there was to be a shipment of supplies comin' in that afternoon and he wanted to wait until he had anesthesia and antibiotics.

I guess the supplies never showed because he never returned. Sister Margarette sat by my bed through the night. I think she was fearful that I wouldn't live to see the bonny dawn. By mornin', when the surgeon still hadn't come to perform the amputation, she convinced me to start it myself. Unlike the farmer and his wife, she didn't have schnapps to give me. Wrath from an angry commandant would rain down upon her if she intervened in a medical procedure, so she left a razor on the medical tray sitting by my bed, and ran to get help.

I did what she told me and tried to cut through my skin and bone, although I don't think it's possible to cut through a human body with a straight razor. Still, I gave it a considerable try. I passed out from the pain, and when I woke up, the visitin' German doctor had taken part of my arm and left this hideous stump in its place.

I did my best to look at the positives. I was alive, and I had my guardian angel looking out for me, but when a young man loses a limb, he loses a part of himself—a part of his youth—a part of his manhood.

I remained at Obermassfield for the next month drinkin' smuggled dandelion tea and raw eggs. Sister Margarette visited me daily. We started my rehab with walks around the upper floor of my ward. Then, with permission from the doctors and the Commandant, she took me outside. It was cold, but the air was fresh and clean, and the view of the forests surrounding the compound was beautiful. A couple of times, she even took me downstairs to see my recovering friend, Joseph Reynolds.

After the war, Marty and I tried to find Sister because we wanted to thank her for saving my life. We even wrote to her convent, but it seemed as though she had disappeared. I never did buy young Reynolds a beer, but I did give him a call a few years ago. He managed to make it back to the states, and since he now has a wife and four children, he didn't die a virgin.

Anywho, I'm convinced that the reason I survived that far into my nightmare was that my name was Stauffer and I could speak German passably well. If I had been a Jones, a Smith, or a Miller, I would've died in a large room surrounded by five hundred other men. And if my Margarette had not developed a fondness for me, I would have departed as a two-armed man, rottin' in my own blood, pus, and vomit.

Hey Doc, if you were here, I'd tell you today's meanderings made me feel worse.

…..…..*…..*

November 7, 2019
Dear Diary,

I awoke to another annoying text from Mike. I have concluded that 'excessively aggravating' is the only type of message he's capable of sending anymore. This one read: *How are things going with your union attorney? Be sure you're staying on top of things.*

Doesn't he understand that I'm not talking to him? I was so angry I wanted to throw my cracked phone across the room. I was planning my response when Dr. Greene's number appeared on my caller ID. I wasn't in the mood for his nonsense either. I let his call go through to my messages, then listened.

"Hi, Patricia. I am expecting you at three. Be here even if you don't feel well. Remember cancellations without twenty-four hours' notice result in a full appointment fee."

He hadn't even asked how I was feeling or said goodbye.

What an ass!

I needed a new therapist, a nice grandmotherly lady who understood what I was going through. How could a pompous, thirty-something man have a clue about how to help me?

It's a good thing that Mrs. Stewart was a doll. She put me in a good mood before I had to see Greene. She greeted me warmly and then presented me with a cup of tea and a fresh-baked snickerdoodle. We talked while the doctor finished with his previous appointment.

"Do you think he tortures all of his patients?" I asked the gracious receptionist.

At first, she looked confused. Then I think my annoyance dawned on her. "Patricia, he's worried about you. Your situation keeps him up at night. Go easy on him, because he has a lot on his mind."

I took a sip of tea and contemplated her statement. "Like what?"

"He broke it off with his fiancée a few days ago," she whispered.

"What?" I asked. "Why?"

She didn't answer my question; instead, she said, "He's a good doctor and a good man."

Perhaps it's Mrs. Stewart's fresh-scrubbed face, her 1950s wardrobe, or that she drugged her baked goods, but she has a way of getting you to spill your guts. Maybe she's the one who should earn the big bucks.

I leaned forward and, in a voice too loud to be a whisper, said, "Do you know when I had the flu, he told me I had to pay for my missed appointment?"

She tsked and wagged her finger. "No. He told you if you canceled today without twenty-four hours' notice, you had to pay for your appointment."

"What if I had been throwing up or couldn't get out of bed?" I pointed out.

"Were you throwing up?"

"No," I confessed.

"You didn't have the flu, did you?" she asked, even though she seemed to know the answer.

Delores Stewart—two.

Patti—zero.

I hung my head in shame. "No, Mrs. Stewart. How did you guys know?"

She winked. "Because the flu hasn't hit the area this season."

I sighed. When had I turned into such a big fat liar? Oh, I know. A few weeks ago, when I almost died, then had to start talking to a therapist who resembled a sexy surfer in a suit.

I helped myself to another sodium thiopental-infused cookie.

Mrs. Stewart stared into my soul. "He's handsome. Isn't he?"

I thought it an absurd question, so I lied for the millionth time in the last few weeks. "I haven't noticed."

She raised a bluish-gray brow. "You just told another fib, Patricia Moore, because even a blind woman would notice him."

Of course, a blind woman would notice him. He smells like an orgasm under an orange tree.

"I guess he's handsome," I conceded.

Egads!

The damn things were drugged. I tossed my half-eaten cookie onto the plate. That sweet, innocent-looking lady wasn't getting any more information out of me. I was onto her spy-like ways and magic baked goods. She could have teamed up with Commandant Staufer to get information out of POWS. Even the amazing Professor Stump would have suffered her charms.

Dr. Greene's office door opened, and he ushered out his previous patient. He motioned for me using curling fingers. "Hi, Patricia. I'm so glad you're over the flu. Please come in."

As I walked past him, I gave him a dramatic scowl. "Spare me, Dr. Greene. I know that you know that I didn't have the flu."

He closed the door behind me, and we took our seats.

He picked up his notebook, opened it, and looked me in the eyes. "Then why did you cancel your last appointment?"

So many truthful responses went through my head: *Because I didn't feel like talking. Because I was up the night before doing paperwork I shouldn't have had to complete. Because you make me crazy with desire, and I'm too old for you. Because I'm terrified that I'm getting worse instead of better.*

"Because I was so tired that I didn't feel well, and I wanted to sleep," I truthfully said.

He acknowledged my response with a nod and made a few notes. "I know I was tough on you, but it's my job to get you ready to return to work before December. I'm dishing out a bit of tough love. I've also been thinking that maybe it's time for you to make a quick visit to your classroom. You can do it after the kids leave for the day. Just a few moments is all. I think simply walking into the building could help to alleviate some of your anxiety."

I gaped at him. "That sounds like a terrible idea and I'm not sure how I feel about your version of tough love."

He sighed. "I've noticed that your voice seems to be less scratchy. I assume it's healed and is back to normal?"

I nodded and uttered a soft, "Yes."

He stopped writing in his notebook to stare at me. I shivered and shifted, feeling self-conscious under his scrutiny.

"The bruising on your neck has also healed."

I didn't respond. Probably because my physical wounds had healed, but my emotional scars still ran deep.

Before he could ask me his next question, I interrupted. "My Student Services supervisor, Anne Westbrook, I told you about her, remember? She came into Valentina's yesterday."

He held his breath and stopped blinking.

"I think she was spying on me. Everyone knows Valentina is my best friend, and I spend a lot of time there."

If he didn't take a breath soon, he was going to need CPR.

Lucky me!

"Zoomie almost attacked her. That's how evil she is. My sweet dog that loves everyone growled at her until she left the coffee shop."

The once emotionless doctor had become increasingly impassioned with each session we've had. Currently, his face was red, and his eyes were angry slits. "What did she say to you?"

I hadn't yet heard his angry voice, and it surprised me. I had heard him defensive, disappointed, amused, disinterested, interested, and often very, very annoyed, but never angry.

"Nothing. Zoomie wouldn't let her near me."

He thought for a moment, dialed back some of his fury, then said, "Although it seems very inappropriate for her to be there, it could have been a coincidence. It's a public place."

"Dr. Greene, I'm not naive. It was during work hours. She should have been in the city working."

He tapped his pen against his notepad while he considered my statement. "You need to discuss this with your union."

He was correct. It has been a tough week, so I need to touch base with Leigh Ann.

Dr. Greene refocused us both.

I guess I wasn't administering CPR any time soon. Darn!

"Do you think our sessions are helping you at all?" he asked.

"I don't know. I have good days and bad days, but I'm worried my panic attacks and nightmares are getting worse." I swallowed to stop tears from forming.

His expression was grave. "Do you want to try another therapist? I can recommend a great doctor—"

I cut him off before he could finish. "No! I want you to keep working with me. You're a great doctor."

I know I use fussing, complaining, and sarcasm as defense mechanisms with Dr. Greene, and he's a bit moody with me, but I deserve it. I don't hate him. It's the opposite. I've been frantically trying to hide that I want to crawl onto his lap and whisper lascivious things into his ear.

"Of course," he said. "But if you change your mind."

I'm not going to change my mind. Doctor Jacob is stuck with my crazy, anxiety-filled, moody ass, so he needs to suck it up and fix me fast. We only have three weeks left.

Two things occurred to me today. Just like Pap and the Commandant, my adversary and I share part of our name. I think I'm going to change mine.

No more Anne for me. *Shiver!*

Patricia Elizabeth Moore?

Patricia Marie Moore?

~~Patricia Marie Greene?~~

Good grief! How old am I?

I wish that my grandparents had been able to find Pap's sweet nun. I would have liked to meet her because she sounds incredible. Plus, I'd like to hire a Sister Margarette for myself because my incompetent guardian angel has left me with two annoying shoulder critters who give terrible advice and duel like Hook and Pan. Although perhaps Zoomie is my new angel and protector.

Then there is Doctor Jacob, with his angelic eyes and devil's allure.

Confused,

Patti

Chapter 16

"The only way you get Americans to notice anything is to tax them or draft them or kill them."

John Irving, *A Prayer for Owen Meany*

November 8, 2019

Dear Diary,

The second I met five-year-old Alexia Harris, I had a new best friend.

We stood on my front porch as Neil introduced us. "This is Daddy's friend, Miss Patti."

Her blue eyes sparkled as she smiled at me. "You look like Ariel."

Anyone who thought I resembled a mermaid princess was my friend for life. The three of us climbed into the car and engaged in sing-along songs as we headed across the river and through the woods to the Pennsylvania Horse and Pony show.

Alexia spent a good part of the evening spinning in circles. Her long blonde curls, yellow ribbons, and Princess Belle dress swirled around her. She wore tiny yellow shoes and a gold beaded bracelet. She reminded me of the young Cassie, who had spent years belly dancing up a storm in her coveted Princess Jasmine costume.

Her tiny fingers grasped her father's palm. Her other hand reached for mine, then she skipped through the exhibition hall. She stopped at each stall to say hello to the horse that inhabited it. When we reached the final exhibit, she squealed in delight. "Daddy, can I ride one of the ponies?"

Ten minutes later, she sat atop a pretty little mare, grasping the reins with both hands. Although concentrating with all of her might, she was still able to toss us a smile each time she circled past. Neil used his cell phone to snap pictures of her before reaching for me. I let him hold my hand because it seemed wrong not to.

After dismounting from her pony, Alexia ran to us. "Daddy, Miss Patti, did you see me?"

"Yes, sweetheart. You did great." A proud Neil puffed up his chest, and his eyes twinkled.

I squatted low and tightened a bow threatening its escape. "You looked like a princess. You're a natural horsewoman."

She giggled and pirouetted as she said, "Thank you, Miss Patti."

I beamed because Alexia was the epitome of contagious joy.

Neil lifted her into the air and planted a kiss on her cheek before calling out, "Ladies, it's cotton candy time." He placed her onto her feet, and the two of them raced to the food stands. Not wanting to miss out, I trotted after them.

Soon the three of us were happily covered in sticky pink and blue sugar and on our way to the staging area. We clapped and hooted for the featured performer, a miniature horse wearing bedazzled colored ribbons in his mane. The adorable equine used his hoof to count on command. Then we cheered as miniature horses pulled tiny carts around a track. It was all too perfect, a little girl's—and an aging mother's—dream come true. Before leaving, we stopped at a souvenir stand to buy Alexia a stuffed pony wearing a pink and blue flowered saddle.

On our drive home, we came across an out-of-the-way Italian restaurant, and since sugar highs require solid food, we stopped for pizza. A lit candle decorated the center of each of the round tables, and an ivy trellis and photos of Sicily adorned the walls. We ordered a thin crust pizza with an unusual spicy sauce on top of the cheese. Alexia recounted each of the horses she had met and made her toy pony stomp his hoof to the count of ten. Eventually, she placed her weary head on Neil's lap and fell asleep. So as not to wake the slumbering princess, he and I whispered about memorable summer vacations and past holidays. I never wanted the perfect evening to end.

Neil walked me to my front door and brushed my lips with a gentle kiss. My first romantic kiss in three years warmed my insides.

As I relive my evening, I realize it reminded me of happier times. Fifteen years ago, I watched as Cassie spun circles in her princess costume. The Moore family was holding hands and seeking adventures together. Mike and I whispered our hopes and dreams before kissing and falling asleep as we embraced. Is it so wrong for me to miss those things and want them back? Neil and Alexia are not Mike and Cassie, and I know it's unfair for me to pretend they are. But for tonight, can I go to sleep and dream about soft kisses, intimate whispers, cotton candy, princesses, and ponies? Please?

Sweet Dreams,
Patti

..........*.....*

Recorded by Robert Stauffer I, TSgt on November 24, 1972
Transcribed by Patricia Moore
Helloop Contraption,

Yesterday was Thanksgiving and the kinfolk were here. Lynn announced she's gonna be a mom. Since Bobby Jr's wife also has one in the oven, I will soon have a brood of grandchildren runnin' around. Marty's in her element. She's positively glowin' with pride.

Speaking of grandchildren, Big Red spent the night. Although she colors and reads for hours, she's a feisty one. She's determined to get her way. She's a talker—never stops. She even stares in the mirror talking to her refection. Boy, oh boy! She reminds me of Marty.

I haven't had a headache for a couple of weeks. I haven't had any panic attacks either, but the nightmares never stop. I'd love to dream about my younger years playin' football or about how romantic my marriage was in the early days. Instead, I dream about black puffs, frostbite, the smell of gangrene, and long hours of solitary confinement. Last night I dreamt of the son of a bitch that knocked my teeth in.

On February 13, 1945, six weeks after havin' my arm amputated, I was released from the hospital at Obermassfield. It broke my heart to say goodbye to Sister Margarette. I was still in poor shape and relied heavily on her to help me walk any distance. Even though I was weak and had lost over sixty pounds from my already scrawny frame, I was to be sent to the Dulag Luft Interrogation Center in Oberursel. Rumors were that Commandant Major Rumpel treated the American and British airmen with respect. Sister told me that I'd be fed well during my time there, but I'd also be interrogated by the Luftwaffe, the German air force, from morning till night. Young Joseph Reynolds had already left for the compound the week before.

I set off that morning with the clothes on my back and my book and photo tucked into my pocket. Sister Margarette had helped to keep them safe. I was concerned about how I would fare without her protection and without a commandant who shared my family name. I hoped that the stories about Rumpel were true, and that life might take a turn for the better, but me luck went dry less than twenty minutes after my hospital release.

A roly poly SS agent announced that the trek to our new location was to be on foot. Since the boxcars were often blown up during the Allied bombing, it had become safer to march. It appeared that the SS felt their prisoners too valuable to allow them to be blown up in trains, or mayhaps they were too lily-livered to risk their own lives? I knew I wasn't strong enough to make the long trip because I could barely walk the length of the compound without a nun to lean on.

They lined up the prisoners and gave us our walkin' orders. So far, my best defense had been standin' up for myself, and it seemed to me that any weakness got you into bigger scrapes with the SS because they appreciated both mental and physical fortitude. Since I hadn't any physical grit left, I thought I'd try for some mental. I told the well-fed guard that I couldn't make the march, seeing as how I could barely stand. When he aggressively insisted I walk, I called him a "das Schwein." Seems as though my theory on self-preservation was wrong with this particular bastard, because he used the butt of his rifle to beat me within inches of my life. The brainless fool knocked out most of my teeth, broke my jaw, and then kicked the shit out of me. He continued to scream at my bloody, prone body, "You are on the wrong side of this war, foolish American soldier!"

He was a dumb-ass son of a bitch because beating me until I couldn't move didn't make it easier for me to walk. To add to my humiliation, he had the other prisoners put my decrepit body in a baby carriage, then push me in the damn thing for the remainder of our journey.

Three days later, we arrived in the northwest of Frankfort. At the time, I was too sick and cold to appreciate the beauty of the countryside. I ended the journey quite poorly, with frostbite on both of my feet.

Gute Nacht!

..........*.....*

TO: PAMoore@gmail
FROM: Cassfldhock@gmail
SUBJECT: Hi

DATE: November 9, 2019
Hi Mom,

Checking in to see how you are doing? I received A's on both my Calculus and History exams. Woohoo! I have an English paper due tomorrow, so I have a lot of work tonight.

Is it still okay for Farez to come home with me for Thanksgiving? He loved Grandma and Uncle Jimmy—and you and Dad and Zoomie, too. He thought Pappap was hysterical. Can Dad come over for breakfast and make his omelets? Pretty please?

How was your date with your police officer friend? Tell me all about it. Are you listening to Great-Grandpa's tapes? What adventures is he up to?

I hope you are taking care of yourself. I love and miss you lots!

Cassie

To: Cassfldhock@gmail
From: PAMoore@gmail
SUBJECT: Re: Hi
DATE: November 9, 2019
Hi Cassie,

Congrats on the excellent grades. I'm so proud of you. Absolutely about Farez. I am already planning our meals. Yes, I will invite your father over to make his omelets, but he can't bring his girlfriend.

Your grandmother bought a fifteen-pound turkey for Thanksgiving dinner. There has been a big ruckus because she threw away Uncle Jimmy's prize trout so that she had enough room in the freezer. Chuckle, chuckle.

This morning Neil, Zoomie, and I went for a run. Afterward, Neil gushed about our Friday night date. We went to the horse and pony show. Do you remember how much you loved it when you were little? His daughter, Alexia, is an absolute sweetheart. She dressed like Princess Belle. Do you remember you used to dress like Jasmine?

The tapes are fascinating. I can't tell you how much I miss my grandparents. Your great-grandfather was an amazing man. He told a story about how he thought he was on his deathbed, and he still comforted the other injured soldiers by reciting poetry. I was about five when I first heard him recite the beer sonnet he had written. Your great-grandmother scolded him for talking about alcohol to children. I also remember him reciting the first half of Kipling's poem "The Ladies" to my cousins and me. Your great-grandma walked in on that one and didn't allow him to finish. Boy, was he in trouble! At the time, I didn't understand the poem, so I had no idea why he had landed himself in the doghouse. All I knew was I liked the sing-songy meter and listening to his oration. I'm not sure if you know it, but it's about prostitutes, venereal diseases, and sex. It's pretty raunchy and absolutely hysterical, so I laugh when I think of your great-grandfather's shenanigans. His sense of humor was one of the things I loved most about him. It's probably his fault that I am such an unbearable loudmouth, and I'm relieved to find out that I didn't stand a chance. Tee hee. I'm glad that you inherited your Grandma Moore's decorum.

There is something I find interesting and thought maybe you could ask your history professor his opinion. I have read many accounts of American soldiers stating the German people mistreated them. It was wartime, so I have no doubts that the Axis Powers treated the Allied Forces atrociously, but your great-grandfather didn't share this view. He marveled at the generosity and kindness that the war-torn people showed him. He was adamant that history books not hold the German people responsible for the mistakes of the Nazi party. He didn't have misplaced anger or live his life in bitterness. I think there is a lesson in this. Perhaps it's time for me to let go of some of my negativity and realize that the real criminal in my saga is not a poor misguided sixteen-year-old boy but an incompetent school leader with too much power.

Dr. Greene suggested I visit school. I think I'm going to do it tomorrow. I have made a deal with myself. Once I walk into the building and sit at my desk for a few minutes, I can splurge and reward myself with a new book. Yes! I'm going to drive into the city and face my fears. I think the first trip will be the hardest. After that, it should get easier. At least, that's what my doctor believes.

I miss you so much. I can't wait for Thanksgiving.

Love you super duper amounts on top of piles of a lot.

Mom

Chapter 17

*"To bear up under loss; To fight the
bitterness of defeat and the weakness of
grief; To be victor over anger; To smile
when tears are close..."*

Zane Grey

November 11, 2019

Dear Diary,

I slept well this weekend. I'm not sure if I dreamt about pink and blue ponies, but I don't remember any bad dreams. Although, unfortunately, today was a real-life epic failure of a nightmare.

As per Dr. Greene's suggestion, I decided to drive into the city after dinner to sit in my classroom. I promised myself a new book as a reward for my bravery. I think it was a mistake to visit at such a late hour because the halls were pitch-black and silent. I made it as far as the end of the first-floor hallway. The sound of my footsteps bounced off the walls, causing an eerie echo. By the time I reached the middle of the hall, my puffs were short and fast. When I reached the end, I couldn't catch my breath at all. I was fearful I would hyperventilate, then pass out. I could picture myself lying on the ground unconscious when the scary dude with the chainsaw found me. Or even worse, immobilized when, early the next day, Tanner Jones came across my comatose body on his way to class. I retraced my route to the entrance at a speed that would have rivaled one of Pap's thoroughbred racers. I sprinted across the empty parking lot, locked myself in the front of my car, then propped my torso on my steering wheel. I stayed in my uncomfortable position until my breathing stabilized, then I drove home with a banging in my chest.

No new book for me.

On the bright side, I don't have to reward myself by spending money I don't currently have.

Chicken shit,
Patti

…..…..*…..*

Recorded by Robert Stauffer I, TSgt on November 26th, 1972
Transcribed by Patricia Moore
Helloop Contraption,

My stay at Dulag Luft was a strange sort of wispy nightmare. The camp was northwest of Frankfort and was surrounded by forests and mountains that remained unscathed by the devastation most of Germany experienced. Before the war, the property had been a stately poultry farm. I liked to refer to my temporary chalet as the Chicken Castle. Even with its barbed wire and goon towers, there were small glimpses of its previous grandeur. The hospital sat inside a fairytale-style Tudor with an arched doorway and a five-story clock tower. Lest someone forget where we were, large white rocks covered the lawn, spellin' out *Prisoner of War Camp*.

Upon my arrival, I was strip-searched and then taken to the interrogation center located inside the stone castle. Under Rumpel's watch, there had been a mammoth orchestrated escape the previous year. Although still treated with dignity, for the most part, prisoners found themselves sentenced to solitary confinement to prevent another Great Escape.

A man named Professor Nagel interrogated me. The professor appeared unhappy about the bloody state I arrived in. I gave him my name, rank, and serial number, and then he had questions for me.

"What happened to you, American airman, Robert Stauffer?"

My newest injuries didn't allow me to articulate much of anything.

"I hear that the Schutzstaffel did this." He tsked. "This is no good; how can you talk if they break your jaw? My, my, will Martha Brickell and your parents Horace and Sarah be sad to hear this has happened to you."

Our training had prepared us for the things that might befall us if captured, so I knew that the Luftwaffe would have researched my family. Still, it sounded like a threat, hearing my loved ones' names come from the bastard's lips.

He held my edition of Kipling in one hand and my picture of Marty in the other. "Martha is quite lovely. Maybe if you cooperate with me, you will see her again? You would like that, ja?"

I wanted to punch the SOB.

"May I read your book, Robert? I like to read Kipling stories."

I tried to mutter, "Be my guest," but it was inaudible and hurt like hell.

"Are you a learned man, Mr. Stauffer? I will tell you what, you will borrow my Faust, and I will borrow your Kipling. Now you will go to your room, and I will send a medic to look at you. Once you are better, you will return, and we will talk. You will tell me about your missions, and I will take good care of you. Ja? Robert Stauffer, we will be good friends, just like you and Commandant Staufer were. We Germans must stick together." Then he dismissed me.

I wish I'd had a voice so I could have told him to go to hell, that we would never be friends, and I would never talk to him. You'd think that my recent bonk on the noggin would have knocked some sense into me. The son of a bitch was playin' with me like a squirrel with a dog. He had my picture and book. I may have had a crippled, twisted body, but my brain was still workin', and I was pissed.

I spent most of my holiday in solitary confinement at a building called The Cooler. My suite was much cleaner than the rooms at Obermassfield. Travelers feasted on porridge, toast, and a fresh egg daily. Unfortunately, I could barely swallow and wasn't able to partake of the delectable vittles. Since vegetables put hair on your chest, I was in danger of becoming one hairless bastard.

A young British medic checked on me daily. The problem with my fancy inn was there wasn't a surgeon on staff, and the stitches on my stump were comin' loose. The medic was concerned about another infection. My jaw also needed tending to, and my hip needed reset. That damn SS agent had left me poorly.

Nine days into my vacation at Oberursel, I got word that I was to report back to the Professor. I grabbed his Faust—which I hadn't read because it was written in German—hoping to trade it for my Kipling.

Nagel stood all pink-faced and fresh-scrubbed in front of me. "Hello, Robert Stauffer, have you been treated well?" he asked.

I supposed besides solitary confinement, I wasn't bein' treated too horribly. I'd been given clean clothes, was warshed, and had a full-sized blanket to myself.

"We must send you back to the hospital at Obermassfield and a surgeon will fix your arm. I am sorry your stay here must come to an end. Here is your picture of your beautiful Martha Brickell, and here is your book."

Then that crazy professor started to recite one of my favorite poems:

"Now this is the Law of the Jungle-as old and as true as the sky:

And the wolf that shall keep it may prosper, but the wolf that shall break it must die.

As the creeper that girdles the tree-trunk the law runneth forward and back—

For the strength of the pack is the wolf, and the strength of the Wolf is the Pack."

If I could have opened my jaw, it would've hit the floor.

"That is a good one, Robert Stauffer. Ja? Don't you think?"

He handed me my things, and I handed him his Faust.

Then that crazy professor said, "Robert Stauffer, think of Goethe's words, 'Haben wir uns oder dir aufgezwungen?' Did we force ourselves on you, or you on us?"

Even if my face hadn't been busted up, I wouldn't have discussed philosophy with the bastard.

"You will be back, Robert, and we will talk more. Ja? You will help me, as I have helped you. Good luck, American airman, take care. I will see you soon."

He had given me back my treasures. He hadn't burned them. He hadn't beaten or threatened me, and he had recited Kipling. Those interrogators were masters at their jobs. I thought that the Luftwaffe were slightly better humans than the SS and Gestapo goons, but I wasn't gonna let my guard down. After years of mulling it over, I think he gave me that book to see if I could read German. However, I'm not entirely certain, since I've never understood power hungry individuals, or Nazi bastards.

A couple of years ago, I found out that the professor really was a literature teacher, and he turned himself in to camp liberators. I guess he now teaches German and British Literature at the University of San Diego or some such place. In Germany, I simply thought he was a crazy Professor of Interrogation. It goes to show you, sometimes a man gets in over his head. It also gets me to thinkin', maybe in another lifetime, in another world, and in another time, a German Nagel and an American Stauffer could have been friends.

Anywho, back to my sightseeing adventure. I was loaded onto a train with my personal goonish escort and was soon back at Obermassfield.

Make no mistake: Containment Camp, no matter how much the Luftwaffe prided themselves and how well read the professor was, certainly wasn't Club Med.

Take er' easy.

Chapter 18

---

*"Marriage: a friendship recognized by
the police."*

Robert Louis Stevenson

November 12, 2019

Dear Diary,

Dr. Greene scrawled in his notebook as he listened to the account of my failed attempt to walk into school. His fervent writing, which had once been unsettling, was now oddly comforting. I still hadn't learned if his furrowed brow and grim expression meant he was concentrating or frustrated. One thing I knew for sure, his smile was spectacular, and he needed to do it more often.

He frowned, leaned back in his chair, and studied me before saying, "Today, I'd like to talk about self-care. You have your running and reading, and writing in your journal seems to be comforting. Trying something new can also be a great way to facilitate healing. So, I'd like you to think about exploring something that you haven't yet tried."

I considered his suggestion. Sex with my therapist was something I had never done. *Don't say it aloud, don't say it aloud!* screeched Ms. Angel.

"What about a dance class? You're a great dancer," he said.

I bit down on my lip at another reference to my dancing like a madwoman at the pirate party.

"Is there a type of dance you want to learn?" he asked.

I didn't feel up to expanding my horizons at that moment, but the next thing I knew, I had agreed to try out a salsa class at the local YMCA.

It was my turn to ask a question. "What about you, Dr. Greene? Is there something fun you want to try?" *Like sex with a redhead?* shouted Mr. Devil. It took a lot of discipline to keep that statement from gracing the airwaves.

He tapped his pen on the notepad. "Let me think about that. Let's get back to you."

I rallied my classroom voice. "It is the opinion of this intuitive teacher that Doctor Jacob Greene takes himself and his job too seriously, and he should have more fun!"

I wanted to hear him laugh until his ribs hurt or see him smile for more than a brief moment. I wanted him to wear a comfortable sweatshirt, and I wanted to know what made him happy.

He nodded and gave me one of his beautiful but brief smiles. "Perhaps the intuitive teacher is correct, but back to her."

I sat forward in my seat. "I know. I bet you want to eat that entire tray of pecan tarts on Mrs. Stewart's desk and wash it down with a medium-rare Porterhouse."

I smiled, and he chuckled.

"Bingo. I knew it." I lifted my index finger in the air to indicate I had an idea. "You want to ride the Great Bear roller coaster at Hershey Park at least ten times in a row. Until you are so buzzed and dizzy, you can't stand up."

He laughed again and said, "Yep!"

"And"—I lifted my eyes to the ceiling, then pointed at him. "You want to go to a deserted island, strip naked, and jump into the waves."

It sounded like an okay thing to say in my head. Not so much when it came out of my mouth.

He cleared his throat and returned to his Ways to Torture Patricia List. "Something else I think we need to talk about is your relationship with your ex-husband."

"There's nothing to talk about. We were married for twenty-seven years. I got depressed after my teaching transfer. Mike started to treat me like a china doll. I told him to knock it off or leave, so he left without hesitation. He couldn't get away from me fast enough. He got a girlfriend. I worked myself to death in a stressful job while he lived at the gym. We still have a kid together, and Zoomie still loves him. That's everything. See, nothing to talk about." I had summarized my decades of marriage into eight sentences.

"He doesn't have a job?" Doctor Greene asked.

"He's a human resources manager for a communication company. He works long hours," I explained.

"So, Mike doesn't just live at the gym. He also has a career?" Greene clarified.

"Well, yes," I conceded.

"Is his job stressful?"

I thought about the question. "Yes. I think so. He was promoted to management a couple of years ago, and it seemed like maybe it got more stressful, but he didn't talk about it much."

"So, a couple of years ago, Mike's stress at work increased with new job responsibilities, and you had an unexpected transfer to an extremely stressful job the year before that, and then you got divorced?"

I frowned and nodded.

"How was your marriage before you both had career changes?" he asked.

I thought before answering. "I loved Mike so much. I was devoted to him. When we had Cassie, life seemed perfect. Then one day, things weren't perfect, and we were angry with each other all of the time. I guess maybe it was changing a tiny bit before that, but honestly, I can't remember."

"So, about three years ago, things changed, and you both became angry?" he asked.

"None of that matters because he sprinted away, and as you saw, he has a girlfriend that's half his age. And you don't need to point it out. I know I have issues with my ex-husband's girlfriend and her age."

Greene nodded, then declared, "His loss."

It took me a moment to process what he had said. Was the doctor insinuating that I was a catch? That any man who rejected me was making an error? Tina had mentioned that Greene was into me. I had dismissed her statement, thinking it laughable, because how could a stunning thirty-something man find a moody fifty-year-old woman attractive? Still, sometimes I felt that Dr. Jacob Greene might be flirting with me. Plus, he had broken off his engagement.

He's not flirting with you! You've lost it, you crazy old woman.

Bonkers! Bonkers! Bonkers!

Bats in your belfry, old ancient one.

Nutball, looney tune!

Hurry up! Someone strap her to the gurney.

Pfft. Saying, 'his loss' hardly qualifies as flirting.

A voice interrupted the back and forth parley between my shoulder companions. "Patricia, did you hear what I just asked?"

I shook myself from the war zone blowing up my psyche.

Greene peered up at me from his notes. "I've noticed that your maiden name is Easterling."

I knew what he was about to ask. Tina, Missy, and countless others had posed the same question dozens of times.

"Why do you still have your ex-husband's last name? Why haven't you gone back to your maiden name?"

Since I had a lot of practice saying it, my quick answer was articulate. "The name on my teaching certification with the state is Patricia Anne Moore. It's a lot of paperwork to change a name on a certification."

Greene didn't look convinced.

"You are hanging onto your ex-husband. I think your unhealthy attachment is keeping you from moving on with your life. It's time to cut the cord and for you to be more independent. You need to enjoy life, find yourself, and establish your new normal."

I defended myself. "But I'm not talking to Mike right now. I'm mad at him."

Dr. Greene rolled his eyes.

Are psychotherapists even permitted to roll their eyes at patients?

Today I thought a lot about the parallels between my grandfather and me. From what I have read, history books do not look favorably on the Schutzstaffel, or SS as Pap referred to them. They were considered the biggest scoundrels of the nefarious Nazi party. Interestingly, Westbrook has a lot in common with the SS bastard who beat up Pap, and both made monumental mistakes. If you need someone to accomplish something, you can't keep beating on them until they can't stand. Tanner Jones may have knocked me down, but Anne Westbrook is responsible for delivering the blows that prevent me from getting onto my feet.

So, there you have it. Anne Westbrook is a Nazi wannabe, and I'm changing both my middle and last name.

Sigh!

On top of my Hitler-like boss and all-wrong name, I have absurd fantasies about a man two-thirds my age. I don't think I'll ever be able to walk into school again, I'm taking a salsa class I don't want to take, and I'm seriously considering "cutting the cord" with Mike. I'm terribly depressed tonight.

      I am sad, sad, sad,
      Patti

…..…..*…..*

Recorded by Robert Stauffer I, TSgt on November 28, 1972
Transcribed by Patricia Moore
Helloop Contraption,

      I arrived back at Obermassfield on Feb 23rd, 1945. I had lost most of my teeth, had rifle butt wounds to my face and jaw, my sutures had come loose, and my stump was infected. The orderly checked me over and said, "Damn, Robert. You're in worse shape than when you left us." I told him the tale of my misfortunes with the ass of an SS agent.

      I was taken to one of the surgery rooms and was still wide awake when one of the doctors stitched me up. Lookin' back, I think I may have been becomin' numb to the pain because, despite the lack of anesthesia, I don't recall feelin' a thing except for a torturous itch in an appendage that no longer existed.

      I had two visitors that afternoon. My angel, Margarette, was by my bed within a few hours, and Commandant Staufer visited before dark.

      "Who did this to you, my friend Robert Stauffer?" the other Staufer asked.

      "One of your son-of-bitch SS der scheisker, as soon as I walked out the door of this place!" I informed him.

      "Unacceptable, my friend. He will be dealt with," the shiny man promised.

      I didn't argue because I hoped that he was dealt with, although I was pretty skeptical.

      "Were you treated well during your stay at Oberursel?" Staufer asked.

      "It was a goddamn picnic!" I told him.

I spent the next two weeks with my nun by my bed. She brought me the news that the tide of the war was changing. She read to me daily and took me for my walks. I was still fairly weak when the orders came that I was to be transported to Stalag 7B until the end of the war.

My hell continued to escalate to intolerable levels over the next six weeks, and I find it difficult to discuss my life at Memmingen. The agony of parachuting from an exploding fortress from twenty-two thousand feet and having my arm amputated felt like drops in a rusty bucket compared to weeks of my insides eating me alive.

Pip. Pip. No Cheerios!

…..…..*…..*

TO: PAMoore@gmail
FROM: Lmartin@PEA.com
SUBJECT: Grievance
DATE: November 13, 2019
Patricia,

I have received a response from the Superintendent. We are scheduled to meet with the School District solicitor, Dr. Anne Westbrook, and District administrators on November 25th at 10:00 a.m. Let's plan to meet at 9:30 at the administration office. I have received your list of concerns, and all of your paperwork is in order.

It has come to my attention that Dr. Westbrook plans to ask for your resignation. Do not allow her to intimidate you into resigning. Please feel free to contact my office if you have questions.

Sincerely,
Leigh Ann Martin Esq.

TO: Lmartin@PEA.com
FROM: PAMoore.gmail
SUBJECT: Re: Grievance
Date: November 13, 2019

Leigh Ann,

I will be there on the 25th. Thank you for your help during these challenging times.

Sincerely,
Patti

..........*.....*

November 13th

P: My therapist says I'm too dependent on you, and I need to cut the cord.

Mike: You mean the shrink that looks like a prep school pretty boy?

P: He is a psychotherapist, and I think he looks like a surfer.

Mike: I think he looks like a pretty-boy-asshole.

P: He is only an asshole 20% of the time. The other 80 he is a decent guy. And how do you know what he looks like?

Mike: Whatever. Screw him! We had a kid together, so I will always be here for you.

P: I think maybe I should go back to my maiden name.
P: Hello! You there?

Mike: How are things going with the Union Rep?

P: ~~Screw you too.~~
P: ~~Why did you have to run off with Shelly?~~
P: ~~Stop nagging me.~~

Mike: Hello! You there???
Mike: Pat, answer me!!!
Mike: Fine, if you want to change your name, go for it.

P: ~~Mike! Please help me. I think I just hit rock bottom, and I'm so damn scared.~~

Mike: Hey, Pat! Please talk to me.

Chapter 19

"Men may rise on stepping stones of
their dead selves to higher things."

Zane Grey

November 14, 2019

Dear Diary,

Today I showed up at my session to find Mrs. Stewart and Dr. Greene sitting in the waiting room, drinking tea and eating baked goods. The doctor wore one of his death grip ties and a dashing wool overcoat. The receptionist wore a big grin.

"Hi, Patricia. Have a chocolate chip cookie. I baked them this morning," Mrs. Stewart said in her innocent grandmotherly voice.

No way was she plying me full of those scrumptious little truth bombs. I was onto her. "No thanks, Mrs. Stewart," I replied.

Her shoulders slouched forward. "Are you sure?"

Since I have a soft spot for treats and sweet elderly ladies, I sighed and said, "Okay, just one."

Greene stood. "We have a field trip. Let's go."

"A field trip? Where?" I asked.

"I'll tell you on the way." He placed his hand between my shoulder blades and aimed me toward the door. Then he called over his shoulder, "We'll be back in an hour and a half, Delores."

He sent her a thumbs-up, and she tossed him a wink.

I scowled at them both. I probably don't need to point this out; however, I feel the need to emphatically declare that I didn't appreciate their cryptic communication.

I wondered if my insurance would cover a double appointment, and if it didn't, I was a bit cash poor so I said, "An hour and a half, but our sessions are only forty-five minutes? And what if I have plans at four?"

"Do you?" Greene asked.

I squished up my face and crossed my arms over my chest. "No, but what if I had?"

Greene grinned. "But you don't, so let's go."

"Cookies for the road?" Mrs. Stewart asked.

The doctor turned back to grab two. I followed him and grabbed one. Mrs. Stewart lit up, then we waved and left the office.

I suspect my stubborness in the waiting room may have been to hide my excitement. A few minutes later, I was sitting in a fancy red sports car on the way to a surprise with the man who starred in my fantasies. A mini case of brattiness felt like the only protection I had from the rejection I would face if my doctor had any inkling of how incredibly attractive I found him.

In our sessions, we were about five feet from each other. There was less than a foot between us in the car, and our proximity magnified my senses. That distinct musky pine and citrus smell that rendered me defenseless enveloped me. I was mesmerized by his hands on the steering wheel. Interestingly, they were calloused and hardened, while the rest of him appeared pampered. I wondered if he was a lumberjack in his spare time. If so, it would explain the muscular thighs that threatened to split his pants at any moment. My eyes wandered back and forth between his masculine hands and his delicious lap. Eventually, they settled on his profile. When he turned in my direction, I noticed his eyes were a brighter blue than usual, and his cheeks seemed to have an extra pinkish hue.

I attempted to disguise my excitement and goofy girl feelings. "Where are we going, Dr. Greene?" I cringed at my high pitch.

"Your school," he answered cheerfully.

"What? My school?" I stammered because no way was my school one of the numerous fantastic places that I envisioned accompanying this man. "I thought maybe we were going for ice cream, or to the museum, or bowling."

"Bowling?" he asked. "Do you like to bowl?"

I glared at the side of his head. "No. I hate bowling with its gutterballs and smelly shoes. But I'd rather bowl than go to school!"

He glanced at me again before looking back at the road and making a promise. "After we go to school, I'll take you for ice cream."

My pouty face was momentous enough that Mrs. Stewart probably felt it back in the office. We rode into the city in silence. My trip to school earlier in the week had been traumatic. I wasn't sure I wanted the doctor to see me that pathetic. Telling him how I felt was one thing. His being an actual witness to my demise was more than I could bear.

We pulled into the parking lot and sat, staring at the *Home of the Tigers* sign that hung above the main entrance to the school. The final bell had announced the end of the day fifteen minutes earlier. Only teachers' and coaches' cars remained in the parking lot.

He broke the silence. "You told me how hard it was for you to do this earlier in the week. I thought I'd come with you, and we could go in together."

"Great idea, Doc." I stole my grandfather's name for his VA doctor when he was annoyed with him, and swathed him in some go-girl attitude for good measure. "The school is always on lockdown, and we can't get in without a card key, and since I didn't know we were coming, I didn't bring mine."

"I called, and the office is open for another hour, so we should be able to get in," he informed me.

There were still people in the building that could open doors for us, but I felt belligerent. "Well, we still can't get into my room without a key."

"Come on," he said. "We'll figure it out. You need to do this."

I knew he was correct. I had to deal with my fear and visit my classroom. I shook my body the way Zoomie flings rain from his fur. Then I left my attitude outside the school and walked into the building, accepting my mission.

Lilly Anne, the front office secretary, greeted us with her heavily powdered cheeks and lip-sticked smile. "Patti, so good to see you. How are you? We miss you."

"Hi, Lilly Anne," I said. "I'm just checking on my classroom. I forgot my room key. Could I borrow one?"

She motioned for us to follow her to the counter. The doctor and I stayed on one side as she went around to the other and rummaged in a drawer.

Once she finished with her task, she looked at us. Her eyes focused on Greene. They went wide, brightened, and her eyelashes fluttered. Lilly Anne, a sucker for biceps, beamed.

He smiled back.

Boo hiss! said Mr. Devil.

Lilly Anne leaned across the counter. "Patti, I gotta tell you, your classroom is a mess. They can't find a substitute, and the kids are misbehaving. Anderson is losing his mind. Anne Westbrook hasn't done a thing to help out."

"The woman is a menace," I said.

Lilly Ann sang out, "Can I get an amen?" before placing the key on the counter.

I stared at it—and stared at it—and stared at it.

Dr. Greene picked it up.

Knowing Lilly Anne, she probably purposely licked her lips. "Who's your friend?"

"Not my friend. A textbook salesman. You know what a pain in the ass they can be." I shot Greene a toothy grin.

He choked out a laugh, thanked her, then scooted me out the door.

"Remember, slow, steady breaths. You're StumpStrong. You can do this," he whispered into my ear as we started down the first corridor.

He stayed a step behind me as I took in my surroundings. Everything was the same as when I left—the same as it had been for the three decades that I had wandered those halls. We passed by rows of army green lockers and open classroom doors. Most of the teachers who devoted themselves to their livelihood were still there, exhausted and laboring despite the lack of respect and resources. Missy's door was open, and I knew she was correcting papers and writing lesson plans. We watched as a custodian cleaned graffiti from a wall. Then we continued our trek to the stairs that lead to the basement. The dungeon was where they locked away the lost kids, the kids nobody wanted or cared about, and me.

I wasn't as anxious as I had been the first time I undertook my mission. Maybe it was the doctor's presence, or perhaps it was that the halls weren't as dark. Maybe it was because I had already done this once before. This time I also had the reminder that I was StumpStrong. It wasn't easy because my heart was racing, but my breath was slow and steady.

I looked down that dark stairwell and froze. *No way! I can't do it.* I decided to get the key back and toss it to the secretary before I sprinted to the car.

"Can I have the key?" I asked.

Dr. Greene peered down that stairwell, then studied me and gave me an emphatic, "Nope!" In fact, I think he clutched the key in his palm tighter.

I reached for his hand, and he pulled away. We wrestled for a bit as I tried to confiscate the key. He won the skirmish, bypassed his coat pocket, and shoved it into his pants pocket.

I guess he figured I might try to retrieve the key from his coat. He should have wiped that smug look off of his face, though, because if he thought that I might not reach my hand into his pants, he was wrong. In fact, I would enjoy it. He was messing with the wrong horny woman. I poked at his pocket, and again we wrestled.

"Patricia," he said sternly, his voice dropping a few octaves. "Knock it off and come on." He pushed my hand away and started down the stairs. A feeling of indignation mingled with the profound ache in my body. I wanted to continue to tussle with him until we were both naked.

How in the heck can you be thinking about a man at a time like this? Ms. Angel asked.

She was correct. After further consideration, I realized that my tingly pang was probably fear and not the desire to seduce the mountain in front of me. We made it down the stairwell without further incident.

When we reached the landing, Greene's expression became one of compassionate seriousness. "Where's your classroom?"

I walked a few feet into the dark corridor, stopped, and pointed.

The doctor removed the key from his pocket, opened the door, and entered. I peeked over his shoulder to view a mess. There were books and papers all over the place, and the chairs and desks weren't in their predictable rows. It wasn't at all how I had left it.

Dr. Greene sat at one of the student desks and used curling fingers to motion for me to join him. Finally, I entered and sat in my chair, and looked around. The room wasn't as terrifying as it had become in my memories and nightmares. It was merely my classroom. Nothing more, nothing less—well, messier than I had left it—actually, a lot messier.

I'm not sure if Greene watched me, looked around at the room, or stared out a window. He seemed to make himself invisible, but I knew he was there and that I wasn't alone.

Once my heart rate returned to normal, I rifled through the papers on my desk. Then I walked around, examining the piles of things scattered about. I took a moment to clean up the trash that littered the floor.

I sat down and closed my eyes. I imagined Tanner Jones standing in front of me, calling me a bitch. I pictured the endless piles of paperwork. Then, I thought about the disrespectful comments, the cell phone battles, and trading in sleep for lesson planning. I asked myself if I was ready to deal with the understaffing, the lack of services for my students, the unrealistic expectations of parents, and the fear of being hurt in my classroom? I considered it all, and I didn't run out of the building, I didn't huddle in the corner crying, and I didn't hyperventilate.

"I'm ready to go," I said.

We locked my classroom door and retraced our path. Once outside the school, I took in the fresh air, then sighed in relief. I had done it. I'm not sure I could have done it without the doctor. I don't understand our strange dynamic, but I think his company made me stronger. Unless it was my mantra and the memory of my grandfather that had given me a newfound determination.

I turned to Jacob. "Thank you," I whispered.

"You did it," he responded just as softly.

Jacob Greene was standing close to me, and my gratitude needed an outlet. I leaned toward him, my arms opening to embrace him in a hug when my lone female student accosted me.

"Missus! Oh, my God! I miss you!"

Instead of hugging Jacob Greene, I hugged Diamond Washington.

"Oh, Missus. We all hate Tanner for making you leave. It sucks without you. It's boring, nobody teaches us nothin', and I haven't learned a thing since you left. And some of the boys are real pigs. Everybody lets them be bad. Tanner beat Nate up last week. He didn't get in trouble, and Nate even got a bloody nose."

"Hi, Diamond," I said. "What are you still doing here?"

"I was walkin' past and saw you. I waited for you to come back out so I could say hi. I miss you," she said.

"I'm sorry, Diamond. Who is teaching you?"

"I told you, Missus, nobody's teachin' us nothin'. They put a different teacher with us every day. Ms. M&M sometimes comes down and eats lunch with me. She says I need a girl to talk to, and she's nice and doesn't let the boys call me a fat, ugly whore."

"Oh, Diamond. I'm so sorry."

Diamond wasn't fat, ugly, or a whore. They were merely cruel words meant to torment her. How could anyone allow such hurtful name-calling?

"Well, that one principal, the tall bald guy, comes in. He makes sure we have food and that nobody gets beat up when he's with us."

Missy and Anderson were good eggs. They were doing the best they could to help out during my absence.

"Does a lady with blonde hair named Dr. Westbrook ever come in?" I asked.

She thought this over. "No. I don't know any blonde lady, and no doctors ever come in."

I studied Greene, who grew angrier by the second.

Diamond used her most powerful weapon of persuasion—her pleading brown eyes. "Can you come back? Cause nobody's gonna help me get upstairs with the good kids if you don't. Do you think they're abusing me? Letting those boys be mean and not teaching us anything?"

When I didn't answer, she turned to my companion. "You think they're abusing me, mister?"

Greene continued to take his frustration out on the pavement as he shuffled anxious feet and singed the ground with angry eyes.

"Diamond, I'm having some health problems, and this is the doctor who is helping me get better. I'm not better yet, but I'm working hard, so maybe after Thanksgiving vacation, I might be able to come back."

"Really?" she cried out.

"Maybe. I'm not sure, but I'm trying."

"Is this your shrink cause Tanner made you lose your mind?" she asked.

I didn't see any point in lying to her, so I nodded to the affirmative while Dr. Greene continued to stare at his feet.

"I hate Tanner, and if that fucker touches you again, I'm gonna kill him," she declared.

I cringed at her language and her threat. As much as I would have loved for her to stand up for me, I said, "You don't want to go to jail because of Tanner. Do you hear me? You're doing great, and you won't let him change that."

"Okay, missus, I might not kill him if you come back, but if you don't come back, I'm gonna kill the fucker."

"Diamond," I said, doing my best to look into her soul. "Sometimes, it is the adults that aren't doing their jobs that make kids misbehave."

Diamond huffed. "It isn't your fault Tanner's an ass."

"No," I said. "But maybe it's his parents' fault. And maybe the systems set up to help him are broken."

She shrugged and hugged me again. "Bye, missus. Bye, Missus' doctor." She waved and strutted across the parking lot toward the main street.

Dr. Greene looked a demented angry as we drove away from the school. "Tell me about Diamond."

I figured it would be okay to tell my therapist about my student since he had to keep anything I told him confidential.

"She's a sweet kid who has had a rough life. I don't know much about her dad, and her mom works two jobs to keep food on the table. Diamond got herself into trouble for fighting. But she only got into the altercations because she was trying to protect herself. She doesn't tolerate nonsense from anyone. I never thought she belonged in an alternative setting. I think she got sent there because nobody advocated for her."

"Without you, there still isn't anyone to advocate for her," Jacob deduced.

"I guess not. The thing is, all of the kids in my class made a mistake. Most of them are decent humans who need a little bit of TLC. Others have severe behavioral issues, some are volatile and have more needs than a public school can provide, but they mix them all together. The powers that be don't seem to understand that a child with learning problems in survival mode is different from one with sociopathic tendencies. Then they shove them into a tiny room with a teacher who doesn't have the correct resources, and then they cut what few services there are until there is nothing. I ask myself, 'why?' all of the time. The obvious answer is that they want to save money, but I can't help but think it's more than that. I mean, it seems to be sheer incompetence." I paused. "Right? Pure incompetence?"

"Patricia..." I felt like he wanted to tell me something, but he didn't finish his thought.

I waited before asking, "What were you going to say?"

He let out a long exhale before answering. "The incompetence probably stems from a lack of funding and society not caring enough to invest in education." His sigh was so heavy I thought he might fall through the floor of his expensive car. "Diamond is correct. It is almost like child abuse to do that to those kids."

"I'm not sure. I've never thought of it as abuse, but maybe it is. I know I feel helpless to do anything," I replied.

We finished the drive across the bridge that separated the intimidating city from my impervious borough in silence.

"Hey," he said, pulling into a Dairy Queen parking lot. "I promised you ice cream. Will this do?"

Five minutes later, I sat in the car beside Jacob, lapping up my creamy peanut butter and M&M concoction. The fact that my belly was already full of Mrs. Stewart's cookies did nothing to curb my appetite for more sugar. I enthusiastically told him about the evenings we gathered around my grandfather's baby grand. My grandparents would lead us in song. I don't think playing one-handed dulled Pap's passion or talent. I don't think the fact that Grandma sang slightly out of tune bothered any of us. I recalled them ending our sessions with the same little ditty, "She's got freckles on her butt—she's nice." Then Grandma would giggle. I think this was as risque as she ever got. Pap enjoyed her semi-raunchiness immensely, as did her grandchildren. Our prim and proper grandma had joyfully sung out the word, "butt"— or was it "but?"

I learned that Jacob's hobbies were reading, woodworking, and swimming. He was currently building a bookshelf. He was on his college swim team, he still swam in the adult league at the YMCA, and butterfly was his strongest event. His favorite book was *One Flew Over The Cuckoo's Nest,* and he loved to watch old Marx Brothers movies.

Feeling like Jacob and I had connected on our field trip, I took a chance. "Mrs. Stewart told me that you broke up with your fianceé. Do you want to talk about it?" I held my breath and waited.

His cheeks puffed up. I think he was holding his response in his mouth. Eventually, he said, "Different life paths."

There was a comfortable lull in the conversation right before he taunted me by pushing on my shoulder and asking, "Can you really recite 'Gunga Din'?"

I answered him by busting out my best Cockney accent. I sang out the entire ballad, finishing with my favorite stanza:

"So I'll meet 'im later on
At the place where 'e is gone—
Where it's always double drill and no canteen.
'E'll be squattin' on the coals
Givin' drink to poor damned souls,
An' I'll get a swig in hell from Gunga Din!
Yes, Din! Din! Din!
You Lazarushian-leather Gunga Din!
Though I've belted you and flayed you,
By the livin' Gawd that made you,
You're a better man than I am, Gunga Din."
I smiled and took a seated bow.
"Bravo! Bravo!" Jacob clapped.

Pap was right. All those hours memorizing Kipling had paid off. I had received accolades from the sexiest man in the world. I was beyond ecstatic because I had just eaten ice cream and pretended to be on a date with the man who gave me goosebumps.

This afternoon I turned a corner and overcame a considerable roadblock. I was able to walk back into school, and my precious Diamond reminded me of the reasons I became a teacher. I have no intention of allowing Westbrook to force me to resign. In fact, I think I'm ready to return to work. Most importantly, I feel like celebrating because today was the first day of the rest of my life.

Ecstatic,
Patti

Chapter 20

*"All battles are fought by scared men
who would rather be somewhere else."*

John Wayne

November 15

Missy: Hiya GF. You have plans tonight? Nope! Ha! Well, now, you do! We are going to refresh our self-defense techniques. Next time you'll knock that little bastard on his ass. I'm picking you up at 6:30. Invite Valentina and that kooky coffee shop chick with all the piercings.

P: I did self-defense years ago. A lot of good it did me. Besides, we can't knock kids on their asses.

Missy: Stop feeling sorry for yourself and get your ass out of bed.

P: My cash is a bit low until I go back to work, so I better pass.

Missy: No worries because I won four lessons in a raffle. You know how I love free things! Bonus-the instructor is hot as hell! 🔥🔥🔥

P: I can't go tonight. I forgot. I have a date with my friend Neil.

Missy: Liar, Liar, pants on 🔥 You would never forget you had a date. See you at 6:30.

P: I can't believe you are stooping so low as to force me to do a stupid self-defense class. What kind of friend are you?

Missy: Wish you could see my cheesy grin and the middle-finger I saved especially for you. Searching for my fuck you Patti emoji 😂

P: Hey, Tina. Missy McMann wants to know if you and Chelsea want to go to some self-defense thingy tonight at 6:30? She won the lessons. I know it's late notice, so no worries if you can't go. Sounds like a nightmarish waste of time to me.

Valentina: We are so in! Where should we meet you?

P: My house. Missy is picking us up 🙄

P: Tina and Chelsea can go. See you at 6:30. FYI. I plan to be pissy, and I can't promise I will still be your friend after.

Missy: Beggars can't be choosers! And you are going to have fun if it kills us all.

P: I ran into Diamond yesterday. She said you are looking out for her. Thanks!

Missy: I love that kid! Westbrook needs to be strung by her toes over an open 🔥 See you tonight.

…..…..*…..*

November 16, 2019

Dear Diary,

Ladies and gentlemen, welcome to your Friday Night Fights!

First up for Team Patti and the Pathetic Pansies, hanging out in the wrong corner, wearing her paint-stained sweatpants and pit-stained sweatshirt, weighing in at two hundred pounds plus. With three thousand wins because she does not accept losses, it's Ms. Happy M&M!

Next up, still, in the wrong corner, wearing way-too-tight black leggings, a low cut t-shirt, a push-up bra, and a full set of salon tips is the super sexy Miss Be My Valentina or Die.

Ladies and gentlemen, we haven't left the wrong corner. Smelling of week-old coffee beans and weighing in too heavy due to body jewelry, our next competitor will make you want to knock yourself out when you see her purple print zebra pants and lime green sweater. Please put your hands together for The Kooky Klutz and her intimidating spiky pigtails.

Are you ready to meet our final in-the-wrong-corner competitor? Wearing non-descript yoga pants, a grey sweatshirt, and a messy ponytail, with a record of no wins and three trillion million losses, is Patti.

Give it up for Team Patti and the Pathetic Pansies.

(Crowd boos)

Now, in the right corner, wearing the perfect white pants, weighing in at the ideal weight, with all wins and no losses, we have four-time Golden Glove winner and Olympic wrestling team qualifier, Mr. Dan the Hot Man Miller.

(The crowd goes wild)

Well, maybe there was no crowd booing and cheering, but the rest of the scene was spot on. Mr. Dan had his work cut out for him.

I should have known we were in trouble when Missy passed hooch around the van in the Recreation Hall parking lot.

"Drink up, ladies! First, we need to get Patti relaxed. Then we need to teach her how to kick ass!" she declared.

"Woohoo! Then we need to get her laid," Tina yelled before taking a huge swig and handing the bottle to Chelsea.

"Go, kooky girl," Missy encouraged her.

Chelsea seemed to like her new nickname. She was wearing her Cheshire cat grin when she handed me the bottle.

"This is so going to suck!" I muttered.

I'm sure I looked as disgusted as I felt. First of all, I hate whiskey. Second, I did not care to drink out of a bottle that other people had put their lips on. Third, I especially did not want to drink after Chelsea. Most importantly, I did not want to get laid or to admit that I wanted to get laid. Whichever, me getting laid was not a goal I wanted any part of because perimenopausal women don't need to get laid.

"Drink! Drink! Drink!" the three stooges chanted in unison. I pinched my nostrils and took a sip.

"Holy shit," Tina and I said at the same time, but for entirely different reasons. My throat was on fire, and Tina's loins were on fire.

"Is that him?" Tina asked.

We peered out the SUV windows to check out what had caused Tina's panties to dampen. A large, tattooed man with copper-colored hair was walking across the parking lot toward the building. Despite the November chill, he was wearing thin white pants and a white T-shirt. His colorful, muscular biceps were on display.

"Yep," said Missy. "Told you. Hot! Let's go." She took another swig and shoved the bottle under the front seat.

"Hey, guys. I don't think this is a good idea," I said.

Unfortunately, my friends had simultaneously slammed the car's doors, and like mesmerized sheep, followed the large tattooed man.

"Wait," I yelled across the parking lot. "Anyone wanna go get dinner?"

"You're broke, remember?" Missy called back.

The three of them disappeared through the door. The last thing I saw was smart-ass Valentina waving goodbye.

"Damn! I need new friends," I whimpered. I pouted for a good five minutes before I followed them into the building.

A dozen lust-struck women sat in a semi-circle surrounding Dan. They hung on his every word as he filled their heads with dread. Apparently, there were billions of sociopathic perverts behind every shrub waiting to attack weak, unprepared women. Just the knowledge I needed with my current assault-induced anxiety. Drool dripped from my mesmerized friends. I, for one, was skeptical. He may have had the body of a Greek god, the cheekbones of a Roman statue, and hair the color of a copper penny in the sun, but I concluded he had been on a bathroom break when brains were handed out.

I was about to take my seat on the mat when the big man said, "Hey, Red. Come here."

Crap monsters!

"Big Red—"

I cringed when he used the nickname my grandfather had bestowed upon me. Especially since I knew that his 'big' was laced with sarcasm.

"—is the smallest person in the room. But, with some confidence and skill, she can protect herself against someone my size," he promised.

"I hate you," I mouthed to Missy.

"Go, Big Red!" Missy cheered.

"Big Red! Big Red!" the class chanted as I walked to the gigantic man. As anyone with fire-colored hair will tell you, the redhead in the room is a target and the first to be humiliated in a room full of other perfectly acceptable potential victims. I have found that being the shortest person in the room doesn't help.

"What's your name?" Mr. Biceps asked.

"Patti," I answered.

"Go, Patti!" the room cheered.

"Turn around, Patti," he commanded.

I hesitantly turned. I didn't want to have my back to him, even if it was a pretend attack.

"So, what would you do, Patti, if a man came up behind you and did this?"

As he locked his forearm around my neck, I attempted to face him so that I could punch him in the nose. Bigger, faster, and stronger than me, he grabbed me and flipped me onto the ground. Then, his monstrous thighs straddled me. He locked my arms to my body, leaving me defenseless. Gasps came from the female onlookers. I wasn't sure a good instructor should be tossing around a half-a-century-old woman like a sack of potatoes, but I wasn't sure about much these days.

"Hey," Tina called to him. "Mr. Dan, Patti got attacked a few weeks ago by some kid in her class twice her size. You might need to take it easy on her."

There were more gasps. If our fear-mongering instructor was correct, almost every woman in that room should have been attacked by one of the gazillions of perverted perpetrators peppering the universe. As I suspected, he was a bit off with his statistics because I seemed to be the only woman out of this dozen who had experienced an attack. Unless I was the only one who had a bunch of big-mouthed friends announcing it to the world.

The pronouncement of my saga seemed to reinforce our instructor's notion that I needed a ton of attention. Although it's also possible that the attention I was receiving was because Chelsea, the person in the room closest to my size, and the hands-down winner of the Klutziest Person in the World Award, was my partner. In the first hour of class, she managed to knee herself in the gut, twist her ankle, scratch my cheek, and slap the instructor. Her misplaced slap landed her in the same floor-splatting take-down that I had experienced earlier. The difference being, I think she enjoyed Dan the Hot Man straddling her.

By break time, I craved another quaff. The four of us used our fifteen minutes of freedom to pass around Missy's car flask. Swigging and loudly singing, "One hundred bottles of beer," revved us up for the second half of class.

By eight-fifteen, we had reached the absurd shenanigans level. We spent the remainder of the class pretending to grab Dan's ass, although Missy wasn't acting. Tina was wildly creative as she struck juvenile poses behind his back. Chelsea remained glued to the mat, giggling. Enjoying my friends' antics was the most I had laughed in years.

At nine o'clock, a thoroughly disgusted Dan dismissed us.

Missy grabbed his ass on her way past, calling out, "Thanks, Mr. Dan."

"Hey, are you ladies drunk?" he asked.

His acknowledgment of our state resulted in uncontrollable female sniggers.

"This is serious stuff. You would think that after what happened to Red here"——he pointed at me——"the four of you would have taken tonight seriously."

This statement was hysterical to four drunk women.

"You ladies cannot drive home. Can someone come and get you?" Dan asked.

"We aren't going home. We are going to Charly's Place," Missy announced. "And you are driving us, sexy man!"

That is how the five of us ended up out in the middle of nowhere, in a scuzzy honkey-tonk bar, dancing, playing pool, and doing shots of whiskey.

We were on our third round of shots. Missy called out "drink," then in unison, we picked up the glasses, chugged, gasped as the liquid burned the entire way down, and slammed the glasses onto the bar.

Drunk, our inhibitions unencumbered, we became fascinated with Dan's cauliflower ears. We took turns touching them and admiring the toughness it would take to allow others to smash up the cartridge in your ears for the sake of sport.

I ran my finger along the bridge of his nose. "How many times you break your nose?" I yelled from the seat next to him.

He leaned his shoulder against mine. "Three. But I have broken ten times that."

"Hey, Mr. Dan, word of advice," I called over the loud music pounding from the jukebox. "I'm also a teacher, and one thing every good instructor knows is, you shouldn't throw around senior citizens."

His eyes narrowed. "Senior citizens?" He gulped from a questionably clean beer mug.

"Patti's convinced she's the oldest person in the world. Too old to be worthy of any enjoyment in life," my BFF, Mrs. Sassy Pants Smith, declared. "She probably needs to get laid."

Dan moved his face in and out. I think he was checking me out from different angles. "How old are you?"

"Fifty," Tina answered for me.

Chelsea toppled forward and landed face-first on the bar. At least we knew that Chelsea, despite her slightly junked-up appearance, was not a drinker.

I stared at the back of Chelsea's head and muttered, "Oh, crap." I lifted her face off of the bar to shove a few napkins under her forehead. I have no idea why I did it, but it seemed to be my way of taking care of the poor girl.

"Fifty! No. Really?" he exclaimed. "Damn, Red! You're a MILF, for sure."

I ignored his comment since I was concerned about my strange friend's comatose status. "Do you think sshe iss okay?" I slurred.

He studied her. "Nothing a nice long nap won't cure." Then he added, "Hey Red, I'm available." He lifted his arms to showcase himself.

I could do a lot worse, so I considered taking him up on his offer.

A few seconds later, I declined, saying, "I already have more men in my life than I can deal with." Even drunk, I attempted to analyze the statement I had blurted out. I had no idea what I had meant by "more men."

Dan's frown turned into a smile as he addressed Tina. "Hey, pretty Spanish lady, I'm available."

"I'm Dominican and happily married." She gave him a flirtatious wink.

He studied Missy, taking in her girth and baggy clothes. He shrugged. "You may be more woman than I can handle, sweet Mama, but I'm available."

Missy chuckled, her infectious belly laugh causing a wave of joy at the bar. "I'm definitely more woman than you can handle."

I suspect that being sexually harassed by a gaggle of females had his testosterone in overdrive. He looked around at the toothless varieties of fish in his current sea. Shuddering, he grabbed Chelsea's hair and lifted her head off of the bar to say, "Hey, I'm available." A sleeping Chelsea wasn't available. He gently laid her head back on the napkins and sighed.

"Come on." Missy grabbed him. "Let's dance!"

The rest of the night is blurry. I remember dancing with Tina, dancing with Dan, and then dancing with some scrawny homeless-looking dude who smelled like cigarettes and vomit. I also remember that Tina and I played pool with two large hairy men who continued to ply us with beer.

I awoke early this morning to Zoomie trying to rid me of my offensive frat house smell. My mouth tasted like I had consumed a plague-ridden rat, and my body felt like a two-hundred-pound man had body-slammed me, then sat on me.

Oh, yeah!

"No bath, Zoomie," I pleaded. His saliva added to my nasty feeling. "Zoomie, I keep telling you Mommy needs new friends. Maybe a few knitting grandmotherly types! What do you think, boy?"

Despite my protests, my dog insisted I needed to be cleaned and continued with his monumental chore.

When I rolled over to check the time, I saw that my phone had collected messages overnight. Disjointed memories of my evening flooded in, alerting me to the damage I had done. I slightly remembered calling Cody to come and get us. I almost remembered Cody and Dan carrying Chelsea to the car, and I kind of remembered a horrific texting rampage.

I think it necessary to note that hangovers bite, and I need to sleep this off.

Dead!

Patti

..........*.....*

Sometime between November 15th-16th
P: Hi Neil. I took a self-defense class, and I'm drunk.

Neil Harris: Awesome! I hope you got in a few chokeholds before you passed out.

P: Michael Christopher Moore has a tiny cock!

Mike: Since you know that is NOT true, you must be drunk.

P: Hi Dr. Sexy! I want you bad!

Dr. Greene: We need to talk.

Missy: Cha-ching! Wow! Dan is the man!

Cassie: Hi, Mom. Hung over much? Dad says you got drunk last night and sent him lewd texts. 😂😂🤢🤢🤢

..........*.....*

November 17, 2019
Dear Diary,

By the time I got out of bed yesterday, it was past noon.

"Oh, Zoomie. What have I done?" I asked my pup.

Zoomie sneezed.

I staggered into the shower to erase the stink of the night. I walked and fed my pup and threw on a clean sweatshirt and leggings. I needed to see Tina.

She didn't look any better than I felt. She had the lights in the coffee shop turned low. She was barely moving, and I could see from her squinty eyes that she had a headache. A line of people waited for her to take their orders.

"Hi," she whispered when I reached her. "Chelsea isn't in yet. I sent Cody to check on her."

I joined Tina behind the counter so that I could help fill orders. I figured it would give us a chance to talk.

"Oh my God, what happened last night?" I asked.

"Well, I don't think we learned much self-defense, but we had a hell of a good time." She groaned "Maldicion" as she rubbed at her temple. "Missy ended up sleeping with Dan the Hot Man. They can have strapping Viking children." Laughing seemed to exasperate her pain because a moan and another temple rub followed her chuckle.

"Coffee and muffin to go," said a customer eavesdropping on our conversation.

"Tina, I sent texts last night. Humiliating ones," I told her.

Her brow furrowed as she concentrated. "Oh, yeah. You told Mike he had a little penis."

The waiting customer's eyes went wide, and I handed him his coffee and muffin and scooted him on his way.

"Way worse." I leaned close to her and whispered. "I sent my therapist a text telling him I wanted him. I called him, 'Dr. Sexy.'" I groaned, and my cheeks burned me alive.

"Hah! I knew it! I knew you had it bad for him when you came in all flushed after your first appointment. Ouch!" She closed her eyes for a moment. "Next," she half-called, half-whispered to the line of customers.

A young girl who was a regular ordered a double espresso.

"I can't recall ever doing anything more inappropriate or embarrassing. What am I going to do?"

Tina didn't answer because she was concentrating on her hand as she stirred the drink.

It was at that moment that the most horrible thing ever happened. The door opened, Dr. Greene walked in, and his eyes searched the shop, landing on me.

"Oh my God," I moaned.

Tina muttered, "Santo cielo!" It was her way of saying, *Holy crap.*

Greene was wearing jeans and a sapphire blue cable knit sweater that matched his eyes. His un-moussed waves were everywhere. In awe of his physical perfection, I allowed myself to be swept away in one of my touching-the-young-doctor's-pretty-hair fantasies. I returned to earth, remembering that I was smack-dab in the middle of a severe case of humiliation. He took his spot in line and watched as Tina and I struggled to fill orders due to our hungover-haze and Doctor Greene shock. I considered running through the shop, out the front door, to the safety of my covers.

When he reached the front of the line, I held my breath.

"Hi, Valentina. Hello, Patricia. I'll have a large cup of coffee to go."

We silently prepared his order.

Once Tina handed him his cup, he asked, "Valentina, could I talk to your helper for a few minutes?"

"Coffee is on me today," she said. "And I guess so?" She looked to me for confirmation.

I nodded and Dr. Greene thanked her. He poured a lot of cream into his cup. Then we made our way to the shop's most remote corner and sat.

I immediately blurted out, "Dr. Greene, I'm sorry. I'm embarrassed. My friends and I got a little drunk at self-defense class, and I think I meant to send that text to my cop friend." My brain was foggy, and that was the only thing I could come up with.

"You call your cop friend doctor?" he asked.

I stuttered. "I don't know. I was drunk. Maybe I meant to tell you—" I searched for something, anything, that wasn't the truth. "That I wanted you to know how good I did in self-defense class?"

I was a hot mess!

"Back up. You were drunk in self-defense class?" He sniffed at me like I was a trash receptacle during a heatwave.

I was a hopeless hot mess!

I scrunched up my nose. "Well, probably only buzzed, and that was Missy's fault. We got drunk afterward. I'm kind of having trouble recalling much after the bottle of hooch and the three shots, maybe four. I'm not sure, and the beers."

I was a hopeless, humiliated hot mess!

As if on cue, Cody and Chelsea walked into the shop. Chelsea looked like death in sunglasses.

"See." I pointed. "Chelsea is hungover too."

He looked at her and chuckled. Even though I was in pain, his laugh sent shivers up my spine.

I was a hopeless, humiliated, horny hot mess!

He reached over and touched the scratch on my face. A volt of electricity, a million watts strong, careened through my body. When he pulled his hand away, his eyes were wide, alerting me that he had also felt it.

"What happened? I mean to your face." I suspected he was specifying the scratch so that I didn't think he meant the lightning bolt that had passed between us.

"Chelsea's love tap." I did some type of twisted grin-grimace as I recalled Chelsea's leap through the air as she did her best Kung Fu Panda impression and removed a patch of skin from my cheek.

He looked over my head. "No worries, I'm sure you just wanted to tell me you were having fun."

Relief flooded through me. I had covered, and it was going to be okay.

He focused his eyes on mine. "More than likely, you were drunk and texting a lot of people." He stood and I thought he was going to walk away. Instead, he bent over and leaned close. "Unless you do want me, Patricia Easterling." His voice had dropped a few octaves and was the most incredibly sexy sound I had ever heard. It sent my breath to the moon, and I felt a scorching flush cover my neck, overtake my cheeks, then work its way to the top of my head.

Then, coffee in hand, Jacob Greene confidently strolled into the sunlight like he owned the world.

"You're the one that told me to have more fun. You're such an ass," I said to the closing door. "And I want you so much I'm losing my mind," I whispered to the air.

Embarrassed beyond words,
Patti

Chapter 21

"Healthy, lusty sex is wonderful."

John Wayne

November 18, 2019

Dear Diary,

Although I'm physically feeling better after Friday night's debauchery, I'm an emotional wreck.

I haven't been able to stop Jacob Greene's comment from bouncing around and careening into my brain. Specifically, the one in which he said, "Unless you do want me, Patricia Easterling." Now, I know for certain he has been flirting with me.

Crazy? Right?

The man has been fueling my obsessive schoolgirl crush, and it isn't helping my mess of a life! I can't decide if I'm furious or turned on. Since I'm a wack-job, it's probably some sort of dysfunctional combination.

Moving on.

Neil dropped by my house this afternoon to go for a run. I opened my front door to his sweet smile, a pumpkin pie, and the news that the district magistrate confirmed Tanner Jones' appointment for next week.

Four miles later, Neil and I sat on the couch, glasses of water and spicy pie spread out on the coffee table. Zoomie sat between us with his head propped on Neil's lap. That is, until Neil promised him a piece of crust if he would relocate to the floor. Like mother, like pup—Zoomie is a sucker for desserts.

Neil grasped my palm as he stared into my eyes. "Patricia, we need to talk."

I considered excusing myself to the restroom. I even contemplated stuffing another piece of pie into my mouth so that I couldn't say something stupid and anxiety-inducing. If there is one thing that fifty years on this giant globe has taught me, "We need to talk" is rarely a good thing. Determined to be brave, I choose not to run away or shove copious amounts of food into my body. Instead, I let Neil hold on to me as he confessed his feelings.

"Look, I'm crazy about you, and I need to know how you feel about me. I want to ask you to do more with Alexia and me, but I don't want her to get hurt if this isn't going anywhere." He squeezed my hand tighter. "And it was hell getting over my divorce. I don't want to hurt that much ever again."

I was acutely aware of the pain Neil referenced. He deserved better. I knew it was time to rip off the band-aid, so I took a moment to compose myself.

You have to do this, Patti. Stop being a huge-ass pussy! I scolded myself. I mentally counted to three, then ripped! I didn't take a breath until I had blurted it all out. "Neil, you've been a good friend to me, and I loved being with you and Alexia, but I think that being with the two of you reminded me of being with my family during our good times, and that isn't fair to either of you."

His pretty eyes took on a faraway look, and the soft shade of blue faded to a pale gray as he said, "I see."

I didn't want to lose my champion or the precious little girl who had recently become my friend, but he deserved honesty, and I needed to move on. I reminded Neil of the numerous reasons he should not choose me as a girlfriend. For starters, there was my failed marriage. Add to that my work-induced anxiety, my current lack of income, my nightmares, and my age.

Besides being sweet, Neil is stubborn. My cautionary tales did nothing to dissuade him.

He pushed a stand of hair behind my ear, saying, "None of that matters because your smile lights up the room. I think you're beautiful. I love when your hair is all over the place; it takes my breath away. You make me laugh when you talk to yourself. Everything about you is honest and real. I can always tell what you're thinking, except for when it comes to how you feel about me."

What was he talking about? "Honest and real"? I had turned into an unscrupulous liar trying to hide my feelings from everyone. I removed my hand from Neil's and looked to Zoomie for advice. Zoomie chewed on an old tennis ball, not concerned in the least with my problem.

I sighed before continuing. "Neil, I'm going through a tough time, and my emotions are all over the place."

"I know, you feel vulnerable since your attack. That situation at your school is ridiculous, and your supervisor should be fired for putting you in the basement with those kids and no support. And I know you don't see it, but you aren't too old for me. Hell, I'm in decent shape, and I have to work to keep up with you when we're running, and you still dance like you're a teenager."

I squinted one eye and cringed. I wasn't in an accepting-compliments kind of place and lumping them together in one long diatribe overwhelmed me.

"There's more," I told him. "I think I have feelings for someone else. I'm sorry. I don't have any kind of romantic relationship with him, but it isn't fair to keep it from you."

His bruised look broke my heart. So did his next comment. "Mike is lucky to have you."

But Mike had Shelly, not me. I had been referring to Jacob Greene. At least, I think I meant Jacob. My attempt at stoicism was fruitless. I dabbed at a lone tear and fought with my mouth until the corners turned upward.

Neil stood, bent to pat Zoomie, then looked at me and forced a smile. "I'll see you at the magistrate's on the twenty-sixth. That kid needs help, and we'll try to get it for him."

After sealing his promise with a peck on my cheek, Officer Neil Harris walked out the door. The loneliness that he had kept at bay washed over me like a black tidal wave. I allowed myself some time to grieve before issuing a mental slap and focusing.

Neil's revelations made me explore some of the ideas whirling around in my mind. What if Doctor Jacob felt the same way? Did he think my smile lit up the room? Did he think my messy hair was beautiful? Did he find my absurd comments when I talked to myself endearing? I knew one thing. The energy that passed between us when we accidentally touched was like a surge of electricity.

But, Mike?

Mike??

Mike???

There is so much to consider. I'll go before the magistrate this week to tell her what a disturbed sixteen-year-old-boy did to me. I'll ask her to throw the book at Tanner, but if the school had done right by him, would this have happened? If his parents had done right by him, would this have happened? If society cared about its lost children, would this have happened?

Am I partially to blame?

The thing is, I can't ignore Tanner's actions. With his violence escalating, he can't stay in the classroom. At five feet three inches tall, one hundred thirty pounds, and fifty years of age, I can't prevent his assaults, even with Dan the Hot Man's lessons. What if next time Tanner hurts my Diamond?

How can I help any of these kids if they lock us away and give us nothing?

I know there is a solution. I just don't know what it is—yet.

Pap, what would you do? Help me to deal with my aching heart and the "der hurensohn."

Tired,
Patti

..........*.....*

November 19, 2019
Dear Diary,

Last night Pap appeared in his favorite tweed blazer and answered my prayers. He told me to "buck up" because I was "cuchi-cuchi dancing," learning to "beat someone about the face and eyes," and spending time with my "convivial" girlfriends. He seemed to think I had "demonstrated pluck" by entering my classroom. He was quite chatty, adding that my soulmate and I had to "screw our heads on straight." He reminded me that it had been a week since I had experienced an "accursed nightmare." Since Pap was always correct, I listened. I concluded that bucking up meant no more pity parties and taking complete control of my life. However, I ignored the comment about my soulmate since I no longer had one.

I'm not sure what got into me. Pap certainly wasn't encouraging wanton behaviors, and Zoomie, with his incessant sneezing, insisted I had on entirely too much perfume. For some reason, I felt shockingly bold. I was ready to seize the reins of my life, and step one was seducing my sexy doctor.

I dressed in my emerald blouse and high-heeled boots. I strategically left my top button undone and carefully applied heavy black eyeliner and smoky eye shadow. Then I did a hair toss that made me dizzy, righted myself, and strutted into that office.

Mrs. Stewart greeted me. "Hi, Patricia, you're early. Did you predict I have fresh brownies?" She held her fancy silver platter under my nose. A drug dealer tempting an addict had nothing on this artful woman.

"Not today, Mrs. Stewart."

She stared me down with puppy dog eyes.

I wasn't falling for her wily ways. I was on a mission that sugar-laden confections had no part in.

I picked up a magazine and pretended to read, but ended up staring at an article titled *Ten Ways to Simplify Your Life*. I read the first line at least fifteen times and still didn't have a clue what it was saying.

Finally, Dr. Greene's office door opened. A young man exited and made his way to Mrs. Stewart's tray.

"Hi, Patricia," Jacob said, ushering me in.

His astute eyes studied me as I passed.

"What's the special occasion?" he asked.

"What do you mean?" I replied, pretending not to understand.

He closed the door behind me. "You look particularly lovely today."

"I'm going shopping after I leave here," I declared.

"Shopping?" He smiled, and his eyes sparkled.

What an arrogant ass! He knew precisely why I had gunked make-up and musk all over myself, and I was going to force his hand.

He picked up his pad and began his scribbling. "Have you had any nightmares recently?"

"No nightmares."

"How are you feeling now that you've had a chance to process our trip into the school last Thursday?"

"I think it went well."

"Not very talkative today." It was not clear whether he intended the statement to be a question or an observation.

I shrugged.

"Okay." He sighed. "Do you want to talk about Friday night?"

"What about Friday night?"

"Well, you went to a self-defense class with your girlfriends. Apparently, you got drunk and sent me a text."

I refused to allow my words to reflect my horrific humiliation. I pulled my shoulders back. "You're the one who told me to have fun."

He flashed me one of his exceptionally gorgeous smiles. "Yes. I guess I did." The line of his lips straightened, and his voice became stern. "About the text?"

I lifted my chin. "I thought we established the text was an accident. You have a short memory."

I could tell my taciturn responses frustrated him because his jaw tensed, and his cheeks became a telling shade of purplish-red. The thumping of his pen against his notebook created a ticking time bomb metronome.

When the tapping ceased, the silence that lay between us became charged with a scorching current. Like a magnet drawn to an opposite pole, I made my way to where he sat. He held his breath as he studied my every move. I leaned in close and relieved him of his notebook and pen, tossing them onto the floor. The second I heard Jacob Greene's hiss, I knew he was mine.

Our gazes locked, and he allowed me to take control of the situation. I encouraged him to stand, and taking his hand in mine, led him to the settee where I usually sat. I pushed into his chest, and he plopped down. His muscular frame overwhelmed that small sofa.

Although I was out of practice, my fantasies had prepared me for my next daring move. I gracefully climbed onto his lap to straddle him. His sapphire eyes turned into searing flames. With my face inches from his, I twirled one of his waves between my thumb and forefinger. His ensuing growl sent shivers traveling the length of my spine to the nape of my neck. The flutters changed directions and landed with a thud in my aching girl parts.

One of Jacob's hands grabbed a fistful of my hair, while the other dug into my waist. I settled into position, shifting my hips back and forth until the curves in my body matched his. We meshed like perfectly fitting puzzle pieces. I felt his body tense, then relax, as he reacted to me. I leaned in and planted a searching kiss on his lips. Tasting of peppermint and chocolate brownie, he kissed me back. His touch caused a sensation akin to a million tiny butterflies tickling my insides. I finally knew the truth. Jacob Greene wanted me as much as I wanted him.

I took his bottom lip between my teeth and gently nibbled. He nibbled back. Then I kissed a trail to his ear to whisper, "I do want you, Jacob."

The thrill of saying his name tipped my desire over the edge, and it appeared to have the same effect on him. A moan, guttural and wild, escaped from him before his insistent hands pulled my hair, and his hungry lips stole my air. Reason and restraint gone, our hands, lips, and tongues were everywhere.

The moment was perfect, except for the fabric that kept our skin from touching. I unbuttoned his shirt to run my hands over the smooth chest that had become my obsession. I painted a trail of licks and kisses from his neck to his belt line. I stopped to peer up at his heavy-lidded eyes. My short halt allowed him to take over. With my legs still straddling him, he stood and effortlessly carried me across the room, where he tossed me onto his desk. His handsome face was contorted with desire and drawn tight when he reached for my top button. At first, he was too consumed with passion to take his time. Finally, he stopped his frantic effort and smiled. It was an odd sort of grin that didn't fit the wild look in his eyes. His expression changed before his tongue made a brief appearance. He grappled with the rest of my buttons and pulled my shirt open, exposing my torso.

He moaned out a "Christ."

I tilted my head to the side, exposing the sweet spot between my neck and shoulder. Jacob got the hint and gently suckled on the area before growling into my ear, "Patricia, I want you too. So damn much."

Those words from my usually well-spoken therapist obliterated the small amount of restraint I had left, and my treasured blouse found its way to the floor. He continued his sensual assault on my neck before tending to the area above my breasts, then found his way to my waist. I wanted him to continue. Unfortunately, my jeans were in the way.

"Jacob," I whispered, taking immense pleasure in saying his name.

He responded with a low, raspy, "Patricia," right before climbing onto the desk.

We were simultaneously reaching for the clasps on the other's pants when the session timer went off. I jumped. He moaned. Then he scooted off of me and pulled me to a seated position.

He buttoned his shirt while he spoke. "I'm sorry. I have another appointment."

I was mindless and boneless, and incapable of dressing myself. Additionally, watching him tuck his shirt into his waistband mesmerized me. Since I was gawking instead of putting on my clothes, he slid my blouse over my shoulders. Then his large fingers fumbled as he secured four emerald buttons into place.

"Patricia." He snapped his fingers in front of my eyes in an attempt to focus me.

My hormones remained in overdrive. The hum of his electricity was alive and coursing under my skin. It was the first time in three years that I'd had any sort of physical encounter with a man—other than a sweet kiss from Neil— and it had been cut short by an annoying buzzer.

"Look, Patricia. You have to go."

Finally, I snapped to attention. In front of me stood my sexy young therapist with messy hair, flushed face, and swollen lips.

"You look like you just had sex," I told him.

He made a sound that was half-laugh, half-sigh. "Too bad I didn't."

I tried to right his disheveled waves.

He smiled and kissed my nose. "You know you're making me lose my mind. Your hair is so sexy, like you just walked out of a windstorm."

Don't hair plus windstorm equal rats' nest?

As if he needed to prove his point, he wrapped a strand around his finger. "Sometimes you button your blouse wrong. It takes all my willpower not to reach over and fix it."

Now I knew why he had grinned while unbuttoning my shirt. It served me right for purposely showing cleavage. How often had I dressed like an uncoordinated drunk?

Note to self—make an appointment with the eye doctor about my aging vision!

He continued, "I love the way you dance with total abandon."

I suppose I had made quite an impression at the Harvest Walk, since this was the millionth time he had brought it up.

"When I accidentally brush up against you, I feel this bolt of electricity that's so strong it knocks the wind out of me."

Ha! I knew it! He had also felt those earth-shattering jolts.

He ran his finger along my cheek. "I see the longing in your eyes when you look at me, and I want to make love to you all night long."

Crap monsters.

He had seen the longing in my eyes?

Embarrassing!

Of course, I wanted to take Jacob in my arms and school him in those things older women teach younger men. A woman married for almost three decades has to know something. Right?

"Your hair, your voice, your hands, you make me crazy too, Jacob. And your smile, well, I can't even think when you smile at me." I stopped blabbing so that I could satiate my desire to nibble on his bottom lip.

Damn!

He smelled like both heaven and sin.

"Come visit me tonight. Please?" I begged between our gentle bites. "You have my address, right?"

Mrs. Stewart knocked on the door and called, "Your next appointment is waiting for you, Dr. Greene."

Jacob grunted. "Damn Delores and her stopwatch." He brushed my lips with one last kiss before opening the door to usher me out.

It pains me to write this, but Jacob never showed. I waited in my two-decade-old red negligee, mindlessly watching Netflix. What had I been thinking? What had made me behave so brazenly? Mike is the only man I've slept with, so I don't even know how to seduce a man who isn't my husband. Once again, I have made an absolute ass of myself.

I fell asleep on the couch for about thirty minutes before a beep from my phone awoke me. Jacob wrote to inform me that he couldn't make it.

I didn't respond. I took a shower, reluctantly washing away his smell that still clung to me. Even cold water didn't remove the scorching imprints his hands left behind. I crashed into bed, feeling like a rejected schoolgirl.

I've been trying not to cry. I can't ask Grandma or Pap for guidance on this indiscretion because they'd roll over in their graves at my deplorable behavior.

I have three words—stupid shoulder devil!

I suppose it's a good thing Jacob never showed because it can't be ethical on his part. Right?

Poke, poke! Besides, he isn't your soulmate.

So, now my doggone white-clothed companion decides to pipe up.

"Too late, angel lady!"
A rejected slut,
Patti

…..…..*…..*

November 19th
Dr. Greene: Please forgive me. I won't make it.

November 20th
Dr. Greene: Are you awake?

Cassie: Good Morning Mom. Love you. Have a great day. Kiss Zoomie for me.♥

P: Love you more.♥♥

Cassie: I talked to Dad. He's excited to go to Grandma and Pappap's for Thanksgiving dinner. On Saturday we are going to Nana and Pappy Moore's. Will you come? I told Dad...NO SHELLY! Love you the most.♥♥♥

P: I will think about it. Love you more than the absolute most. ♥♥♥

Mike: Good morning.
Mike: Hi Pat!
Mike: Helllooooo.
Mike: Answer me goddammit!!!

P: What do you want?

Mike: We need to talk.

P: Why?

Mike: I'll be over when I get off work so we can talk in person.

P: I have a salsa class, so it will have to be after 9:30.

Mike: Salsa? With the cop?

P: ~~None of your business.~~
P: No. Neil and I decided not to see each other anymore.

Mike: See you tonight at 9:30.

Dr. Greene: I'm sorry. Please come to your appointment tomorrow and make sure you go to your dance class tonight.

Chapter 22

"Hoping for the best, prepared for the worst, and unsurprised by anything in between."

Maya Angelou, *I Know Why the Caged Bird Sings*

November 20, 2019

Dear Diary,

When I awoke this morning, the first emotion I dealt with was my embarrassment over behaving like a wanton bimbo. Jacob texted again in the middle of the night while I was sleeping. I have not yet responded. My body continues to ache for his touch, but I'm not heartbroken. I've felt heartbreak before. A rejection from Jacob doesn't come close to the hurt that I experienced because of Mike. As much as I want Jacob, the truth is, he and I are taboo, and I know it. I'm fifteen years older than him, and he is my therapist.

There is also the matter of the message Pap called out in last night's visit. "Hey, Big Red. That's the wrong one."

I assume he meant man.

"Hey Zoomie, for a woman who humiliated herself yesterday, I'm feeling pretty good this morning. I'm ready to face Westbrook and fight for my job. I'm ready to help Tanner Jones, and I'm ready to return to my classroom. What do you think, bud? Do you think Mommy might be getting her shit together? You think I'm StumpStrong?" I scratched between his ears. "Wanna go for a run?"

Zoomie wagged his tail, barked, and kissed me. *Yes, Mommy. So much, and you are perfect,* he seemed to say.

I popped from my mattress, brushed my hair and teeth, threw on leggings and a sweatshirt, and took Zoomie for a run. Afterward, we stopped by the coffee shop for breakfast. Chelsea's skunk eyes let me know she was angry with me for ending my relationship with her uncle. She conveniently dropped my muffin on the floor. Zoomie didn't mind. He thought the dirt and blueberries combined to create a delectable flavor.

I sat with a cup of coffee and made a plan for *Patti Takes Control of Her Life: Steps 2 through 6.*

Step 1: Seduce the therapist had been a bust, but things had to improve. I wrote down what I wanted to say to Anne Westbrook. I considered what I thought the magistrate needed to know to help Tanner. I drafted a request to convince Anderson to include Diamond in the regular student population. I wrote down a few things I needed to say to Mike. I decided I was going to throw away all of my misshapen elastic-less underwear. Any undergarments that looked like they belonged to a homeless bag lady were going in the trash. I attempted to figure out what I wanted to say to Jacob Greene. I felt like I needed to tell him a million things, but beside his name, I wrote a note to myself: *So embarrassed! And so damn proud of myself for finding my spunk!*

I pulled my shoulders back in triumph. The brave old Patricia had peeked her head out of the sand and taken a chance.

Believe it or not, I was looking forward to my salsa class. I showed up at the YMCA a few minutes early. A glutton for punishment, I strolled past the natatorium and peeked at the pool. My intuition was spot on. Doctor Jacob stood on the deck in a red speedo. His waves were wet curls, and his well-formed muscles were prominent from having just been used. All of Jacob was exposed for the eye to behold. I couldn't look away because he was magnificent. Just yesterday, I had run my hands and lips over his perfect physique, but today we were a million miles apart. He turned to witness my ogling. Caught, like a major stalker, I considered running and hiding. Instead, I stared him down until he tossed a lucky towel over his shoulders and walked my way.

We couldn't hear each other through the thick see-through partition. Swinging my hips and executing a rocking step, I mouthed to him that I was going to salsa class. He acknowledged that he understood, and if I read his lips correctly, said, "Have fun." Even that glass barrier couldn't stop the sparks that passed between us. Finally, I waved and walked away. I needed to get to class. Besides, I was fearful that people might notice the tiny red-haired lady and the practically naked man staring lustfully at each other.

The class had started, and we had warmed up and were in the process of being paired off when Jacob, wearing a gray knit beanie over his damp waves, walked into the studio. "I'll be her partner, Adrian," he told the instructor as he took me in his arms.

"Back for another class with a different pretty lady?" Adrian asked.

The nonchalant way my dance instructor announced this meant he either had no idea or didn't care that this statement could have been a complete home-wrecker. Instead of a wife with a rolling pin about to beat her cheating husband, I was the pathetic other woman with a sense of humor. I laughed at the realization that Jacob had been in this class before.

I suspect I had a smart-ass twinkle in my eye when I asked, "Another pretty lady?"

"My ex-fiancée and I took the class this summer," he explained.

I nodded and let him lead me around the floor. He danced sensually, holding my body close to his as we swung our hips to the music. He took every opportunity to touch my face and look into my eyes. "I'm sorry I didn't visit you last night," he whispered.

There wasn't an appropriate response to this statement, so I didn't try to give one. I chose to focus on the feel of his hand on my waist and the rocking motion of our hips.

"At first, I chickened out," he confessed.

I assumed that he decided I was undesirable, and I still didn't have a response.

"Although I did come. I sat outside your house," he said.

I stopped moving to gape at him.

"You are my patient, and it's wrong, so I talked myself out of coming. But then I couldn't stop thinking about you, so I drove to your house, sent you a text, and waited outside for a while."

We continued our steamy dance while a fire sizzled between us. Eventually, I whispered in his ear, "You move well, Jacob." I swirled under his arm and pressed my back against his chest.

He embraced me and positioned his lips next to my ear so that he could confide the rest of his secrets. "Have I ever told you that I have a thing for redheads?"

I tilted my ear to hear him better.

"I was done the second you walked into my office with that hair, your gorgeous eyes, your captivating storytelling, and your silly scraped knee. I spent our first few meetings pretending like I didn't notice any of it, but I did. I noticed everything about you."

Crazy!

That explained his indifference during our first few sessions. Had he found me as attractive as I found him the entire time?

Double crazy!

He spun me so that I faced him. I felt his grip tighten as a raw, needy rumble vibrated into my ear. "Can I visit you tonight? I promise I won't chicken out this time."

Meanwhile, a fantasy in which Jacob pushed me to the wall where I was helpless to his advances consumed me. Since he had cornered me and I couldn't escape, I succumbed to his seduction. I wrapped one leg around him as he lifted me off the ground and had his way with me in front of everyone in the room.

Dang!

I snapped my attention back to my even sexier reality—my enticing crush begging for a booty call. I wanted to say "yes" to his visit more than I had ever wanted anything, and I never wanted my searing dance to end, but it did.

"Jacob, not tonight. Mike is coming over to talk to me. I think he wants our family to be together for the holiday."

"Okay." His words indicated he accepted what I was saying, but the look on his face was that of a wounded child.

"I'm so sorry. I want you to," I told him. "I've been a bit ashamed thinking I had come on to you and you rejected me."

"No way," he said. "All I have thought about since yesterday is how much I want you. Call me when Mike leaves, and I'll come over. I promise."

I bit my lip. "Tonight isn't a good time."

I wanted to make love to Jacob Greene more than I wanted to breathe. But, if I called Mike and told him not to come, he would show up anyway. If I tried to send him away early, he would sit on the couch petting Zoomie. Mike would look into my eyes and know I was up to something. And what if Jacob blew me off again? Could I take the humiliation a second time?

Nope!

I am getting my life together. I don't need a wavering man even if he is a sexy god. Besides, there is that niggling, nagging voice coming from the lady in white. *Patricia, Patricia. No. Don't do it. Mike!*

For the first time in my life, I forced myself to put my family before my carnal desires. Although I'm not sure I had ever had carnal desires up until meeting Jacob Greene. But still—

I grabbed my possessions from the shelf in front of the studio and waved to Jacob, calling over my shoulder, "See you tomorrow at our session." Then I walked away from my fantasy.

I arrived home to find Mike's car already parked in front of the house. I slammed the front door and stomped down the hallway to find him sitting in the living room petting Zoomie.

My prediction was correct. Mike had let himself into my house, he was lounging on my couch, and he had ruined my chances of having mind-blowing sex with someone that wasn't him!

I stared him down. "Make yourself at home." Sarcasm oozed and dripped, coating the oriental rug.

"Thanks, I did." He flashed me a satisfied smile.

Annoyed on a trillion levels, I scowled and plopped down beside him. "I'm thinking about going to your parents. I haven't decided for sure."

He sat forward. "That isn't what I want to talk about."

I thought for a moment. "Cassie already texted me. Yes, you can come to Thanksgiving dinner, for Cassie's sake, so that her family is together."

"So, you don't want me there at all?" he asked.

I needed to avoid his trap. I chose my words carefully. "No, Shelly! You got that? Do not even think of bringing her! I'm not eating Thanksgiving dinner with my ex-husband's skanky girlfriend."

Yep, my meaning was clear—emphatic *No*s when it came to the bimbo. There was to be no negotiation on the topic.

"About that," he said.

I sharpened my claws and growled.

He cleared his throat, and it took him three attempts to confess. "Well, I broke up with Shelly the day I picked you up at the hospital."

I shook my head in confusion. "But you were with her at the Harvest Walk. *"*

"Because she asked me to go with her, but we had already broken up. You saw how well it went."

I smirked as I recalled what a disaster his date had been.

"The truth is, I can barely stand her." He sighed. "At first, I liked her. She made me feel young and desirable. Well—" He scrunched up his face. "And she made you jealous."

It hit me all at once. My ex-husband was an infuriating idiot. "Wait a minute. You have been hanging out with some bimbo you don't even like to make me jealous?"

"Umm. Yes."

I suspected he thought I would reward his honesty because he reached for me. Furious, I pulled away.

"What the hell, Mike? You tormented me to make me jealous?"

If I were a violent person, I would have punched him in the nose.

"Look, I tried to tell you weeks ago after the Harvest Walk. Remember, you locked me out of the house and sent me away?"

I closed my eyes and let out a long, slow exhale. Then words poured out of me like blood spurts at a decapitation. "You're the one who shut me out of your life and then walked away. You left me alone and depressed. You left me defenseless in a job that is killing me." At the beginning of my tirade, my voice had been loud and aggressive. By the end, it had become soft and defeated. "You walked away like it was nothing, without ever looking back."

I finally understood my actions. I had sent Mike away, but I had never wanted him to leave. I had wanted him to care enough to fight for us. Now, it seemed so very wrong, and I could see it had been an act of desperation.

He had rarely ever raised his voice in our decades of marriage, and it was now in an octave I hadn't heard since Cassie had once lied about having done her homework. "That's unfair, Pat! You are stubborn and bull-headed, and you have to have the last word. There's no way I could have convinced you to take me back unless you thought it was your idea. Besides, you're the one who shut me out. And you, defenseless? Cut the crap. You are a freaking bulldozer with a will of iron."

"Get out, Mike!" I was one breeze short of a tornado.

"Pat, stop throwing me out the door every time you disagree with me," he begged. "It isn't fair. You tell me to leave, then punish me when I do."

My heart ached so much I thought it might stop beating right then and there as a red-faced Mike waved his arms about.

"Get out. You can come to Thanksgiving dinner for Cassie's sake, but other than that, I don't want to talk to you," I bellowed.

Mike grabbed my face between his hands so that I had to look into his eyes. "Pat, listen to me. I love you, and I know you still love me. Why are we wasting the time we have left?"

I had waited years for him to remember and then remind me of how we felt. He let go of my face. I muttered an "Oh, Mike," then dropped my forehead into my hands. Neither of us spoke for a few moments. Finally, I lifted my head and looked at him. "I don't think I ever stopped loving you, but I'm hurt and angry. I need you to leave so I can think. Please?"

He moved closer and wrapped his arms around me. I was done fighting. I gave in, rested my head on his chest, and cried long, painful sobs.

His tears coated my temple. "I'm sorry, Pat. I'd take back everything if I could. I'm sorry about what happened to you at work. It's killing me to watch you go through this. I want to make everything okay, and I feel helpless. I'm sorry for all the times I wasn't there for you, but you pushed me away. You wouldn't tell me what was wrong or what you needed. You weren't behaving like the same feisty girl I married. I didn't know what to do."

He let go of me to grab tissues from the end table. He returned and wiped my eyes before taking care of his own.

"Mike, I'm not a twenty-one-year-old carefree college girl anymore." I blew my nose. "You can't ignore me every time I'm not who you want me to be. I was so overwhelmed when my job changed that I didn't know what I needed, but now I know. I needed you to be there for me and to fight for me."

"I know that now too, and I don't just want the twenty-one-year-old Pat. I want you at twenty-one, thirty-one, fifty-one, one hundred and one. I want all of you."

I needed him to leave because I had finally started feeling like my old self. I couldn't have him messing with it, and I needed to think.

He kissed my forehead. "I love you, Pat, and I'll do whatever it takes to make things right." He let go of me. "I'm leaving tonight, but I'll be back tomorrow, and the next day, and the day after that. I won't ever let you push me away again. I am going to fight you—for you." Before leaving the room, he turned to me. "Go ahead. Get the last word in. Give it to me good."

I didn't say a thing.

He wore an oddly wry smile. "How ironic, a communication specialist who can't communicate with the woman he loves."

I thought about reminding him of the cobbler's son who was shoeless but said nothing.

"I love you, Patricia Anne Moore, more than I have ever loved anyone or anything. I'll be back tomorrow," he declared before walking down the hall toward the front door.

"Please don't go, Mike," I whispered after the door closed.

Grandma? Pap? Annoying shoulder creatures? Anyone?

Help,
Patti

..........*.....*

November 21, 2019
Dear Diary,

Last night my grandparents scolded me in my dreams. Grandma waggled her finger and gave me an earful about what a "pain in the ass" men are. Pap laughed, then told me I was getting closer to "getting it right." Grandma insisted that even though she wanted to slap Mike upside the head, she wanted me to do a better job of communicating with him. Pap asked if I was looking out for Diamond. You can't get too upset with nagging ghosts because they mean well. Besides, I suspect it is way more frustrating if they stop visiting you.

Thanksgiving is one week away. If both Jacob and Dr. Long approve, my return to work is less than two weeks away. I have the meeting about my work situation and an appointment with the magistrate all within the week. My ex-husband, the man who broke my heart, wants to come home, and my therapist wants to have sex with me. At least I can go to self-defense class tomorrow. Hopefully, Dan the Hot Man will let me punch something.

I tried to make myself look presentable and attractive for my therapy session, but my eyes were still red and swollen from crying. I curled my hair and did my best to hide the evidence of my tears. While dressing, I heard Mike's comment bumping around in my head. "You are a freaking bulldozer with a will of iron." Toward the end of our marriage, Mike treated me like a weak child that needed to be cared for. I thought he saw me as helpless and fragile— that is, until he simply started to ignore me. Why was I just now finding out he thought me capable and bulldozer-ish?

Then there was Jacob.

Once the door closed, Jacob held fistfuls of red hair as his lips pressed against mine. He found his way to my ear to coo, "Patricia, I thought about you all night. I canceled my next appointment."

I shivered because his words came from somewhere far below his voice box. His taste, his smell, and his hands all over me were too much, and I caved. Soon his shirt lay on the back of his swivel chair, and I sat on top of his desk. Testosterone oozed out of him, drugging me as he kissed me and lowered me onto my back.

My little red shoulder critter cackled a devilish chuckle before saying, *Oh God, yes!*

The annoying angel jumped up and down on my right side, screaming *Mike! Mike! You love Mike!* I finger-flicked that overbearing do-gooder off my shoulder, and she tumbled to the floor, splattering into a white puddle. Then I kissed my psychotherapist with the abandon of a child enjoying a lollipop.

Hearing the raw desire in Jacob's voice when he said, "Christ, Patricia," was downright dangerous.

Again, the little red character urged me on. *Don't be a saint. Mike slept with another woman, and Jacob is here and now.*

"Jacob," I purred right before that stupid Seraphin pulled herself together and climbed up my torso, through my ear, and into my brain. As Jacob's hands reached for the top button of my jeans, I pushed him off of me. "No. I can't!"

At that moment, not only did the most handsome man I had ever seen look deliciously drugged, he hovered above me, also looking hurt and confused.

"Dr. Greene, I mean Jacob." I no longer knew what to call him. "It's Mike."

"Oh." He rubbed his forehead and pulled his swivel chair around. He sat so that he faced me as I looked down on him from my perch on the desk.

His voice was gentle. "Tell me."

"Mike came over last night. He wants us to work things out. He said he still loves me."

"What do you want?" Jacob asked.

"I don't think I ever stopped loving him, and our divorce wasn't all his fault. I'm also to blame, but I'm confused and angry."

Jacob clasped his hands together and rested his chin on his knuckles. The moment seemed to last forever. Finally, he sighed and grabbed his shirt from the floor.

"None of that takes away from how I feel about you. I love Mike, but I'm crazy about you. I've never wanted a man so much in my life." I was desperate, so complete honesty seemed to be my only recourse. "I don't understand my feelings."

He acknowledged my confession with a nod.

"I'm so overwhelmed by you, Mike, Neil. Remember, I went for three years without a single man paying attention to me."

"I doubt that, but go on."

I wondered what he meant by the statement but never asked.

"I think I need to give my marriage and family another chance. Don't you?"

He swung his shirt behind him, slid his arms into the sleeves, and buttoned it.

"Are you upset?" I asked.

"Not at all, and what you are feeling for me is lust." His eyes met mine, and he forced a smile.

"I think it's more than lust. You're my friend. One I pay, but a friend, nonetheless." He was more than a friend. He was a mentor, a protector, and a confidant. Come to think of it, I had never seduced and straddled a friend before. I no longer knew what to call him.

He moved so that he now sat on top of his desk, beside me. "What a pair we are."

I took in a deep breath and sighed it out slowly.

"You know your loyalty to your ex makes you all the more desirable to me, and of course, I'm a louse."

I placed my hand on his forearm. "Don't say that. You're not a louse."

"Yes, I am, because if you don't take your hand off of me, I'm going to rip your clothes off and throw you down on the desk."

God, yes, I thought before backpedaling. "You know, one day earlier and I would have begged you to."

"Your damn ex-husband and his timing." Jacob laughed right before his energy became heavy.

I knew that there was more he wanted to say.

He jumped off the desk. "Come here." He took my hand, escorted me to my seat, then sat in his leather chair.

We were in our usual spots, indicating we were about to have a serious session, but his posture was wrong. His legs were wide, and he leaned forward. He didn't have his notebook, and he wasn't scribbling. Instead, he was rubbing his temples.

"Is there something you want to tell me?" I asked.

"I am a louse because I've been flirting with you knowing it's wrong."

"I'm a big girl," I told him. "I know what I'm doing."

"Yes. That's true. But there's something else I want to tell you."

Moments ago, he was flushed. Now he looked pale and sickly. I wondered what was upsetting him. Did he have a million girlfriends? Did he try to bed everything with breasts?

"So..." He paused, obviously searching for the correct words. "I know Anne Westbrook. She was one of my patients."

I thought I had heard him wrong. "What?"

"Anne was one of my patients. She isn't anymore. I stopped treating her, even before you came to me."

I gawked at him.

He continued, "I didn't realize that she was your supervisor at your first session. I guess I should have, but I didn't make the connection until your second visit, and by that time, as I told you yesterday, I was already fascinated with you. Truthfully, I just wanted to help you." As an afterthought, he added, "And I thought it would be okay since she wasn't my patient anymore."

I didn't like how the conversation was going, so I decided not to say another word until I understood what he was getting at.

"Anyway. She had a few sessions with me. I recommended that she see someone who dealt specifically with her issues. She was belligerent about my suggestions, and she got into a scrape with Delores over paperwork. On top of that, Delores claimed she was a 'dishonest witch' because she caught her snooping at her desk. Anne never came back, and I was glad of it because I didn't like her."

"I told you she's an Ice Queen of a bitch." I tried to laugh, but it came out as an odd snort. "Why didn't you just tell me?"

"Patient confidentiality," he replied.

"Wait, but you aren't treating her anymore, right?" I asked.

He looked at the ground before focusing on me. "I'm not, but I still shouldn't be telling you this."

Coming clean was killing him. He looked defeated and beaten down. Anne Westbrook could do that to the most Herculean of men.

I felt the need to be closer to him, so I slid to the edge of the settee and leaned in his direction. "You better start at the beginning." I didn't mean it as a threat. It was more of a plea to a man I had shared the most intimate moments with to finish coming clean.

"When Delores processed your paperwork, she saw where you taught. She made the connection immediately." His brilliant blue eyes had lost their sparkle.

"Mrs. Stewart is a sharp one. I hope you pay her well. Go on."

He nodded and continued. "Delores said, 'I hope that dishonest witch isn't harassing Patricia.' My facial expression must have given away your situation. Delores always thought Anne was a fraud. Her sister had heard some rumor about Anne leaving her last position under a cloud of controversy."

"I think they were rumors. Nothing substantiated as far as I know. However, it wouldn't surprise me. She seems incompetent to me," I said.

"Anne was drinking a lot and was making mistakes at her previous job. It seems that there was an agreement that if she resigned before her contract was up, they wouldn't proceed with her termination."

I thought about the times Anne's behavior was off, and when she smelled of fermented fruit body sprays. I considered how oblivious to time constraints and disorganized she was and the joke I had made about her being drunk. "Is she an alcoholic?"

Jacob nodded.

"Holy guacamole," I said. "I think she was drunk years ago when I introduced myself to her. Do you think she thought I knew, and that's why she transferred me to the basement and overworked me?"

"Perhaps. It sounds like something Anne would do. Plus, she is mismanaging resources because she's trying to save money. Anyway, I recommended that she see a drug and alcohol counselor. The truth is, I believe in people having second chances and that people can change. If I didn't, I wouldn't be in this profession, and just because she drinks doesn't make her a bad person. I guess I had hoped that even though I wasn't the correct person for her to talk to, and that she was unlikeable, maybe she had taken my advice and seen someone who could help her." Jacob ran his hands through the same hair I had mussed. "I think she is a deplorable person, though. Drinking aside."

"So, you feel guilty that you couldn't tell me all of that. You don't need to. I understand confidentiality. Information about my students is also confidential," I told him.

"There's more. Delores insisted that something else was up, so she drove to the administration office with a tray of cookies and got to the bottom of it."

"I knew it! They're little truth bombs," I blurted out.

Jacob studied me with a confused expression. "What?"

"Nothing," I said.

Again, Jacob ran his fingers through his disheveled hair. "According to the secretary that Delores befriended, the school board knows what a mess Anne is making of things, but her decisions are saving them money, so no one asks too many questions. Any time anyone makes waves, she gets rid of them somehow. Then nobody pays her too much attention."

So, there it was, the thing I had been trying to put my finger on for years. It was so obvious and yet so insane it was hard to believe. Anne Westbrook was afraid that I— opinionated and intuitive Patti Moore, the woman who had tried to stand up to her—had discovered her secret because I had seen her drunk. She thought that I would go to war and expose her. She had locked me away to keep me silent. Tanner Jones had foiled her plan when he called attention to me. In temporarily taking my voice, he had given me power!

"Jacob," I said. "I know I should have told you, but the truth is, I've kind of been in denial. Westbrook wants me to resign. I think that's why she showed up at the coffee shop. I think she wanted it off the record when she tried to intimidate me."

Jacob frowned. "I'm so sorry, Patricia. It's been eating at me that I knew about her issues and I couldn't tell you. I think it has added to my obsession with you."

Obsession with me?

Double holy guacamole.

Jacob stood and walked to stare out the window. It was as if he was searching for some answer behind those heavy blinds as he kept his back to me. Maybe he was simply struggling to face me. Clues to his knowledge of Anne's issues were slamming at my memories. How could I have been so stupid? There was his reaction the first time I said her name, the excessive concern he had for me, the time he was late for our appointment because he was "doing research."

"Jacob, the time that you became upset about the file left on your desk—why?"

He faced me. He didn't need to search his memories to recall the incident I was referencing. He responded immediately. "Delores left Anne's file on my desk because she likes you." He smiled for half a second before his grave expression returned. "I wasn't running late. Delores let you into my office early. She set the file out to give you a hint to discover what was happening on your own. The thing is, you never noticed it. Instead, you sat stewing and festering." He gave a derisive laugh. "You know, you're always angry with me." He frowned. "I thought if I could help you get past your anxiety, you'd be okay, and I'd handle the rest."

"The rest?" I asked.

"That I would figure out a way to deal with the fact that your supervisor is drinking herself to death and the powers that be are ignoring it."

I walked over to where he stood. "Have you figured it out?"

He scrunched up his face and shoulders, and for a brief moment appeared to be a tiny man. "You could use the information I gave you to save your job and help your students."

"Then someone might discover that you told me. You mean you would risk your practice for me?" I asked.

"I already risked my professionalism when I decided to kiss you," confessed Doctor Jacob.

So, there you have it. What do I make of that? My doctor threw away his treasured moral code to kiss me. Anne Westbrook is a fraud. She is destroying everything she touches, calling it educational law and best practices. No one questions it as long as she saves the school money. I believe it has become politically incorrect to confront her if she throws the term "Special Education" in. Nobody wants to be the one to make a Special Education faux pas. If I expose her, I risk hurting Jacob. I can't allow her to continue to wreak havoc with my life, the lives of children, and my co-workers. And I can't allow her the satisfaction of forcing me to resign.

Grandma and Pap, what should I do?
In over my head,
Patti

Chapter 23

"When however small a measure of jealousy is mixed with misunderstanding, there is always going to be trouble."

John Irving, *A Prayer for Owen Meany*

Recorded by Robert Stauffer I, TSgt on December 1, 1972
Transcribed by Patricia Moore

HElloop Contraption,
Stalag 7B in Memmingen was hell.
I arrived in early March of '45, all six feet of me, weighin' in at a strapping one hundred ten pounds. I had lost over eighty pounds durin' my months of captivity and looked more skeletal than human. I was strip-searched, and my picture and book were confiscated. They had survived two months of hell, only to be destroyed by a shithead of a beast. The bastard ripped Marty up right in front of me. Then he tore all of the pages out of my book and tossed the binding into a rubbish can. The son of a bitch made a show out of it.

"Say goodbye to your girl. You will never see her again! You will die in this camp, American airman."

Rip! Rip! Rip!

"What a silly book! I spit on your silly stories!"

Rip! Rip! Rip!

The bastard's flair for dramatics would have been laughable had I not been witnessing my last tie to home bein' callously destroyed in front of me. It took everything I had to hold myself together. I shoved down my tears because I couldn't appear weak. But damn, I was about as strong as runny pudding.

There were thousands of prisoners livin' in the overcrowded barracks and the makeshift tents that littered the compound. The lazarette, where I spent the majority of my time, had one American doctor and most days over seventy patients. I'm not sure why, but Memmingen had more medical supplies than the other places I had been, although understaffing remained a critical complication.

The morale I kept up for most of my captivity wavered because my body was deteriorating, and the SOB had destroyed my good luck charms. Still, I held on to the hope that I would get home, see my family, and earn my teaching degree. I also had my daily goals. I tried to walk a few feet more each day, and I practiced usin' my left hand to write. In the long hours of boredom, I pretended there was a piano in front of me and learned my scales using only one hand.

Despite the intolerable, filthy conditions and extreme hunger, the camaraderie of the other prisoners was remarkable. We occasionally got news from the front on the makeshift foxhole radios ingeniously made from a razor, a paper clip, and a pencil. There was an overall feeling that the war would soon be over, we would defeat Hitler, and we'd be goin' home to our loved ones.

Not only was the overwhelming hunger a challenge, but there was the torturous boredom. Occasionally, when my strength allowed, I joined a card game or played dice. On Sundays, we walked the grounds. It took me weeks to muster the strength to join the others for a short walk. At one end of the camp, there was a large field where we were occasionally permitted to play games. The sports equipment was limited, so creativity ensued, and every available item became a football. My physical ailments never allowed me to join in on a game, but toward the end of my stay, I was able to limp to the fields and cheer the participants on.

On a good week, I received two Red Cross parcels that I had to share. Since peas make you pretty, I was becomin' an intolerably ugly son of a bitch. We were fed a form of barely edible bread made of sawdust, butter made of coal, and bowls of porridge that had all sorts of critters crawlin' in them. Marty used to make that cream of wheat muck for the kids. I couldn't even stay in the kitchen while they ate it. But in 1945, I choked down porridge made from bugs and sawdust, and whatever other poison those bastards fed us, because my body was eating itself from the inside out and I was wastin' away.

Anywho, the men sent on work detail were the lucky ones. They had to work twelve to fifteen-hour days, but at least they were off of the compound, not bored, and fed fresh farm food. I, on the other hand, spent long boring days at the lazarette consuming the bugs and dirt, playing my pretend piano, and tryin' to get my strength back.

In mid-April, the Commandant received an order from Berlin instructing him to execute every last prisoner in the camp. Although many of the guards were adamant that the Commandant follow orders, he refused, telling the men that they were to continue as usual, and anyone who didn't follow his orders would be shot on sight.

On April 28, 1945, General Patton's men, ridin' atop tanks, rolled into camp, liberating us. I recollect the jubilant celebrations like they were yesterday. Thousands of men were cheering and dancing in the streets as Patton's men showered us with cigarettes, food, and weapons. The commandant and his guards surrendered peacefully. I suspect that was the plan all along. Someone tossed a can of baked beans at my feet then handed me a gun. I gave the gun back to my liberator, calling out, "This war's over to me." After eyeballing me, that same man cut my can open with the biggest knife I've ever seen. Then I sat down on a rock, propped my beans between my knees, and dipped my fingers in. Best damn beans I ever ate!

That's all she wrote!

…..…..*…..*

November 22, 2019
Dear Diary,

I'm trying to improve the bad habits I've developed during my medical leave. So today, before the crack of dawn, my alarm went off, causing Zoomie to whimper.

"Alarms are the devil's work. This was a bad idea. It's too cold!" I complained.

My pup agreed and listened to me fuss on and on.

Grandma and Pap consumed my dreams last night. Thank goodness, because I needed their advice. Grandma told me to fight for my marriage and family. Pap told me to fight for my job and students. Then twice, he said, "Remember, give someone enough rope!"

I received Pap's message loud and clear. He didn't believe in revenge. He felt that if you stepped back and let a person be, their true nature would emerge. If they were guilty, they would eventually hang themselves, and you walked away with a clear conscience. This meant that I shouldn't mention the things Jacob confided to me about Westbrook. I didn't need to hurt the doctor. I just had to stand up for myself and my students.

I leaned over and rubbed my buddy. "Did you have fun with your daddy last night?"

Zoomie panted, then rested his nose on the bed and closed his eyes.

I think my pup was tired from the previous evening because he had played fetch with Mike for hours. Overwhelmed from my day, the low-key evening watching the two of them toss and retrieve was comforting.

Once I was finally warm and awake, I called the man who had been beside me every day without fail.

"Hi, Dad. How are you?" I asked.

A cheery voice responded. "Hi, Kiddo. You finally called me. I guess you do love your dear old dad."

"Of course, I love you. You goofy old man."

"Are you back at work yet?" he asked.

"No, Dad," I responded.

"They put that kid in jail yet?" he asked.

"No, Dad."

"Want to come out tonight and play a game with me?"

My dad loves card games.

"I can't tonight," I explained. "I have plans with my friends, but I want to tell you something. Are you sitting down?" I paused in case he wanted to brace himself. "Mike and I are going to try to work things out."

"Work out what?" my dad asked.

"Our relationship." Then I sighed, since I knew what my father's response would be.

"What's wrong with your relationship with Matt?"

I half-heartedly rolled my eyes. "You know? Our divorce?"

"Oh, that. You aren't really divorced," my dad said.

"Yes, we are, Dad, you just can't accept it."

As usual, my father sounded out his laugh. "Ha, ha, ha, ha. Then he became serious. I like Mike. He can fix my TV remote control, and he likes the Steelers. He loves you, and he's a good dad to Cassie. I'm glad you're working things out, Patti. I don't want you to be a lonely old lady."

"Thanks, Dad. I'll see you for Thanksgiving Dinner. Can you let Mom know that Cassie, Farez, and Mike will all be there?"

There was a taunting tone in my father's response. "I won't see you until Thanksgiving? What if I have the big one before then?"

"Dad, you're fine." The most amazing part of my statement being, I believed it this time.

"I'll tell your mom. She'll be happy. Bring Boomie," he said.

I pretended to be exasperated. "It's Zoomie, Dad."

"That's what I said, Boomie."

"Fine! Chrisie, Fred, Matt, Boomie, and I will be there."

My dad and I were both chortling when we said goodbye. I hung up, fixed a cup of tea, and curled up with a book.

After the drama of the week, it was nice to have an uneventful day. Even self-defense class felt subdued. The girls and I were on our best behavior. I had sworn off alcohol forever, and Tina and Chelsea pledged to join me in my lifelong goal of liquid abstinence. Missy was trying hard to control her fun-loving, albeit obnoxious ways. She had had a taste of Dan the Hot Man and seemed set on not jeopardizing a second chance at his goods. We learned to deflect a punch, get ourselves out of a chokehold, and how to damage the parts of a man that would bring him to his knees. After class, we forwent Charly's Place for tea and cookies at my house.

I longed to fill my friends in on the sexy encounters with my psychotherapist but decided not to. I ached to ask them for advice about handling the secret I had learned about Westbrook, but I didn't. However, I did confide that I wanted to try again with Mike, and my girl power gang swore to disembowel him if he hurt me. I suppose that over the years, I had complained so much about Mike that my friends no longer remembered I shared in the blame.

It was almost eleven p.m. when Mike showed up, dispersing my party.

Missy tapped two fingers to her eye and then pointed those fingers at him.

Tina let loose with a lengthy diatribe in her native tongue. I have no idea what she said, but it sounded scary.

Chelsea shot him skunk eyes, made extra intimidating by her sparkly magenta eyeshadow and thick kohl eye pencil. "She gave up my uncle for you. You better be worth it," the barista said right before she turned and walked face-first into the column separating the living room from the front hallway.

A rattled Mike stood before me. He nervously extended a package. "Peace offering for breaking up your party and for everything I've ever done."

I motioned for him to come into the living room and join me on the couch. Zoomie took his happy spot between us as I opened my present.

I stared into the gift bag on my lap. "A new phone?"

"The newest model for the one you have," he said. "That cracked screen has to be making you crazy."

I smiled. "It is."

"I can help you set it up if you want," he said.

I considered his offer. How easy it would be to let Mike control every part of my life and take care of everything for me.

"I'll try myself first. If I can't do it, I'd like it if you helped me." I wasn't going to make the same mistakes with my second chance. This time around, we would communicate, compromise, and be equal partners in everything.

"Sounds good," he said.

We sat in silence, my head on Mike's shoulder, Zoomie's chin on his lap. Around midnight my soulmate, Michael Christopher Moore, kissed me on the forehead and said, "See you tomorrow, Pat."

"Thank you for the phone," I called after him.

I sat a few more minutes before dreamily strolling to bed.

Perhaps I'm not going to die a poverty-stricken, lonely old lady after all.

Peaceful,

Patti

..........*.....*

Recorded on January 2, 1994 by Pap Stauffer
Transcribed by Patricia Moore
Helloop Big Red,

Though she be mini, she be mighty. And you, Big Red, are mighty. Never doubt that you are huge, immense, a force to be reckoned with, with a prodigious heart to match. I knew it the second you came out of your mother's womb, pint-sized and screamin', and demandin' to get your way. You reaffirmed this every time I was with you.

I remember the time I saw you sitting on your grandmother's lap, looking exactly like her, readin' that comic strip. At the tender age of four, you didn't let up until you learned to read it perfectly. By the end of the day, you were readin' the *Daily News* to us. I also remember how proud I was when you stood up to the neighborhood bully who was twice your size. You walked over to her, stuck your finger in her face, and read her the riot act.

I'm in awe of the way you persevered with your studies, never giving up until you achieved perfection. Your grandmother and I are extremely proud that our granddaughter is a teacher. It's the toughest job there is. You have a chance to mold young minds and change the world. Sometimes the system will bog you down, but don't ever think you don't make a difference.

I'm happy you found Mike. He's a good man and will make a good father to your children. There will be tough times. Don't give up. Stick it out. When you look back at your life, the rest is superfluous details. Your family and if you're lucky, one or two good friends, will be the only things that matter.

Patricia, you have never backed down from any challenge. You are my jumbo-sized granddaughter in a tiny package, bustin' at the seams to take on the world. I'm proud of you, and I love you.

Big Red, take the world by storm! Give it hell! And always love with all your heart!

Pap

Chapter 24

"All that five thousand kids lived in those five thousand houses, owned by guys that got off the train. The houses looked so much alike that, time and time again, the kids went home by mistake to different houses and different families. Nobody ever noticed."

Ken Kesey, *One Flew Over the Cuckoo's Nest*

November 25th

Jimmy Junior: Call Mom and Dad. They are worried. Dad wants to know if you want him to take you to your work meeting so he can dish out some knuckle sandwiches.

P: Hey little brother, Pap left you a message on one of the tapes. "Be true to yourself, Junior." He said to follow that dream you have and never let anyone talk you out of it. What dream is that? :) He said more. I wrote it down for you. Tell Mom and Dad I'm fine. There is no need for knuckle sandwiches today.

Dr. Greene: Stay StumpStrong! Make your demands. Don't back down!

P: Thank you Jacob. I couldn't have done this without you.

Mike: I love you, my feisty, beautiful bulldozer. Are you sure you don't want me to go with you? I can take the morning off work.

P: I need to do this on my own, and I love you too!

Missy: You got this GF! Rumor is the Wicked Witch of the West got herself into trouble over something.

P: Wow! Wonder what she did this time? I'll let you know how it goes.

Missy: No idea...but I think it's big. I'll try to find out. Give 'em hell!

Valentina: Buena suerte! Chelsea can watch The Cup. I can take you to your appointment.

P: Thanks, but I need to do this by myself. I will let you know how it goes.

Cassie: Good luck today. I love you.

P: Love you the most!

…..…..*…..*

November 25, 2019
Dear Diary,

Today I dressed in my most conservative blue suit and pinned my unruly hair back so that I looked neat and official. I even dug out my monogrammed briefcase that matched my black pumps. Then I met Leigh Ann Martin, attired in her pinstriped suit, in front of the school administration building. I think we made quite the fierce duo.

"Ready?" Leigh Ann asked.

I gave her a chin lift with a sharp down to the affirmative and declared, "Yes! I am." I had been ready since Diamond Washington accosted me with hugs in front of East City High School.

Leigh Ann and I fist bumped. Then we walked into that building like confident warriors.

Before entering the conference room, I took a deep breath and repeated my mantra. "StumpStrong!"

I expected to be met by a horde of school officials; however, there were only four. Anne Westbrook, Principal Anderson, Superintendent Mitchell, and the school solicitor sat around a rectangular table in a cold conference room. Although Anderson sat beside Anne, his reassuring smile indicated he supported me. Mitchell shook my hand, then sat next to Westbrook. Leigh Ann talked directly to the solicitor as she told him that the classroom was out of compliance and they would lose every grievance she was about to throw at them.

The school solicitor moderated, saying, "Ms. Moore, let's start by reviewing your first concern."

I took my notes from my briefcase and again said, "StumpStrong."

"What did you say, Patricia?" Superintendent Mitchell asked.

I have no idea why I tapped my hand on the table three times before saying, "I said that I have no intention of resigning."

"Resigning?" Mitchell asked, shuffling through the papers in front of him.

Anderson cradled his chin between his thumb and index finger and looked thoughtful.

Westbrook leveled a squinted-eye scowl on me.

I pulled my shoulders back and reviewed the list in front of me.

I know it may be hard to believe, but I was articulate. So much so that I shocked myself. I requested every item I needed to make my students successful. I demanded additional staff, a well-rounded curriculum, and that all the support services be reinstated.

Then I made my most important demand. "I want Tanner Jones, and any other student who has a documented history of violent behavior in school, evaluated. If the public school isn't equipped or staffed well enough to provide the support that these particular kiddos require, I want to investigate alternate options. We need to make the best decisions for every student's programming. Brushing problems under the rug to save money isn't ethical. I can't be a part of covering up safety concerns or violence."

Anne Westbrook was an emotionless square, all tight lines and sharp corners. Any time she cleared her throat to speak, Mitchell glared at her. Anderson had a faint smile on his lips, and the solicitor nodded as he listened and took notes.

When it was time for my final demand, I said, "And I want to finish the year in the Alternative Classroom to fix this mess that Dr. Westbrook has created. That gives the administration nine months to find a replacement for me. Then I want to be reinstated in my old assignment, the class I feel properly trained to teach."

I stopped talking to check myself. That wasn't the demand I had written on the paper in front of me. When had I decided that I wanted to finish out the year in Alternative Education? "Hmm," I mumbled. It was the first time I was consciously aware of it, but apparently, I wanted to stay and make things better for my students.

"We will reconvene in thirty minutes," the solicitor announced.

Before closing the conference room door, I looked over my shoulder. I shuddered because Westbrook personified silent frostbite in a suit.

Leigh Ann and I watched the clock in a small waiting area until Anderson peeked his head around the corner. "Good job, Patricia. We're ready for you."

Upon entering that chilly room, the first thing I noticed was Dr. Westbrook resembled a prune. She appeared to have shriveled to half her size. Was it that I had stood up to her? Was it Mitchell's glares? Perhaps it was the combination?

The solicitor explained that the district planned to resume the student's support services. Art, music, and physical education would be added back into the curriculum, I would once again have access to a social worker, and my teaching assistant would be reassigned to my classroom. This was the just beginning.

Once I completed the paperwork to have the students who had met their academic and behavioral requirements transitioned back into the regular education setting, I could hand it in to Anderson. This meant Diamond and two other students would be given a chance to prove themselves.

The solicitor announced another win. "Dr. Westbrook will begin the process to have Tanner Jones put in an out of district classroom placement, where he will receive intensive behavioral interventions. This is temporary, as the plan is to move him back to his home school eventually. But Patricia won't be in a classroom with him until he has had a full psychiatric evaluation with a licensed psychiatrist and has completed the recommendations."

"What about getting my old teaching assignment back?" I asked.

This time Superintendent Mitchell spoke. "If the school board approves, we will look for a candidate to take your spot for the next school year. There are no guarantees because the board has to approve, and then we still have to find a qualified candidate."

The crazy thing was, I wasn't upset by his pronouncement. Now that I had the resources to do my job, I wanted to stay in the alternative classroom and make a difference.

"We'll meet again in mid-January to see how everything is going and to discuss any other changes that need to be made to provide a suitable and safe learning environment for your students." I knew the school solicitor was finished because he closed his notebook and shoved it into his briefcase.

I would never know the truth, but I had a feeling that the school district's attorney had advocated for me. Anderson winked at me. Leigh Ann looked satisfied. Mitchell's angry eyes focused on the withering Wicked Witch of the West. It was at that moment that I noticed someone had turned on the heat.

Elated, I climbed into my car and drove to Dr. Greene's office. I didn't have an appointment, but I needed to see him. He was with a patient, so I sat with Mrs. Stewart, talking, drinking a cup of tea, and eating homemade peanut butter fudge. Dr. Greene's next patient walked through the door, reminding me that he was a busy man who might not be able to see me between appointments.

When his office door opened, it took Jacob a moment to process that I was in his waiting room. His eyes went wide with what I interpreted to be a combination of surprise and confusion.

"Patricia? What are you doing here? I don't think you set up any more sessions after last week?"

"I'm sorry. I know I don't have an appointment, and I see you are busy. I'll talk to you another time?" I got up to leave.

"Levon," he said to the man sitting beside me, "could you give me a moment?"

"Sure," Levon said between nibbles of fudge.

Once we were alone, Dr. Greene asked, "Why are you here right now?" He was standing so close that I thought he might reach over and touch my face.

Since I didn't entirely trust myself to do the right thing, I took a step back and away from him.

"Jacob, we did it!"

His eyes narrowed.

"I got almost everything I asked for, and I never brought up anything you shared with me about Westbrook. I won because I was in the right, and it was what was best for the kids."

He grinned. "I knew you could do it! Congratulations. Are you going back to your old classroom?"

"Not this year. Maybe next. I asked to stay for the remainder of the school year to get the classroom running smoothly. Who knows, I might want to stay longer. I have my teaching assistant back, and all of the student's services are to be resumed. Also, Tanner is being sent to a different classroom temporarily."

"Only temporarily?"

"Yes. But he is to have intensive behavioral interventions, and he has to have a psychiatric before returning. That means Tanner has to have a full evaluation with a psychiatrist. Maybe the doctor might recommend another placement."

Dr. Greene nodded. Of course, he knew what a psychiatric evaluation was.

"And not a single person brought up my resignation. I think Westbrook was hoping I would hang it up so that we didn't have to have today's meeting."

"I'm proud of you," Doctor Jacob said.

My cheeks grew warm. For once, I didn't begrudge my pale thin skin for betraying my feelings. "I'm sorry that I came without an appointment, but I needed you to know. I'll let you get to your next patient."

"I'm glad you came," he said.

"I don't know how to thank you." I had given considerable thought to how I might show my gratitude, but nothing came to mind.

"I'm happy you fought back and that you're feeling strong. That's reward enough." He gave a smile of triumph. "Are you ready to return to work?"

I happily sang out, "Yes!"

"I'll send a recommendation to Dr. Long that you return after the Thanksgiving holiday. Your weekly visits are over, but I want you to schedule a follow up for two weeks after   you   return   to   work." I would miss him, so the follow up gave me something to look forward to.

"Don't forget. It's important. Two weeks after you return, you are to set up an appointment with Dr. Long."

My heart fell because the appointment was with my general practitioner, not Dr. Greene.

I peered up at him. "But I can still see you if I need to, in the future, if I struggle with anxiety attacks and pushing strange men in grocery stores and coffee shops?"

There was an interminable moment of silence, and a million miles seemed to separate us.

His voice sounded sad when he said, "Of course. You can contact me anytime about anything."

"Thank you." I reached for the door, my arm halting in mid-air at his question.

"Are things going well with Mike?"

I beamed. "Yes. Very!"

Then I took what I thought might be my very last glimpse of the man who had protected and guided me during these weeks of soul searching. I waved and pulled his office door closed. Then I hugged Mrs. Stewart, grabbed a piece of fudge, walked to my car, and called Mike. I blabbed on and on, telling him every detail of my victorious day. Then I invited him to a celebratory dinner for two.

Mighty,
Patti

…..…..*…..*

November 26th
Neil Harris: See you at the courthouse at 11:00.

P: I had my meeting with the solicitor at work yesterday. Tanner is to be removed from my classroom and sent to a special school temporarily. I don't think we need to proceed with today. Is it too late to cancel?

Neil Harris: Just checked. That info was forwarded to Judge Marlow. She still wants to review the case. There are additional assault charges. Another from school, and one from the community that involves a weapon. He is being charged with 3 counts of Aggravated Assault causing serious bodily injury.
Neil Harris: Do you still want to drop charges? Because he would still be looking at 2 counts.

P: Holy Guacamole! I assume the one from school is the one a student told me about. He punched a kid in class and gave him a bloody nose. The other was in the community? His behaviors are escalating.

Neil Harris: Yeah. He walked into a guy's yard and beat him with a tree branch. I guess the guy told him he couldn't hang out on his property and smoke.

P: I need to attend. Don't I?

Neil Harris: Yeah. We need to get him help.

P: Ok. See u at 11.

…..…..*…..*

November 26, 2019
Dear Diary,

I'm still processing yesterday's meeting with school personnel. I had convinced myself that it would never go my way, but it did. I'm planning to return to work after the holiday, Tanner will receive the help he needs, and I will have the support I require to keep my classroom safe and my students learning. I'm astonished, although not speechless. I've never been speechless, not even when I had a vocal cord injury. But I digress.

Since there was a plan in place for Tanner, I considered skipping his appointment with the district magistrate, that is until Neil texted me and convinced me to go. I met Neil in the lobby of the courthouse. He explained that since Tanner was a juvenile, we would be in a small conference room. His trial was public, but the magistrate chose to move juvenile cases out of the courtroom and into a smaller, less intimidating setting. The only people in attendance would probably be the magistrate, Neil, a probation officer, Tanner's parents, and me. His third assault victim was still in the hospital.

Neil was wrong about one thing. Tanner's parents weren't there. The second shock of the morning was that Tanner wouldn't be sent to a special school because he was assigned to a juvenile detention center. The magistrate was horrified to find out that the school district had not expelled him and had allowed him to torment and assault classmates. The probation officer assigned to Tanner did most of the talking. It was probably a good thing because I'm unsure I would have been able to keep Anne Westbrook's incompetence a secret.

After the hearing, Neil walked me to my car. I didn't feel joyful or vindicated. I felt at odds with what had transpired.

"Neil, his parents weren't even there? He has so many issues. His parents failed him. The school failed him, and society failed him. What if the juvenile probation system fails him too? What kind of chance does he have?"

Neil placed his hand on my shoulder. "You didn't fail him. You tried to educate him and give him a chance. Handing him over to the justice system at this point is the correct thing to do. It's best for him, society, and the other students in the class. Don't beat yourself up."

I thanked Neil and hugged him before getting into my car. Neil was amazingly magnanimous. I had bruised his heart, yet he remained a steadfast friend.

I arrived home to find a landline message from Principal Anderson, asking me to call him immediately. I panicked, thinking that the school district might be reneging on the promises made twenty-four hours ago. But I was the brave new Patricia, or the brave old Patricia, depending on how I chose to look at it. Either way, I was once again facing life's challenges head on, so I called him back immediately.

There was a slight quiver in my voice when I said, "Hello, Alan. It's Patricia Moore, returning your call."

His voice sounded cheerful. "Hi, Patricia. Thanks for getting back to me right away. I'm glad you'll be back on my staff soon. We need you here."

"Thank you. I'm looking forward to returning."

"I'm calling to let you know that Dr. Westbrook gave her notice following our meeting yesterday."

I felt an odd combination of shock and joy. "She did? Why?"

"You weren't the only teacher concerned about her incompetence. Last week she lost a grievance that cost the district money."

I muttered a "Hmm." That must have been the rumor Missy had been alluding to.

Anderson continued. "Good thing she resigned because last night, she was pulled over for a DUI. Her second one."

I gasped because I hadn't expected to hear that.

Anderson continued. "Anne was vindictive and cruel; I never liked or trusted the woman. I think she had it out for me, and I think she had it out for you. I think she was making up mandates and laws that don't exist but as long as she was saving us money, she got away with it. The second she cost money, she got herself into trouble. I think she covered up the incident in your room so the school board didn't question her mismanagement. I also suspect she didn't want to go to them to ask for the funding to send Tanner somewhere else after her screw ups. Those placements are expensive. And her drinking, pft!"

I had always known Principal Alan Anderson was a smart guy.

I simply said, "I agree with you, Alan," and swallowed the rest of my opinion.

"Anyway, your doctor's note was faxed this morning. You're cleared to return to work. Enjoy your holiday. See you next Tuesday."

My guardian angel was back from her three-year vacation. Lucky for her, I wouldn't continue with her termination procedures. Good thing because Zoomie had been working overtime trying to look out for me. Not that he seemed to mind.

I sent Jacob a text to let him know that Anne had hung herself with her own rope.

Pap was right, as usual. Professor Stump should be king of the world!

Then I made myself a cup of tea and curled up in bed with my book.

I think I will finally have a long, restful sleep.

Relieved,

Patti

Chapter 25

"The caged bird sings
with a fearful trill
of things unknown
but longed for still
and his tune is heard
on the distant hill
for the caged bird
sings of freedom."

Maya Angelou, *I Know Why the Caged Bird Sings.*

November 27, 2019

Dear Diary,

Jacob Greene showed up at my house this afternoon. He was dressed in jeans and a sweatshirt and standing on my front porch, looking yummy.

"Hi, Jacob. What are you doing here? Is everything okay?" I asked.

He leaned an arm against the door frame. "Hi, Patricia. Everything is perfect. I've decided to close my practice."

I'm certain my mouth gaped in a most unflattering pose and I responded with an inarticulate, "What? No! Why? Please come in so we can talk."

I opened the door and ushered him into the kitchen. He declined my offer of tea and coffee but accepted a glass of water.

Once seated at the table beside me, he continued his story. "I'm going home to Maryland. I'm going to take over the family business so that my father and uncle can retire."

"The family business?" I asked.

"Yes. We build and repair ships and boats."

I snapped my fingers. "I knew it. I knew you were a seaman."

Jacob laughed. "Yes. And you were also right about those damn ties strangling me." Then he became serious. "I'm indebted to you because you are the one who helped me make this decision."

I experienced a twinge in the pit of my stomach because I wasn't sure I had helped him in the least. Convinced I ruined his life, I asked, "What do you mean?"

"You made me realize I wasn't enjoying life or having any fun. Do you remember you asked me if there was something new that I wanted to try, and the time you asked me what might make me happy?"

"Yes. You promised me you would think about it." I held my breath, waiting to see how badly I had screwed up his life.

"I kept my promise. I thought long and hard. I realized I wanted to be at home, with my family, working with my hands and close to the sea. That's what makes me happy. You know, I spend my life helping others fix their lives. You were the first person who asked me what I wanted. I've been suffocating, and you were the only person who seemed to notice."

"I imagine that's because of my teacher's intuition." And that I had an obsessive crush on him. "But your practice? You are such a great psychotherapist."

"No, Patricia, I'm not. I screwed up. I got emotionally and physically involved with a patient. I allowed Delores to snoop. I got in so far over my head."

I wanted to comfort him as he confessed his sins. Wasn't I partially responsible for all of them? His hand was sitting on the table, so I reached over and placed mine on top.

"I doubt you could have stopped Mrs. Stewart no matter what you did."

"True," he said.

"Jacob, I'm a fifty-year-old woman who is capable of her own decisions. You didn't coerce me or take advantage of me. And other than some kissing and groping, nothing else happened."

He thought this over.

"You know what the magnificent Professor Stump would tell you?" I asked.

Jacob's eyes brightened. "What advice would Technical Sergeant Robert Stauffer with the legendary stump give me?"

"He would say that even good men can get in over their heads. He would tell you that family is all that matters and the rest is superfluous details, and that you should follow your dreams." I thought another moment. "He would also tell you it wasn't your fault you kissed me because I'm a force to be reckoned with." I flashed him a smiley-face-emoji-style grin.

The once austere Jacob Greene belly laughed, and it was glorious.

"What will happen to Mrs. Stewart?" I asked.

"Mr. Writestone needs a new secretary to help with his online business. She starts working for him after the holiday."

I clapped my hands. "Good for Mr. Writestone and Mrs. Stewart. I hope they will be happy working, and whatever else-ing, together."

Jacob chuckled again.

"What about your ex-fiancée, Claire?" I asked.

He shook his head. "Claire is a sweet woman, but she wants a doctor, not a shipbuilder. It was becoming more and more apparent that our lives were traveling different paths."

I nodded. Although I had made a joke about being a "force to be reckoned with," I still didn't understand how a man Jacob's age could find a woman my age attractive, so I asked.

"It's not so abnormal. I've told you before. You're beautiful and spunky. Besides, I know a lot of men my age who like women your age. Ashton Kutcher liked Demi Moore. Every man I know likes Jennifer Lopez, and boy do I like Julianne Moore and Susan Sarandon."

I still didn't get it, so I responded with a sigh and, "Maybe you just like the name, Moore."

He thought my comment over and grinned.

"Is this our goodbye?" I asked.

"Unless you want to visit me. Bring Zoomie, and you can vacation on my houseboat. Did you know I have one? You're a hell of a sexy pirate lass. We could recite poetry, and dance, and make love out on the water—all night long."

I tried not to flutter my eyelashes, but I'm pretty sure I did. "How tempting. Are you asking me to run away with you, Doctor Jacob Greene?"

"Yes. But it's just Jacob Greene from now on. I can't promise you a forever kind of thing. But I know for right now I want to spend time with you." He put his other hand on top of our hand pile.

I used his own words against him. "I think what you are feeling is called lust."

"Perhaps, but what a fun reason to run away together."

His smile was wicked, and his offer tempting.

The past few years had been hell, and he was offering me temporary freedom. This was my invitation to leave it all, to run away to the sea, and to make love to him. He didn't care that I was so much older than him. He didn't care that I had been struggling with my mental health. He knew me at my worst, and he still wanted me to join him on his boat.

There were no cartoon shoulder characters, inept guardian angels, or ghostly grandparents telling me what to do, or not do, this time. I had to make a big girl decision by myself.

"There's a part of me that thinks it would be exciting, but I can't. My family, my friends, and my students?" I had trouble catching my breath. "Jacob, I still love Mike."

"I knew you would say no, but anytime you want to leave it all for a little while, find me."

I bit my lip.

"Bye, Patricia. Please understand, I'm relieved. I want to be back on the water where I belong, and you reminded me that I want to be near my family." There was no regret or sorrow in his voice.

We walked to the front door.

"Wait, I have something for you." I ran upstairs and returned carrying a book. "Here." I handed him my copy of *Of Human Bondage*. "Please keep it."

He smiled and tucked the book under his arm.

Standing at my front door, I thanked him one last time for helping me rediscover my strength, and he thanked me for reminding me of his roots.

The last thing Jacob Greene called to me before he climbed into his fancy red car was, "You know, I'll never, ever put on a damn tie again. They'll have to put me in a coffin first."

After Jacob's visit, I distracted myself by baking a pecan pie, a broccoli and cheese casserole, and a bacon-heavy breakfast quiche for the Thanksgiving feasts. I had finished cooking and sat down to rest when Mike, another present in hand, sauntered into the living room.

He kissed me on the cheek, then held out a sparkly gold bag containing a ball of white fur. Mike was all mischievous eyes and grinning lips. I reached in and pulled out two fuzzy bunnies that had little blue eyes, felt ears, and pompom noses. I put them on and shuffled around the living room as a juiced-up Zoomie barked and pawed at them. Mike's eyes lit up as he watched the game going on in front of him.

Finally, I stopped playing to say, "Mike, you didn't forget!"

About twenty years ago, I had asked for a pair of bunny slippers for Christmas, and it seemed as if every pair available was in a toddler size.

"Of course, I didn't forget. I forget a lot, but I never forget anything you say to me." His grin stretched from ear to ear.

I plopped myself onto the couch and stuck my legs into the air. I experienced pure child-like joy as I watched my twin bunnies dance at the end of my feet.

The next thing I knew, Mike had grabbed me by my ankles and yanked my body to the center of the couch. He pinned me down, crushed me under the weight of his body, and kissed me.

Still ecstatic from my perfect present, I kissed him back.

"I miss you, Pat, so damn much," he panted in between kisses.

"I love you, Mike," I whispered, sliding my hands beneath his shirt.

Then, grasping my hand, he led me to our bedroom, where we made up for our three-year battle. Three years is a long time to have pent up emotions and frustrations. Three years is a long time to go without having sex, even for an old shriveled-up raisin. I laugh as I write this, because perhaps I'm not an antiquated piece of machinery after all. They say fifty is the new thirty, and the events in the Moore bedroom earlier this evening may be proof of that.

As Missy would say, "Cha-ching!"

Patti

…..…..*…..*

Thanksgiving Day
Dear Diary,

This morning, after continuing to make up for lost time, Mike and I stayed in bed talking. Our pup, happy to have us together, relinquished his spot beside me so that I could lay my head on Mike's chest. Eventually, I got up to look at myself in the mirror. I felt radiant and wanted to see if it was reflected in my image. It startled me to see my grandmother's face peering back at me.

I crawled into inviting arms. "Hey, Mike. I look like my grandmother, don't I?"

"Yes, but with red hair. And she was beautiful, Pat."

I knew what he was thinking. He didn't want this to turn into one of my I-look-like-an-old-lady speeches. It didn't. I felt positively pretty. "She was beautiful, wasn't she?" I snuggled closer to my man.

Mike nuzzled my neck as he spoke. "What happened to us, Pat? We were so in love."

"I think we started to take each other for granted," I replied.

He nodded in agreement.

I luxuriated in the feel of my fingernails scraping through his coarse chest hair as we talked. "Mike, you nagged me and treated me like a child. Then like a spoiled brat, I had to have the last word."

He used a finger to gently trace circles on my shoulder as he courageously, after many silent years, opened his heart.

"I only ever wanted to take care of you. I never meant to treat you like a child. I wanted to treat you like a queen. Once upon a time, you had so much spunk. You didn't allow anyone to walk on you, and a few years ago, I thought you changed. You seemed sad and defeated. The more defeated you seemed, the more I wanted to protect you. When I couldn't figure out how, and you pushed me away, I left. I wanted to have my girl back. But now, I see she didn't go anywhere. I wasn't looking hard enough."

I stayed silent so that Mike might keep talking.

"I felt like you had stopped loving me, and it hurt like hell. Here I was, this out of shape middle-aged man, my daughter was growing up, I was losing my family, my home, my dog, the love of my life. You are unbelievably stubborn, so I guess I thought if I kept pushing you, you would shut me out completely. I thought the best thing I could do was walk away and let go of you, but I never could, never completely."

I closed my eyes and nestled my head into the crook of his neck. Even after a night of sweaty lovemaking, I could still smell the remnants of his aftershave. Torn between my need to listen to him talk about his feelings and my desire to lick the last of the clean scent from him, I decided to do both. I also concluded that I was so spoiled that I had never tried to see things from his perspective.

I kissed his ear. "Dr. Greene thinks I had a mid-life crisis, on top of everything else."

Mike tilted his head to expose more of his neck to my kisses. "I think we both had a midlife crisis, and damn they suck!"

"What does that say about our characters, that we would both give up so easily when things got tough?" I asked.

My parents and grandparents, if they had ever gone through a midlife crisis, had stuck together. What was wrong with us?

He answered. "It says we're human." Then he moaned as I nibbled at his ear.

"Everything's going to be okay, though, isn't it?" My finger trailed behind my tongue as I explored the man I loved.

"Yes," he promised, as he continued to take in my rose and gardenia —mixed with musky lovemaking—scent while kissing the top of my head. "I won't ever treat you like a child again. A queen, but not a child. Who cares that we're getting older, because I want to grow old with you."

I think those were the most romantic words he had ever said to me. "You're the man I want to grow old with, Michael Christopher Moore." That was the exact moment I was no longer afraid of aging. I had my soulmate, and I planned to spend the rest of my life waking up beside him. "I might still need to get in the last word, but I won't ever send you away again," I promised.

Mike's kisses had traveled from the top of my head, across my ear, and were cascading down my neck when he added, "You can try to send me away, but I won't go."

Mike and I were gearing up to satisfy our starving libidos once again when Zoomie jolted to a seated position. He had gone from contentedly dreaming about terrorizing woodland creatures to alert guard dog status in a nanosecond. He let out a long, happy howl before rocketing from his spot at the foot of the mattress and bounding down the stairs.

"Cassie is here." I kissed Mike before leaping out of bed. I threw on my pajamas, robe, and bunnies.

Mike remained propped against the headboard, his head resting on his arms, with his powerful chest bared and beautiful. The smattering of gray curls that grew among his thick brown chest hair only served to add to his masculinity. The fifty-year-old Mike was as appealing to me as he had been when he was a twenty-year-old frat boy. His luscious head of hair was disheveled, and there was wickedness in his twisted grin. He was sexy, and he was mine. I felt a potent shot of lust that I had to ignore for the moment.

"How are we going to explain this?" He used an outstretched palm to reference his naked body in our bed.

"We'll manage. Get dressed." I smiled as I aimed his pants at his devilish grin. Then I ran down the steps as fast as my oversized furry feet would allow.

Cassie greeted me in the foyer. "Mom, you finally got your slippers."

I hugged her. "Present from your dad."

"Dad?" Cassie said, her eyes focused above me.

Mike stood in the stairwell. His bare feet and tousled hair gave us away in an instant.

"What's going on?" she asked.

I ignored her question. "I made a bacon quiche. I just have to heat it."

Mike helped Farez carry the suitcases to their rooms as Cassie and I prepared the coffee and placed brunch in the oven.

"Mom, what's Dad doing here already?" she asked.

I motioned for her to sit at the table beside me while I explained. "Your father and I have decided to try to work things out. Are you okay with that?"

"Okay with it? Of course, I am. Are you kidding? Even though you are both absurdly stubborn, everyone knows you guys still love each other. I don't think Dad can even stand that horrible Shelly lady."

It was settled. I had my family back.

Dinner at my parents' was perfect. Mom worried that the meat was dry, that the potatoes were lumpy, and the stuffing was overcooked. They were all perfect. Dad made a lot of corny jokes and relentlessly teased everyone. It was also perfect. Mike and I formally announced that we were giving our marriage another try.

"About time," Jimmy Jr. announced, shoving his mouth full of stuffing.

Everyone snuck Zoomie scraps of turkey until he passed out in a tryptophan-induced coma beside my also comatose, football-watching dear old dad.

After dinner, Cassie and Farez each took an end of the turkey wishbone and pulled. Cassie walked away with the bigger piece.

"My wish already came true." She pointed at her father, then smiled at me.

Yes, the afternoon was perfect!

_____

I ended my day on the couch with my feet propped on Mike's lap. Cassie, Farez, and Zoomie bounded through the front door, loaded down with twigs and branches. Zoomie's loot was so immense that he staggered under its weight.

"What are you three up to?" Mike asked.

"Do you remember when I was little and we made Grateful Trees every Thanksgiving?" Cassie asked.

"Yes," Mike and I said in unison.

Every Thanksgiving that our family had been together, we had listed things we were grateful for and hung them on a handmade display.

We followed the three of them into the kitchen. Cassie rooted around in the craft drawer and produced a ball of yarn, construction paper, a stapler, and Sharpies.

"Let's make one right now," she said.

The next thing I knew, the four of us sat around the kitchen table, consumed with our project, Zoomie at our feet. Cassie arranged the twigs in a crystal flower vase. She cut the construction paper into tags and stapled a piece of yarn to each one.

"I'll go first," she called out.

She had said those same words on countless Moore family Thanksgivings.

She hung five tags on the tree as she called out, "Mom and Dad—Zoomie —Farez—Grandma and Pappap —Uncle Jimmy."

Then she hung one more. "That's Zoomie's squirrel." She had sketched a little critter on it.

Zoomie sprang to attention when he heard his name mentioned alongside his archenemy. Then he smiled at our amusement.

Farez announced, "I have one." He read his neat sentence. "I am grateful to spend today with a wonderful family."

"Aww," Cassie said, kissing him.

Mike hung his perfectly lettered tags on the tree. "The best daughter in the world and the most beautiful wife in the world."

Cassie let out another "aww," then kissed her father on the cheek.

Mike eyed the tags that lay in front of me. "Now, that's a pile."

"What can I say? I am grateful this year."

I truly was!

Cassie helped me place them on the tree. We alternated calling out what was written on each tag before we hung it on the arrangement.

"Cassie!"

"Mike!"

"Zoomie!"

"Mom and Dad!"

"Grandma and Pap!"

"Pap's stories!"

"Jimmy Jr!"

"Missy!"

"Valentina!"

"The Cup!"

"Chelsea!"

"Diamond Washington!"

"Principal Anderson and Leigh Ann Martin!"

"Mrs. Stewart's baked goods!"

"Dan the Hot Man teaching me to kick butt!"

"Neil and Alexia Harris!"

"Ghosts in my dreams!"

"Books!"

"Dancing and running!"

"Second chances!"

"Dr. Greene!"

"StumpStrong!"

"StumpStrong?" Cassie asked. "What's that?"

"It's my mantra, something Dr. Greene told me to say when I feel scared. It reminds me of your great-grandfather," I explained.

"And his stump, and how brave he was?"

"Yes," I said.

"So cool," she said. "I'm grateful for that too."

She grabbed another tag and wrote on it. "StumpStrong," she declared, attaching it to a branch. "That's our family motto. We are StumpStrong."

So, there you have it. I survived the trauma of the past three years and came out StumpStrong.

As Pap would say: "Peas make you pretty," "Vegetables put hair on your chest," and "Every little bit helps, said the old lady who peed in the sea!"

Thankful,

Patti

Epilogue

"Why did you look at the sunset?' Phillip answered with his mouth full: Because I was happy."

Somerset Maugham, *Of Human Bondage*

New Year's Eve 2019

Dear Diary,

Life has been busy. I've been working long hours getting my classroom in order. I had mountains of paperwork to complete on Diamond, Nate, and Carlos. Diamond started her transition to her regular education classes last week. She is determined to stay out of trouble. I have a feeling she is about to accomplish amazing things. Carlos and Nate will start their transitions after the Christmas holiday. A happy Zoomie is back at his second job, helping teenagers build confidence as they read. Neil has been in touch to tell me that Probation continues to work with Tanner's counselors at the detention center. They believe he has been abused and neglected. I hope that society wakes up, puts down their cell phones, tunes off the social media, and invests in raising and educating children. It does take a village, after all.

Get this one! Chelsea fixed her Uncle Neil up with Missy. Missy is so excited that she bought sexy new stilettos. I hope she can stay upright in them after the champagne toast. They have their first date tonight at Tina's New Year's Eve Party. Patti's Pathetic Pansies finished their self-defense classes with Dan the Hot Man and now have a standing Friday night girls' night.

Mike has been going to my salsa class with me. Before our first lesson, I glared at Adrian. I wanted him to know that he had better not make the same faux pas he made with Jacob. Hopefully, he continues to demonstrate better sense than to comment on my change in handsome partners.

Mom and Dad are well. Dad hasn't had the big one, and I don't expect him to anytime soon. He is trying to eat healthier and has taken up daily walks with his crazy lodge buddy, Paranoid Pete. I convinced Mom to go out to breakfast at least once a week with her girlfriends. She calls me every Wednesday evening to tell me about it. Jimmy Jr. enrolled in a business class for the spring semester. I suspect he is taking whatever cryptic advice it was that Pap gave him.

Christmas was wonderful. Mike had an oil done of my grandparents' wedding photo that is spectacular and captures their expressions. He hung it above the fireplace mantel so that when I came down the stairs Christmas morning, it was the first thing I saw. I gave Mike the best present ever! Christmas Eve, I presented him with a shoebox containing an eight-week-old furry princess that Mike named Sugar. Zoomie loves his new sister. He watches her and laughs as she has puppy crazies and runs Sheltie circles around him. They have barking contests at mealtime, bedtime, every time the doorbell rings—well, they bark pretty much every minute of the day.

On Christmas Day, we had an enjoyable visit with Mike's family. I hadn't realized how much I missed them until I experienced an embrace that made me feel like a Patti Burger inside an in-law sandwich.

Cassie also gave me a special Christmas present. We got matching StumpStrong tattoos on our inner wrists. Although Grandma is pretending to roll over in her grave, I think deep down inside, she is smiling in approval.

She and Pap aren't visiting my dreams as often. Pap says that now that Mike is waking up with me, I don't need them. I've told him this isn't true. Pap says not to worry; they will always be there for me.

Last week I received a Christmas postcard from Jacob Greene. He looked ruggedly masculine in a fisherman knit sweater and the same gray knit hat he wore the night we danced. His enormous smile is the focal point of the photo. He has his arms looped over the shoulders of two handsome older gentlemen that look very similar to him—I suspect his father and uncle? The banner on the card reads *Happy Holidays from Greene's Shipwrights*. On the other side, he penned a short message:

Dear Patricia,

Merry Christmas to you and yours. Hope this finds you well. I am exceedingly happy, having given up those damn ties. Remember to stay StumpStrong.

Fondly yours,

Jacob

As for me, I've had a significant epiphany. It happened the day I looked in the mirror and saw my Grandma. Up until that moment, I struggled to find much I liked about myself. Sure, Jacob, Neil, and Mike had all said flowery-sweet things, my friends were loyal and adored me, and I had won my battle with Westbrook, but I still didn't like myself. The thing is, when I looked in the mirror that morning and saw Grandma, everything changed. I recalled how she had held a four-year-old me on her lap for hours because we both refused to move until I had learned to read an entire newspaper. I realized, not only do I look like her, but Grandma and I are alike in our determination and obsessiveness.

I thought about Pap and how he had given me a love of literature and teaching. He also gifted me with his sarcastic wit, his wild mane, and his fortitude. Reluctant warriors, we both survived our wars!

I became aware of the work ethic and loyalty my mother instilled in me. And then there is my dad. We both love with all of our hearts and have that same absurd sense of humor. We obnoxiously guffaw at our inside jokes as the rest of the world wonders why the heck we are laughing.

Finally, there is Cassie. My beautiful daughter shares my priorities. I am immensely proud of her love of tradition and family.

I see these individuals who mean the world to me in myself. My ties to them run deeper than memories, genetics, and blood. I no longer have time for self-loathing. I am too busy connecting to my familial roots. They grow deep, lovingly twine around everything, reach up into the fresh air to breathe, and then stretch toward the sun. Why did it take the tragedy of a near-death experience for me to understand this?

I have to go now. I'm heading to Tina's party. All of my friends and family will be there, and Zoomie has plans to show off his baby sister.

Oh—one more thing. My left shoulder companion and I made a trip to Victoria's Secret, and guess what we purchased? FYI—they are decadent, silky, luxurious, and much deserved!

StumpStrong,
Patti

The End

Acknowledgments

Thank you to Julie Lokun for making me "StumpStrong", and for believing in my project. I couldn't have done this without her.

Thank you to my husband for doing my chores as I sat at my laptop for months, and for talking me through my daily anxiety attacks.

Thank you to my daughter for putting up with me and baking my brain muffins.

Thank you to Moxie, Shelby, Rocky, and Buddha for making Zoomie come alive.

Thank you to my kick-ass editor, Therese Arkenberg.

Thank you to Diana Carlile for my gorgeous cover design.

Thank you to Rhea Sanchez, Ambar Encarnacion, The Squad, and my niece Nicki Lesperance, for being my first readers.

Thank you to my parents, siblings, cousins, and aunt for reminiscing and sharing their stories.

Thank you to my Pap, for his bravery, wisdom, and wit, and for coming to me in my dreams and encouraging me to write this.

And finally, thank you to my grandma, for being my best friend, and for forgiving me for writing this.

Also—

Thank you to Kasimer A. Traynelis, Pilot of *The Sky Queen* and *That's All Jack,* for sharing his memoir with my family.

The crew of *The Sky Queen* and *That's All Jack* missing in Action Misburg 12/4/44:
Kasimer Traynelis, William Howe, Duane Mowry, Paul Basye, James Laws, Stewart Livingston, Robert Stauffer, Ralph Tetu, and finally Henry Bouma Jr. who was killed in action on December 31, 1944.

Chapter Quotes
A Prayer for Owen Meany by John Irving
I Know Why The Caged Bird Sings by Maya Angelou
Of Human Bondage by William Somerset Maugham
One Flew Over the Cuckoo's Nest by Ken Kesey
Riders of the Purple Sage by Zane Grey
Rudyard Kipling: The Complete Works by Rudyard Kipling
Treasure Island by Robert Louis Stevenson
Additional quotes from The Duke, John Wayne

About the Author

With the help of two hyperactive Shetland Sheepdogs, Nicki Pascarella writes Women's Fiction, Romantic Mysteries, Humor, Romance and Paranormal Romance. She lives in Pennsylvania with her husband and teenage daughter. When she isn't writing and editing, you will find her running and belly dancing.